ALSO BY JANET EVANOVICH

THE STEPHANIE PLUM NOVELS

Smokin' Seventeen
Sizzling Sixteen
Finger Lickin' Fifteen
Fearless Fourteen
Lean Mean Thirteen
Twelve Sharp
Eleven on Top
Ten Big Ones
To the Nines
Hard Eight
Seven Up
Hot Six
High Five
Four to Score
Three to Get Deadly
Two for the Dough
One for the Money

THE BETWEEN THE NUMBERS NOVELS

Plum Spooky
Plum Lucky
Plum Lovin'
Visions of Sugar Plums

THE LIZZY AND DIESEL NOVELS

Wicked Appetite

THE BARNABY AND HOOKER NOVELS

Trouble Maker #2 (graphic novel)
Trouble Maker #1 (graphic novel)
Motor Mouth
Metro Girl

NONFICTION

How I Write

EXPLOSIVE EIGHTEEN

EXPLOSIVE EIGHTEEN

A STEPHANIE PLUM NOVEL

Janet Evanovich

DOUBLEDAY LARGE PRINT HOME LIBRARY EDITION

BANTAM BOOKS NEW YORK

This Large Print Edition, prepared especially for Doubleday Large Print Home Library, contains the complete, unabridged text of the original Publisher's Edition.

Published in the United States by Bantam Books, an imprint of The Random House Publishing Group, a division of Random House, Inc., New York.

ISBN 978-1-61793-243-4

Printed in the United States of America

EXPLOSIVE EIGHTEEN

ONE

New Jersey was 40,000 feet below me, obscured by cloud cover. Heaven was above me, beyond the thin skin of the plane. And hell was sitting four rows back. Okay, maybe hell was too strong. Maybe it was just purgatory.

My name is Stephanie Plum, and I work as a bail-bonds enforcer for Vincent Plum Bail Bonds in Trenton, New Jersey. I'd recently inherited airline vouchers from a dead guy and used them to take a once-in-a-lifetime Hawaiian vacation. Unfortunately, the vacation didn't go as planned, and I'd been forced to leave Hawaii ahead of schedule, like a thief sneaking off in the dead of night. I'd abandoned two angry men in Honolulu, called my friend Lula, and asked her to pick me up at Newark Airport.

As if my life wasn't enough in the toilet, I was now on the plane home, seated four rows ahead of a guy who looked like Sasquatch and was snoring like a bear in a cave. Good thing I wasn't sitting next to him, because I surely would have strangled him in his sleep by now. I was wearing airline-distributed earphones pumped up to maximum volume, but they weren't helping. The snoring had started somewhere over Denver and got really ugly over Kansas City. After several loud passenger comments suggesting someone take the initiative and smother the guy, flight attendants confiscated all the pillows and began passing out free alcoholic beverages. Three-quarters of the plane was now desperately drunk, and the remaining quarter was either underage or alternatively medicated. Two of the underage were screaming-crying, and I was pretty sure the kid behind me had pooped in his pants.

I was among the drunk. I was wondering how I was going to walk off the plane and navigate the terminal with any sort of dignity, and I was hoping my ride was waiting for me.

Sasquatch gave an extra loud *snork,* and I ground my teeth together. Just land this friggin' plane, I thought. Land it in a cornfield, on a highway, in the ocean. Just get me out of here!

• • •

Lula pulled into my apartment building parking lot, and I thanked her for picking me up at the airport and bringing me home.

"No problemo," she said, dropping me at the back door to the lobby. "There wasn't nothing on television, and I'm between honeys, so it wasn't like I was leaving anything good behind."

I waved her off and trudged into my apartment building. I took the elevator to the second floor, dragged my luggage down the hall and into my apartment, and shuffled into my bedroom.

It was after midnight, and I was exhausted. My vacation in Hawaii had been *unique,* and the flight home had been hellish. Turbulence over the Pacific, a layover in L.A., and the snoring. I closed my eyes and tried to calm myself. I was back to work tomorrow, but for now I had to make a choice. I was completely out of clean clothes. That meant I could be a slut and sleep naked, or I could be a slob and sleep in what I was wearing.

Truth is, I'm not entirely comfortable sleeping naked. I do it from time to time, but I worry that God might be watching or that my mother might find out, and I'm pretty sure they both think nice girls should wear pajamas to bed.

In this case, being a slob required less effort, and that's where I chose to go.

Unfortunately, I was in the same wardrobe predicament when I dragged myself out of bed the next morning, so I emptied my suitcase into my laundry basket, grabbed the messenger bag that serves as a purse, and headed for my parents' house. I could use my mom's washer and dryer, and I thought I had some emergency clothes left in their spare bedroom. Plus, they'd been babysitting my hamster, Rex, while I was away, and I wanted to retrieve him.

I live in a one-bedroom, one-bath apartment in an aging three-story brick-faced apartment building located on the edge of Trenton. On a good traffic day, at four in the morning, it's a ten-minute drive to my parents' house or the bonds office. All other times, it's a crapshoot.

Grandma Mazur was at the front door when I pulled to the curb and parked. She's lived with my parents since Grandpa Mazur took the big escalator to the heavenly food court in the sky. Sometimes I think my father wouldn't mind seeing Grandma step onto that very same escalator, but I can't see it happening anytime soon. Her steel-gray hair was cut short and tightly curled on her head. Her nails matched her bright red lipstick. Her lavender-

and-white running suit hung slack on her bony shoulders.

"What a good surprise," Grandma said, opening the door to me. "Welcome home. We're dying to hear all about the vacation with the hottie."

My parents' home is a modest duplex, sharing a common wall with its mirror image. Mrs. Ciak lives in the other half. Her husband has passed on, and she spends her days baking coffee cake and watching television. The outside of her half is painted pale green, and the exterior of my parents' house is mustard yellow and brown. It's not an attractive combination, but it feels comfortable to me since it's been that way for as long as I can remember. Each half of the house has a postage-stamp front yard, a small covered front porch, a back stoop leading to a long narrow backyard, and a detached single-car garage.

I lugged the laundry basket through the living room and dining room to the kitchen, where my mother was chopping vegetables.

"Soup?" I asked her.

"Minestrone. Are you coming for dinner?"

"Can't. Got plans."

My mother glanced at the laundry basket. "I just put a load of sheets into the washer. If you leave that here, I'll do it later for you. How was Hawaii? We didn't expect you home until tomorrow."

"Hawaii was good, but the plane ride was long. Fortunately, I sat next to a guy who got off when we stopped in L.A., so I had more room."

"Yeah, but you were also next to Mr. Tall, Dark, and Handsome." Grandma said.

"Not exactly."

This got both their attentions.

"How so?" Grandma asked.

"It's complicated. He didn't fly back with me."

Grandma stared at my left hand. "You got a tan, except on your ring finger. It looks like you were wearing a ring when you got a tan, but you're not wearing it no more."

I looked at my hand. Bummer. When

I took the ring off, I hadn't noticed a tan line.

"Now I know why you went to Hawaii," Grandma said. "I bet you eloped! Of course, being that you don't got the ring on anymore would put a damper on the celebration."

I blew out a sigh, poured myself a cup of coffee, and my phone rang. I dug around in my bag, unable to find the phone in the jumble of stuff I'd crammed in for the plane trip. I dumped it all out onto the little kitchen table and pawed through it. Granola bars, hairbrush, lip balm, hair scrunchies, notepad, wallet, socks, two magazines, a large yellow envelope, floss, mini flashlight, travel pack of tissues, three pens, and my phone.

The caller was Connie Rosolli, the bail bonds office manager. "I hope you're on your way to the office," she said, "because we have a situation here."

"What sort of situation?"

"A bad one."

"How bad? Can it wait twenty minutes?"

"Twenty minutes sounds like a long time."

I disconnected and stood. "Gotta go," I said to my mother and grandmother.

"But you just got here," Grandma said. "We didn't get to hear about the eloping."

"I didn't elope."

I returned everything to my messenger bag, with the exception of the phone and the yellow envelope. I put the phone in an outside pocket, and I looked at the envelope. No writing on it. Sealed. I had no clue how it had gotten into my bag. I ripped it open and pulled a photograph out. It was an 8×10 glossy of a man. He was standing on a street corner, looking just past the photographer. He looked like he didn't know he was being photographed, like someone had happened along with their cell phone camera and snapped his picture. He was possibly midthirties to early forties, and nice looking in a button-down kind of way. Short brown hair. Fair-skinned. Wearing a dark suit. I didn't recognize the street corner or the man. Somehow on the trip home, I must have picked the envelope up by mistake—maybe when I stopped at the newsstand in the airport.

"Who's that?" Grandma asked.

"I don't know. I guess I snatched it up with a magazine."

"He's kind of hot. Is there a name on the back?"

"Nope. Nothing."

"Too bad," Grandma said. "He's a looker, and I'm thinking about becoming a cougar."

My mother cut her eyes to the cupboard where she kept her whiskey. She glanced at the clock on the wall and gave up a small sigh of regret. Too early.

I dropped the envelope and the photo into the trash, chugged my coffee, grabbed a bagel from the bag on the counter, and ran upstairs to change.

Twenty minutes later, I was at the bonds office. I use the term *office* lightly since we were operating out of a converted motor coach parked on Hamilton Avenue directly in front of the construction site for a new brick-and-mortar office. The new construction had been made necessary by a fire of suspicious origin that totally destroyed the original building.

My cousin Vinnie bought the bus from a friend of mine, and while it wasn't perfect, it was better than setting up shop in the food court at the mall. Connie's car was parked behind the coach, and Vinnie's car was parked behind Connie's.

Vinnie is a good bail bondsman but a boil on my family's backside. In the past, he's been a gambler, a womanizer, a philanderer, a card cheat, and I'm pretty sure he once had a romantic encounter with a duck. He looks like a weasel in pointy-toed shoes and too-tight pants. His father-in-law, Harry the Hammer, for all purposes owns the agency, and due to recent scandalous events involving misappropriated money, gambling, and whoring, Vinnie's wife, Lucille, now owns Vinnie.

I parked my junker Toyota RAV4 behind Vinnie's Caddy, and checked out the scene in front of me. The cinder-block shell of the new bonds office was complete. The roof was on. Workers were inside banging in nails and using power tools. I looked from the construction site to the bonds bus, where I could see light creeping out from drawn shades. It all looked like business as usual.

I wrenched the coach door open and climbed the three steps up to the cockpit and beyond. Connie was at the dinette table, her purse on the bench seat next to her. Her laptop computer was closed.

Connie is a couple years older than me and a much better shot with a gun. She was wearing a magenta sweater with a deep V-neck, showing more cleavage than I could ever hope to grow. Her black hair had recently been straightened and was pulled up into a messy knot on the top of her head. She was wearing big chunky gold earrings and a matching necklace.

She stood when she saw me. "I'm going downtown to the courthouse," she said. "I need to bond out Vinnie. He's been arrested, and they won't let him write his own bond."

Oh boy. "Now what?"

"He had a dispute with DeAngelo and took a tire iron to his Mercedes. DeAngelo fired off a couple rounds at Vinnie's Caddy, Vinnie Tasered DeAngelo, and that's when the police showed up and dragged them both off to jail."

Salvatore DeAngelo was the contractor Harry had hired to rebuild the bonds office after it burned to the ground. DeAngelo was better known as the contractor from hell since he did everything *his* way, did *nothing* without a bribe, and worked on DeAngelo Time, which had no relationship to an actual workweek.

"Well, at least it's nothing serious," I said.

"Yeah, but it could be if DeAngelo gets bonded out before Vinnie and comes back and sets fire to Vinnie's bus."

"Do you think DeAngelo would do that?" I asked Connie.

"Hard to tell what DeAngelo would do. That's why I didn't want to leave until you got here to stand guard." Connie handed me the key to the gun cabinet. "You might want to pick something out and keep it handy."

"You want me to shoot him?"

"Only if you have to," Connie said, clomping down the stairs to the coach door in her four-inch cork wedges. "I won't be long. And the files on the table are for you. They're the no-shows for court that came in while you were on vacation."

Oh great, I was supposed to babysit a bus that might at any moment go up in flames. On the other hand, Vinnie was my cousin and employer. And without the bus, we'd be renting space from the adult bookstore or working out of Connie's Hyundai. All that still didn't mean I was willing to get toasted protecting Vinnie's makeshift office.

I took the Failure to Appear files outside, hauled a lawn chair out of the storage compartment under the bus, and set the chair in the shade. This way, I could divert a Molotov cocktail and not get trapped inside a flaming inferno.

I sat in the chair and paged through the files. Purse snatcher, armed robbery, domestic violence, a burglary suspect, credit card fraud, assault, a second armed robbery. I wanted to be back in Hawaii. I closed my eyes and sucked in some air, searching for the smell of the sea and instead catching exhaust fumes and a funky stench coming off the construction Dumpster.

A car eased to a stop behind my RAV4 and two men got out. One of them was Salvatore DeAngelo, a short, barrel-chested guy with a lot of wavy black hair going gray. He was wearing pleated dress slacks, a silky black short-sleeved shirt, and a thick gold chain that was stuck in a mat of chest hair that looked slightly singed . . . no doubt from Vinnie shooting a bunch of volts into him with his Taser.

DeAngelo sauntered over to me and stood hands in pants pockets, jiggling change. "Hey, cutie," he said. "What's up? Any special reason why you're sitting outside? Like, are you looking for street business? 'Cause I might have some business for you, if you know what I mean."

I was thinking Vinnie did the right thing when he Tasered DeAngelo.

"I'm just doing my job," I said. "I'm supposed to shoot you if you firebomb the bus."

"I don't see no gun."

"It's hidden."

"I bet," he said. "Let me know if you change your mind about takin' care of my business. And give me some credit here. I don't firebomb buses in broad daylight. I do that shit at night when no one's around."

DeAngelo turned away and walked into the half-finished bonds office building, and I returned to my files.

The subject of the last file in the stack was a surprise. Joyce Barnhardt. She'd allegedly stolen a necklace from a downtown jewelry store and had assaulted the owner when he'd tried to retrieve it. Vinnie had bonded her out of jail, and she'd failed to show for court three days later.

I'd gone all through school with Joyce, and she'd made my life a misery. She was an obnoxious, sneaky, mean kid, and now she was an unscrupulous, self-serving, man-eating adult. From time to time, she'd tried her hand at working for Vinnie in various capacities, but none of the jobs stuck. Truth is, Joyce made her money through serial marriage, and last I looked, she was doing just fine. Hard to believe she'd stolen a necklace. Easy to believe she'd assaulted the store owner.

TWO

Lula's red Firebird rolled to a stop in front of the bus, and Lula swung herself out from behind the wheel and walked over to me. Her hair was dyed pink and teased into a big puffball that looked surprisingly good against her brown skin, and her body was minimally contained by her orange spandex skirt and white scoop neck tank top. She's a former 'ho who gave up her street corner to work for Vinnie as a file clerk.

"You looking to get some sun sitting

out here?" she asked. "Didn't you get enough of that in Hawaii?"

I told her about Vinnie and DeAngelo, and how I was guarding the bus.

"It's a hunk of junk anyways," Lula said.

"What's up for today?" I asked her. "Are you filing?"

"Hell no, I'm not getting stuck in the death trap bus. I'll go catch bad guys with you." She looked down at the files in my lap. "Who we gonna do first? Anything fun come in?"

"Joyce Barnhardt."

"Say what?"

"She shoplifted a necklace and assaulted the store owner."

"I hate Joyce Barnhardt," Lula said. "She's mean. She told me I was fat. Can you imagine?"

It wasn't exactly that Lula was fat. It was more that she was too short for her weight. Or maybe it was that there was an excess of Lula and not ever enough fabric.

"I thought we'd save Joyce for last," I told Lula. "I'm not looking forward to knocking on her door."

Connie's Hyundai cruised down the street, made a U-turn, and parked behind the bus. Connie and Vinnie got out and walked over to me.

"Is DeAngelo here?" Vinnie asked.

"Yes," I told him. "He's inside the building."

Vinnie growled, doing his best imitation of a crazed badger backed into a corner, claws out.

"Cripes," Lula said.

"It's okay to go into the bus," I said to Vinnie. "DeAngelo only blows things up at night."

We all stood looking at the bus for a moment, not sure we believed that to be true.

"What the hell," Vinnie finally said. "My life's in the crapper anyway."

And he disappeared inside the bus.

"What's with Joyce?" I asked Connie. "Did she really steal a necklace?"

Connie shrugged. "Don't know, but it's gotten weird. Frank Korda, the store owner who pressed charges, is missing."

"When did he go missing?" I asked.

"Later that same day. The nail salon

across the street remembers the closed sign in the front door around four in the afternoon. His wife said he never came home."

"And Joyce?"

"Vinnie bonded Joyce out right after she was arrested. She was scheduled for court three days later, and she never showed."

"I bet Joyce snatched him," Lula said. "She'd do something like that. I bet she got him in chains in her cellar."

"Wouldn't be the first time Joyce put a man in chains," Connie said, "but I don't think she's got him in her cellar. She isn't answering her phone. And I drove past her house last night. It was dark."

"Holy cow," Lula said, staring at my left hand. "You got a white ring on your finger where you didn't get a tan. I didn't notice that last night on the way home from the airport. What the heck did you do in Hawaii? And where's the ring now?"

I made an effort not to grimace. "It's complicated."

"Yeah," Lula said. "That's what you

said last night. You just kept saying it was *complicated.*"

Connie examined my left hand. "Did you get married while you were in Hawaii?"

"Not exactly."

"How could you not exactly get married?" Lula wanted to know. "Either you get married or you don't get married."

I flapped my arms around and squinched my eyes shut. "I don't want to talk about it, okay? It's *complicated*!"

"S'cuse me," Lula said. "I was just sayin'. You don't want to talk about it? Fine. Don't talk about it. Just 'cause we're best friends don't mean nothin'. We're like sisters, but hey, don't bother me if you don't want to tell me something."

"Good," I said, "because I don't want to talk about it."

"Hunh," Lula said.

Vinnie yelled at Connie from inside the bus. "The phone's ringing. Get the friggin' phone!"

"*You* get the phone," Connie yelled back.

"I don't do phones," Vinnie said.

Connie made an Italian hand gesture at the bus. "Idiot."

"I suppose we should do something," Lula said after Connie left to get the phone. "What else have you got there?"

I shuffled through my stack of skips. "Two armed robberies."

"Pass on them. They always shoot at us."

"Domestic violence."

"Too depressing," Lula said. "What else you got?"

"A purse snatcher and credit card fraud."

"I'm liking credit card fraud. They never have a lot of fight in them. They're always just sneaky little weasels. They just sit in the house all day shopping on the Internet. What's this moron's name?"

"Lahonka Goudge."

"Lahonka Goudge? What kind of name is that? That gotta be wrong. That's a terrible name."

"It's what it says here. She lives in public housing."

Forty minutes later, we were in Lula's car, motoring through the projects and searching for Lahonka's apartment. It was midmorning and the streets were quiet. Kids were in school and day care, hookers were sleeping, and the drug dealers were congregating in parks and playgrounds.

"There it is," I said to Lula. "She's in 3145A. It's the ground-floor apartment with the kids' toys in the yard."

Lula parked, and we walked to the door, picking our way around bikes, dolls, soccer balls, and big plastic trucks. I raised my hand to knock, the door opened, and a woman looked out at us. She was my height, shaped like a pear, dressed in tan spandex pants and a poison-green tank top. Her hair was standing straight out from her head like it had been spray-starched and ironed, and she had huge hoop earrings hanging from her earlobes.

"What do you want?" the woman said. "And I don't need any. Do I look like I need something? I don't think so. And don't touch none of my kids' shit or I'll turn the dog out on you."

And she slammed the door shut.

"She got a personality like a Lahonka," Lula said. "She even looks like a Lahonka."

I banged on the door, and the door got yanked open.

"What?" the woman said. "I already told you I don't want nothin'. I got a business goin' here. I'm a workin' woman, and I'm not buying any cookies, moisturizer, laundry soap, or jewelry. Maybe if you had some quality weed, but you don't smell like weed pushers."

She tried to slam the door shut again, but I had my foot in it. "Lahonka Goudge?" I asked.

"Yeah, so what?"

"Bond enforcement. You missed a court date and we need to reschedule you."

"I don't think so," she said. "You got the wrong Lahonka. And anyways, even if I was the right Lahonka, I wouldn't be going with you, on account of I got stuff to do. I got a pack of kids who need new sneakers, and you're cutting into my prime earning time. I got eBay auctions goin' on, and I'm making timely purchases elsewhere."

Lula put her weight against the door and pushed it open. "We don't got all day," she said. "We got a whole batch of idiots to bring in, and I got a lunch date with a Deluxe Mr. Clucky Burger."

"Oh yeah?" Lahonka said. "Well, Clucky Burger this."

And she gave Lula a two-handed shove that knocked her back two feet into me. I lost my balance, and we both went ass-first to the ground. The front door slammed shut, security bolts slid into place, and Lahonka pulled the shade down on her front window.

"Probably, she's not gonna open her door to you again," Lula said.

I agreed. It was unlikely.

Lula hauled herself up and adjusted her girls. "Is it too early for lunch?"

I looked at my watch. "It's almost one o'clock in Greenland."

• • •

"That Lahonka took me by surprise," Lula said, finishing off her second Clucky Burger. "I wasn't on my game."

We were eating in Lula's car because

there was a critical time limit to hanging out in Cluck-in-a-Bucket. Minuscule globules of fry fat floated in the air like fairy dust, and exposure lasting longer than six minutes left you smelling like Clucky Extra Crispy all day. It wasn't an entirely bad smell, but it tended to attract packs of hungry dogs and big beefy men, neither of which I was currently interested in.

I pulled a file out of my bag. "Maybe we want to try the purse snatcher next."

"I don't think that's a good plan," Lula said. "Purse snatchers are runners. That's what makes them good purse snatchers. And I just had two Clucky Burgers. I'll get a cramp if I gotta chase after some skinny, baggy-pants idiot now. Don't we have a bad guy who lives by the mall? Macy's is having a shoe sale."

I checked the addresses. No one lived by the mall.

"I might need a nap after all that chicken," Lula said.

A nap sounded like a good idea. I hadn't gotten much sleep on the plane ride home. For that matter, I hadn't gotten much sleep the whole time I was in Hawaii, what with all the nighttime activity. And tonight I was seeing Morelli, and I suspected that wouldn't lead to a lot of sleep. Morelli and I had things to discuss.

I have a long history with Morelli. We played choo choo when I was six years old. He relieved me of my virginity when I was sixteen. I ran him down with a Buick when I was nineteen. And now that we're both adults, more or less, I sort of have a relationship with him . . . although I'd be hard-pressed to define the relationship at this moment. He's a Trenton cop working plainclothes, crimes against persons. He's six foot tall with wavy black hair, a lean, hard-muscled body, and a world-class libido. He's movie-star handsome in jeans and a T-shirt. If you put him in a suit, he looks like a hit man.

"Are we talking about a catnap or a full-on afternoon nap?" I asked Lula.

"It might be a major nap. And then I got a date tonight with a guy who could be Mr. Good Enough. So I'm gonna need some time to make wardrobe decisions."

"In other words, I'll see you tomorrow."

"Yeah. I'll be here at eight sharp, and we could get an early start."

"You're never here that early."

"Well, I'm gonna be motivated to be a excellent bounty hunter assistant. I can feel it coming on. And I'll be ready to go first thing in the morning after a satisfying night of doing . . . you know. Cross my heart and hope to die."

THREE

Lula dropped me at my car, and I took a fast assessment of the surroundings. Work was continuing on the new office. The bus wasn't in flames. DeAngelo's Mercedes was gone, and Vinnie's Caddy was still parked. All good things.

I thought about checking in with Connie, but decided against it. I hadn't made any captures, and a conversation with Vinnie might include a lot of unpleasant nagging about catching Joyce Barnhardt. I'd get her eventually, but I wasn't up to it right now, so I jumped into my RAV and took off for my parents' house.

An hour later, I was in my apartment building, lugging my basket of clean clothes, plus my hamster cage, down the hall. I unlocked my door, pushed it open with a hip, and staggered into the kitchen, arms full. I set the laundry basket on the floor, and the hamster cage on my kitchen counter.

"Here you are, back home," I said to Rex. "Did you have fun with Grandmom?"

Rex was out of his soup can, looking like he wanted a treat, so I got the box of crackers from the cupboard and shared one with him.

Someone rapped on my front door, and I opened the door a crack, leaving the security chain attached. Two men dressed in bureaucrat-level gray suits peeked in at me. Their dress shirts were long past crisp. Their striped ties were loosened at the neck. Their hair was receding. They looked to be late forties. One was around five foot ten. The other was in the five-foot-seven range.

I suspected they liked their double bacon cheeseburgers.

"FBI," the big guy said, flashing me an ID, then returning it to his pocket. "Can we come in?"

"No," I told him.

"But we're the FBI."

"Maybe," I said to the big guy. "Maybe not. I didn't catch your name."

"Lance Lancer." He gestured at his partner. "This is agent Sly Slasher."

"Lance Lancer and Sly Slasher? Are you kidding me? Those can't be real names."

"It's right here on our badges," Lancer said. "We're looking for an envelope you might have inadvertently picked up."

"What kind of envelope?"

"A large yellow envelope. It contained a photograph of a man we're looking for in conjunction with a murder."

"Wouldn't that be a job for the local police?"

"It was an international murder. And there was a kidnapping involved. Do you have the envelope?"

"No." And that was the truth. I suspected they were looking for the envelope I'd thrown away at my parents' house.

"I think you're fibbing," Lancer said. "We have it on good authority you were given the envelope."

"If I find it, I'll give it to the FBI," I said.

I closed and locked my door, and put my eye to the peephole. Lancer and Slasher were standing, hands on hips, looking mildly pissed, not sure what to do next.

I went to the kitchen and dialed Morelli's cell phone. "Where are you?" I asked him.

"I'm home. I just got in."

"I need to check on two guys who claim they're FBI. Lance Lancer and Sly Slasher."

"I'll be a laughingstock if I plug those names into the system. This is a joke, right?"

"Those are the names they gave. They had badges and everything."

"How fast do you need this?"

"How fast can you get it?"

Morelli grunted and hung up.

I imagined Morelli staring down at his shoe, shaking his head, wishing he hadn't answered his phone.

I dialed my parents' house, and my mother answered.

"I need you to do something for me," I said. "I need the photo and the envelope I threw away when I was in the kitchen this morning. I tossed it in the trash."

"Your grandmother emptied the trash right after you left. Today was garbage pickup. I can look out back, but I think it's gone."

So it appeared I was out of the FBI evidence supply business.

Fine by me. I had better, more important things to do, like taking a nap. I kicked my shoes off and flopped onto my bed. I'd barely closed my eyes and the doorbell bonged. I heaved myself out of bed, padded to my door, and looked out the peephole. Two more men in cheap gray suits.

I cracked the door, leaving the security chain in place, and looked out. "Now what?" I said.

The guy standing closest to the door

badged me. "FBI. We'd like to talk to you."

"Names?"

"Bill Berger, and my partner, Chuck Gooley."

Bill Berger was slim, average height, and in his early fifties. Salt-and-pepper hair cut short. Bloodshot brown eyes. Probably, his contacts were killing him. Chuck was my age. Not fat but a chunky body. An inch or two shorter than Berger. His suit pants had a lot of crotch wrinkles, and he was wearing ratty running shoes.

"And you'd like to talk to me about what?" I said.

"Can we come in?"

"No."

Berger went hands to hips, exposing the gun clipped to his belt. Hard to tell if it was an unconscious gesture or if he was trying to intimidate me. Either way, I wasn't opening my door any wider.

"We have reason to believe you are in possession of a photograph that's part of a crime investigation."

My phone rang, and I excused myself to answer it.

"You've been home less than twenty-four hours, and you're already in some kind of a mess," Morelli said. "Do you want to tell me about it?"

"Sure, but I've got guests right now. More FBI."

"Are they in your apartment?"

"No. They're in the hall."

"That's where you want them to stay. As far as I can tell, the first two guys aren't with the Bureau. There are no Lance Lancers or Sly Slashers on active duty. Big surprise. So who have you got in your hall now?" Morelli asked.

"Bill Berger and Chuck Gooley."

Silence for a beat. "Berger's in his early fifties, black hair going gray, and Gooley looks like he's had the same suit on for two weeks, right?"

"Yeah. Should I let them in?"

"No. Gooley eats out of Dumpsters and fucks feral cats. Let me talk to Berger."

I passed my cell phone out to Berger. Two minutes later, Berger gave it back to me.

"Do you know where the Bureau's located downtown?" Berger asked me.

"Yep."

"I'll meet you there tomorrow at ten o'clock. Bring the photo."

"I don't have the photo," I told him.

"Then bring your lawyer."

I rolled my eyes at him. "You need to practice your people skills."

Berger pressed his lips tight together. "I hear that a lot. Mostly from my ex-wife."

I closed my door and got back to Morelli. "I guess Berger is FBI?"

"More or less. I need to talk to you."

"I figured. I hoped to see you to-night."

"I might be late."

"How late?" I asked him.

"Hard to say. Someone just took six-teen rounds to the head in the proj-ects."

"Sixteen bullets to the head? That seems excessive."

"Murray saw him, and he said he looked like Swiss cheese. Murray said the guy had brains leaking out all over the place."

"Too much information."

"It's my life," Morelli said. And he disconnected.

I went back to bed, but I kept thinking about brains leaking out from bullet holes. Morelli was the only one I knew who had a worse job than I did. Okay, maybe the guy at the mortuary who drains out body fluids was also in the running. Anyway, against all odds, Morelli liked being in law enforcement. He'd been a wild kid and the product of an abusive father. And now Morelli was a good cop, a responsible home owner, and an excellent pet parent to his dog, Bob. I'd always thought he had superior boyfriend, maybe even husband, potential, but his job was a constant, frequently grim, intrusion, and I couldn't see that changing anytime soon. Plus, now there was the Hawaiian thing.

The other guy in my life, Ranger, realistically had no boyfriend or husband potential whatsoever, but he was an addictive guilty pleasure. He had a body like Batman, a dark and mysterious past, a dark and mysterious present, and an animal magnetism that sucked me in the instant I approached his force field. He wore only black. He drove only black cars. And when he made love, his brown eyes dilated totally black.

I rolled all this around in my mind . . . Morelli, Ranger, the brains leaking out. Then I thought about the FBI guys, both fake and real, and the guy in the photo. And none of this was conducive to napping. Not to mention, I'm not on salary. If I don't capture skips, I don't make money. If I don't make money, I can't make my rent. If I don't make my rent, I'll be living in my car. And my car isn't all that terrific.

I returned to the kitchen and went back over my files. I thought I had my best shot with the purse snatcher. True, they were usually runners, but the guy looked fat in his photo, and I might be able to run down a fat guy if he wasn't in top shape. His name was Lewis Bugkowski, aka Big Buggy. Twenty-three years old. He'd robbed an eighty-three-year-old woman who was sitting on a park bench. Forty-five minutes later, Buggy was arrested when he tried to buy six buckets of fried chicken with the woman's credit card and the counter clerk didn't think Buggy looked like a Betty Bloomberg. So besides being fat, Buggy was probably not real smart.

I thought about taking my gun, but decided against it. It made my bag too heavy and gave me a neck cramp. Truth is, I never use the gun anyway. I took pepper spray and hair spray instead. I had my phone clipped to the waistband on my jeans and handcuffs in my back pocket. I was ready to roll.

Buggy lived with his parents just slightly beyond Burg limits. This is always a bummer situation, because I hate snagging people in front of their parents or their kids. I could get him at his workplace, but he hadn't listed any. I drove to Broad, hooked a left, and cruised by the Bugkowski house, a small Cape Cod. Clean. Tiny front yard, neatly maintained. One-car garage. No cars parked at the curb in front of the house.

I dialed Buggy's phone, and he picked up after two rings.

"Lewis Bugkowski?" I asked.

"Yeah?"

"Are you the home owner?"

"Nah, that's my dad."

"Is he at home?"

"No."

"Your mother?"

"They're both working. What do you want?"

"I'm conducting a survey on trash removal."

Click.

Great. I'd found out everything I needed to know. Buggy was in the house alone. I parked one house down from the Bugkowskis, walked to their front door, and rang the bell.

A huge guy answered. He was easily 6'5" and three hundred pounds. He was wearing sweatpants and a T-shirt that could have provided shelter for a Vietnamese family of eight.

"Yuh?" he asked.

"Lewis Bugkowski?"

He looked at me. "Is this about trash? You sound like that girl on the phone."

"Bond enforcement," I told him.

I whipped out my cuffs and attempted to clap one on his wrist. No good. The cuff wouldn't close. His wrist was too big. The guy was a mountain.

I sent him a flirtatious smile. "I don't suppose you'd want to come downtown with me to reschedule your court date?"

His eyes locked on to my messenger bag. "Is that what you use for a purse?"

Uh-oh.

"No," I told him. "I use this for documents. Boring stuff. Let me show you."

He grabbed the strap and ripped the bag off my shoulder before I could locate my pepper spray.

"Hey," I said. "Give it back!"

He looked down at me. "Go away or I'll hit you."

"I can't go away. The keys to my car are in the bag."

His eyes lit up. "I could use a car. I'm hungry, and there's no food in the house."

I lunged for my bag, and he batted me away.

"I'll drive you to Cluck-in-a-Bucket," I said.

He closed his front door and stepped

off the porch. "Don't need you. I got a car now."

I ran after him and latched on to the back of his T-shirt. "Help!" I yelled. "Police!"

He shoved me away, crammed himself behind the wheel, and the car groaned under the weight. He rolled the engine over and took off.

"That's grand theft auto, mister!" I shouted after him. "You're in big trouble!"

I watched Buggy disappear around a corner. I procrastinated a minute, then gave in and called Ranger.

"Where are you?" I asked.

"I'm at Rangeman."

Rangeman was the security company he partially owned. It was housed in a nondescript building in the center of Trenton, and it was filled with high-tech equipment and large, heavily muscled men in black Rangeman uniforms. Ranger kept a private apartment on the seventh floor.

"Some big dopey guy just stole my car," I said to Ranger. "And he has my bag. And he's FTA."

"No problem. We have your car on the screen."

Ranger has this habit of installing tracking devices on my cars when I'm not looking. In the beginning, I found the invasion of privacy to be intolerable, but I've gotten used to it over the years, and there are times when it's come in handy . . . like now.

"I'll send someone out to get your car," Ranger said. "What do you want us to do with the big dopey guy?"

"How about if you cuff him, cram him into the backseat, and drive him to the bonds bus. I'll take it from there."

"And you?"

"I'm good. Lula's on her way to pick me up."

"Babe," Ranger said. And he disconnected.

Okay, so I fibbed to Ranger about Lula. Truth is, I wasn't ready to face him. Especially since he sounded a tiny bit exasperated. I looked down at my naked ring finger, grimaced, and called Lula.

FOUR

"You got soft in Hawaii," Lula said. "You lost your edge. That's what happens when you go on vacation and do whatever the heck it is that you did. Which, by the way, I don't even care about no more."

Lula had picked me up at Buggy's house, and we were on our way to the bonds office.

"I didn't go soft in Hawaii," I said. "I *never* had an edge."

"That could be true about the edge, but you've been out after two felons now, and they both whupped your butt.

So I thought maybe it was on account of being distracted by whatever it is you're distracted by. Not that I care what it is. And notice what a good friend I am, even though you don't care to confide in me and I disturbed my nap to rescue you."

"I'm not distracted. You can attribute both whuppings to pure incompetence."

"Well, aren't you little Miss Down-on-Yourself. I could fix that. You need a doughnut."

"I need more than a doughnut."

"What, like chicken? Fries? Maybe one of them giant two-pounder bacon burgers?"

"I wasn't talking about food," I said to Lula. "You can't solve all your problems with food."

"Since when?"

"I'm thinking about taking a self-defense class. Maybe learn kickboxing."

"I don't need no self-defense class," Lula said. "I rely on my animal instincts to beat the bejeezus out of an offending moron."

That didn't always work for me. I wasn't all that great at beating the bejeezus out of people. My fight-or-flight instinct ran more toward flight.

"Now that I'm up from my nap, I'm in a mood to go after the big one," Lula said. "I want to bag Joyce. Where's she living? Is she still in that hotel-size colonial by Vinnie?"

"No. The bond agreement lists her address as Stiller Street in Hamilton Township."

So far as I know, Joyce is currently single. Although that might be yesterday's news. It's hard to keep up with Joyce. She's a serial divorcée, working her way up the matrimonial ladder, kicking used-up husbands to the curb while negotiating lucrative settlements. She left her last marriage with a net gain of an E-class Mercedes and half of a $1.5 million house. Rumor has it he got the guinea pig.

Might as well have a look at Joyce's house, I thought. Make a fast run out to Hamilton Township, and by the time I got back, hopefully, my car would be parked behind the bonds bus.

Twenty minutes later, we were rolling down Stiller.

"This clump of houses is brand new," Lula said. "I didn't even know this was here. This was a cornfield last week."

The clump of attached town houses was called Mercado Mews, and it looked not only brand new but expensive. Joyce lived in an end unit with a two-car garage. Everything looked fresh and spiffy. No activity anywhere. No cars parked on the street. No traffic. No one tending the azalea bushes. No one walking a dog or pushing a stroller.

"Looks to me like lots of these houses aren't sold yet," Lula said. "They look empty. 'Course, Joyce's house looks empty, too."

According to the file notes, Connie had been calling every day, twice a day, since Joyce went missing. She'd called the cell number and the home phone, and no one ever picked up.

Lula pulled to the curb and we went to the door and rang the bell. No answer. She waded into the flowerbed and looked into the front window.

"There's furniture in here, but no Joyce that I can see," Lula said. "Everything looks nice and neat. No dead bodies on the floor."

"Let's snoop around back."

We skirted the house and discovered the backyard was sealed off with a seven-foot-high wooden privacy fence. I tried the fence door. Locked.

"You're gonna have to kick it in," Lula said. "I'd do it, but I'm wearin' my Via Spigas."

We've done this drill many, many times. Lula was always wearing the wrong shoes, and I was inept.

"Go ahead," Lula said. "Kick it."

I gave a halfhearted kick.

"That's a sissy kick," Lula said. "Put something behind it."

I kicked it harder.

"Hunh," Lula said. "You don't know much about kickin' in doors."

No kidding. We went through this routine at least once a week, and it was getting old. Maybe I didn't need kick-boxing lessons. Maybe I needed a new job.

"One of us is gonna have to alley-oop over the fence," Lula said.

I looked up at the fence. Seven feet. Neither of us was exactly Spider-Man.

"Who's going to alley, and who's going to oop?" I asked her.

"I'd do the lifting, but I just got a manicure. And I notice you don't have a manicure at all. Only thing noticeable about your hands is the missing tan on your ring finger that I don't care about."

"Okay, great. I'll do the lifting, but you're going to have to ditch the Via Spigas. I don't want to get gored by a stiletto."

Lula took her shoes off and threw them over the top of the fence into Joyce's yard. "Okay, I'm ready. Give me a boost."

I tried boosting, but I couldn't get her off the ground.

"You're going to have to climb onto my shoulders," I said.

Lula put her right foot on my thigh, hoisted herself up, and wrangled her left leg over my shoulder. Her spandex skirt was up to her waist, and her tiger-striped thong was lost in the deep, dark recesses of her voluptuousness.

"Uh-oh," she said.

"What *uh-oh*? I don't like to hear *uh-oh*."

"I'm stuck. You gotta get a hand under my ass and shove."

"Not gonna happen."

She wrapped her arms around my head to keep from slipping, and we went over backward. *WUMP.*

"Are you okay?" I asked her.

"Hard to tell with you laying on me. I might need a moment."

We both got up and reassessed the situation.

"My Via Spigas are on the wrong side of the fence," Lula said, tugging at her skirt. "No way am I losing them Via Spigas." She hauled her Glock out of her purse and drilled five rounds into the gate lock.

"Holy cow!" I said. "You can't do that. That's *loud.* Everybody's probably calling the police."

"There's no everybody," Lula said. "This here's a ghost town." She tried the gate, but it was still locked. "Hunh," she said. "Maybe we could dig under the fence."

"Do you have a shovel?"

"No."

"Then you're going to have to decide between your manicure and your shoes," I told her.

"Over you go," Lula said.

She got me to the top of the fence, where I hung for a moment, swung one leg and then the other, and managed to fall without fracturing anything. I opened the gate, let Lula in, and we looked in the back windows. Same deal. No Joyce in sight. Back door was locked.

"I could get us in," Lula said. "I could have a accident with one of these back windows."

"No! No broken windows. And no more shooting at doors. I can get Ranger to sneak me in."

"I bet," Lula said. "Not that it's any of my business or that I care about what's going on with you and Mr. Mysterious. 'Course, if you were dying to tell me, I suppose I'd have to listen."

"The only thing I'm dying to do is get out of here."

We unlocked the gate from the inside, returned to Lula's Firebird, and she drove me back to the bonds office.

"Looks to me like Ranger got your car washed," Lula said, eyeing the RAV4 parked behind the bus. "I can't ever remember seeing it that clean. Ranger's like a full-service dude. He rescues your car from being stolen, and he returns it detailed. I'm guessing you must have made him real happy in Hawaii. Not that I care. I'm just taking a winger here."

It was more like I made him happy, and then I didn't make him happy, and then I made him happy. And then the shit hit the fan.

"He's just a clean kind of guy," I said to Lula.

"Yeah, I could see that."

Lula took off, and I went to my car. The driver's side door had been left unlocked. The key was tucked under the mat. There was no Big Buggy in the backseat.

I punched Ranger's number into my cell phone. "Thanks," I said. "Did you get my car detailed?"

"There was a problem with blood on

your right front quarter panel, so Hal ran it through the car wash."

"Omigod."

"Nothing serious. Bugkowski slipped resisting arrest and smashed his face into your car."

"Where is he now?"

"Bugkowski was screaming like a little girl and drawing a crowd, and Hal didn't have the paperwork to justify a capture, so he had to let him go."

"Did Hal get my messenger bag?"

"Yes. He brought it back here to Rangeman. He didn't want to leave it in an unlocked car."

"Maybe you could mail it to me?" I asked.

I was really, really not ready to see him.

"You can run, but you can't hide," Ranger said.

So true. I hung up and headed for home. I stopped at the supermarket and had my cart half filled with groceries when I realized I had no money, no credit cards, no ID. It was all in my messenger bag . . . with Ranger. Damn.

I returned the groceries and called Morelli from my car.

"About tonight," I said. "Is it going to involve dinner?"

"Not unless you want to eat at midnight."

"Are you avoiding me?"

"I'm not that smart," Morelli said.

I sat for a long moment after Morelli hung up, reviewing my current choices. I could drive to Rangeman and retrieve my bag from Ranger. I could go home and share a cracker with Rex. I could mooch dinner from my mom.

Twenty minutes later, I was at my parents' house and Grandma was hustling to set a plate at the table for me. My mom had been making minestrone this morning, and that meant there'd also be antipasto, bread from the bakery, and rice pudding with Italian cookies.

"The table is set for four," I said to Grandma. "Who's coming to dinner?"

"This real interesting lady I met last week. I joined one of them bowling leagues, and she's on my team. You might want to talk to her. She's some kind of relationship counselor."

"I didn't know you could bowl."

"Turns out it's easy. You just gotta throw the ball down the alley. They gave me this shirt and everything. We're the LWB. That stands for Ladies with Balls."

My father was watching television in the living room. He rattled his newspaper and muttered something about women ruining bowling. He was watching national news and a bulletin came on showing a picture of a man found dead at LAX. He'd been hit with a blunt instrument, had his throat slashed, and he'd been stuffed into a trash can.

Ugh. As if this wasn't horrific enough, I was pretty sure it was the guy sitting next to me for the first leg of the Hawaii flight home. I'd spoken to him briefly in the beginning but slept for the rest of the trip. I'd been surprised to find his seat empty when we reboarded. My impression had been that he'd planned to fly into Newark. I guess this explained his absence.

The doorbell rang. Grandma rushed to get it and ushered a brown-haired, pleasantly plump, smiling, forty-something woman wearing an LWB bowling shirt into the living room.

"This is Annie Hart," she said. "She's the best bowler we got. She's our ringer."

I knew Annie Hart. I'd been involved in a Valentine's Day fiasco with her a while back and hadn't seen her since. She was a perfectly nice woman who lived in LaLa Land, firmly believing she was the reincarnation of Cupid. Hey, I mean, who am I to say, but it seemed far-fetched.

"How wonderful to see you again, dear," Annie said to me. "I think of you from time to time, wondering if you've resolved your romantic dilemma."

"Yep," I said. "It's all resolved."

"She got married in Hawaii," Grandma told Annie.

My father shot straight out of his chair. *"What?"*

"She had a ring and everything," Grandma said.

My father was wild-eyed. "Is that true? Why didn't someone tell me? No one ever tells me anything around here."

"Look," I said, holding my hand in the air. "I'm not wearing a ring. I'd be wearing a ring if I was married, right?"

"You got a ring *mark,*" Grandma said. "Of course, I guess there could be other explanations. You could have the vitiligo, like Michael Jackson. Remember when he turned white?"

My mother put two platters on the dining room table. "I have antipasto," she said. "And I have a bottle of red open."

My father went to the table shaking his head. "Vitiligo," he said. "What next?"

"Annie's been helping Lorraine Farnsworth with her love life," Grandma said, forking into a slice of hard cheese and prosciutto.

My mother looked over at Annie. "Lorraine is ninety-one years old."

"Yes," Annie said. "It's time for her to make a decision. She's been seeing Arnie Milhauser for fifty-three years. It might be time for her to move on."

My father had his head bent over his antipasto. "Only place she's gonna move on to is the bone farm."

"She's doing pretty good for her age," Grandma said. "Sure, she rolls her share of gutter balls, but heck, who don't."

"She's doing better now that we got her the longer tubing to her oxygen tank," Annie said.

Grandma nodded. "Yeah, that helped. She was on a short leash before."

I had my phone clipped to the waistband on my jeans, and it beeped with a text message. *We need to talk to you. It's urgent. Come outside.* It was signed *The FBI.*

I texted back *no.*

The next message was *Come outside or we're coming in.*

I pushed away from the table. "I'll be right back," I said. "I need to step outside for a moment."

"Probably got to let a breezer go," Grandma said to Annie. "That's always why I got to step outside."

My mother drained her wineglass and poured another.

I went to the front door, and saw they were the fake FBI guys. They were standing at the curb in front of a black

Lincoln. The bigger of the two, Lance Lancer, motioned me forward. I shook my head no. He pulled his badge out, held it up for me to see, and crooked his finger at me. I did another head shake.

"What do you want?" I yelled.

"We want to talk to you. Come here."

"Move away from the car. I'll meet you halfway."

"We're the FBI. You gotta come to us," Lancer said.

"You're not the FBI. I checked. Besides, the FBI doesn't ride around in big black Lincoln Town Cars."

"Maybe we got it on account of it was confiscated," Lancer said.

"What do you want?" I asked him.

"I told you we want to talk, and I can't be yelling to you. It's confidential."

I moved out of the house onto the walk. "I'll meet you halfway," I said again.

Lancer mumbled something to Slasher, and they marched over to where I was standing.

"We want the photograph you got on the plane," Lancer said. "Bad things are gonna happen if you don't give it to us."

"I told you. I don't have it."

"We don't believe you. We think you're fibbing to us," Lancer said.

Good lord. As if the vacation wasn't disastrous enough, now I'm involved in God knows what.

"I don't have it. I'm not fibbing. Go away and bother someone else," I told them.

Lancer's eyes opened wide. "Get her!" he said.

I whirled around and jumped away, but one of them managed to snag my shirt. I was yanked back, clawing and kicking. There was a lot of swearing and ineffective bitch-slapping, and somehow my foot connected with Slasher's boys. His face instantly went red and then chalk white. He doubled over, hands to his crotch, and he went to the ground in a fetal position. I ran into the house, locked the door, and looked out the window. Lancer was dragging his partner into the Lincoln.

I straightened my shirt and returned to the dinner table.

"Feel better?" Grandma asked.

"Yup," I said. "Everything's good."

"Your digestion will improve when we get your romantic problems solved," Annie said.

Little alarm bells went off in my head and my scalp prickled. *We?* Did she say *we*? I had enough trouble going on with the men in my life without Annie getting involved. Annie was a sweet person, but she was only a few steps behind Morelli's Grandma Bella in the Whacko of the Year competition.

"Honestly, I haven't got any romantic problems," I told Annie. "It's all peachy."

"Of course it is," Annie said. And she winked at me.

"I hate to rush everyone, but we gotta get a move on," Grandma said. "Bowling starts at seven o'clock, and you gotta get there early or all the good shoes are gone and only the fungus shoes are left. I'm going to get my own shoes, but I have to wait for my Social Security check."

Rushing through dinner is never a problem. My father doesn't waste unnecessary minutes on bodily functions.

He slurps his soup down boiling hot, has seconds, mops the bowl with a crust of bread, and expects to immediately move on to dessert. This no-nonsense approach to dinner gets him back to the television in record time and cuts down on time spent tuning out Grandma.

"I was talking to Mrs. Kulicki at the bakery today, and she said she heard Joyce Barnhardt was mixed up in something bad and got compacted at the junkyard," Grandma said, helping herself to an almond cookie.

"How awful," my mother said. "How would Mrs. Kulicki know such a thing? I haven't heard anything."

Grandma dunked her cookie in her coffee. "Mrs. Kulicki's son Andy works at the junkyard, and it came from him."

That would be a real bummer if it were true. It was a pain in the ass to get money back on a dead FTA. Especially when the body was incorporated into the bumper of an SUV. Plus, I suppose I'd miss Joyce, in a perverse, sick sort of way.

After Grandma and Annie took off, I helped my mom with the dishes and spent a few minutes watching television with my dad. No one mentioned rings or marriage. My family solves problems with silence and meat loaf. Our philosophy is, if you don't talk about a problem, it might go away. And if it doesn't go away, there's always meat loaf, mac and cheese, roast chicken, pineapple upside-down cake, pasta, potatoes, or baloney on white bread to take your mind off unpleasant things.

My mother sent me home with a bag of cookies, a half-pound of deli ham, provolone, and a loaf of bakery bread. If you come to eat at my mom's house, you leave with something in a bag.

I stopped at the entrance to my apartment building parking lot and did a fast survey. No black Lincoln Town Car in sight, and I was sure I hadn't been followed. So probably it was safe to go to my apartment. I took the stairs, walked the second-floor hall, and listened at my door. Silence. I pushed the door open and peeked in. No fake FBI guys lurking in the kitchen. Most likely, Slasher was sitting somewhere icing down his privates. I'd made a good connection. Imagine what sort of damage I could inflict if I actually knew what I was doing.

I gave Rex part of a cookie, went to my computer, and searched around until I found a news story on the man murdered at LAX. His name was Richard Crick. Age fifty-six. Surgeon. Had an office in Princeton. He'd been in Hawaii attending a professional conference. Police were speculating it was a random robbery gone bad.

I suspected different. Crick had something valuable . . . the photograph. For whatever reason, he slipped the photograph of the man into my bag while I was sleeping. And then either he fingered me before he died, or else a bunch of people figured it out. I had no clue as to the significance of the photograph, and didn't especially want to know.

I tapped Crick into one of the bonds

office background search programs and watched the information scroll down. He'd been an army doctor for ten years. Three were in Afghanistan. Three in Germany. The rest Stateside. He'd gone into private practice when he left the army. Divorced. Two adult sons. One living in Michigan, and one in North Carolina. Squeaky clean until a year and a half ago, when he was hit with a wrongful death malpractice claim. So far as I could see, the claim was still pending. He owned a home in Mill Town. The latest appraisal was $350,000. He owed $175,000 on his mortgage. He drove a two-year-old Accord. No other litigation. No liens. No reports of bad credit. All in all, a pretty boring guy.

No point to sneaking into his house and his office and looking around. I was coming to this game late. The fake FBI, the legitimate FBI, local police, employees, and relatives would already have combed through everything.

I remoted the television on and surfed around, finally settling on the Food Channel. I fell asleep halfway through a

Food Truck special and didn't wake up until eleven-thirty. I checked my phone for messages, found none, and went to bed.

FIVE

I awoke disoriented. The room was dark. An alarm was going off. I was next to a warm body. Morelli. He reached across me and shut the alarm off. The alarm had been coming from his cell phone.

"What the heck?" I said. "What time is it?"

"It's five o'clock. Gotta go. Early briefing. And I need to go home and feed Bob before I leave for work."

"When did you get here?"

"Around midnight. You were asleep."

"So you just crawled under the covers? I thought we were having issues."

He slipped out of bed. "I was tired. This was easy."

"Easy?" I was up on an elbow. "Excuse me? *Easy*?"

"Yeah, I didn't have to talk to you." He kicked around in the dark, picking clothes off the floor. "These boxers are mine, right?"

"Who else would they belong to?"

"Could be anyone's," Morelli said.

I rolled my eyes and switched the bedside light on. "Does this help?"

He tugged his jeans on. "Thanks."

Now that the room was partially lit, I could see the Band-Aid across Morelli's nose, and his black eye. The fight in Hawaii had been violent but short, terrifying to witness and infuriating to remember. Ranger had needed seven stitches to close the cut under his eye, and he'd cracked a bone in his hand rearranging Morelli's face.

"How's your nose?" I asked Morelli.

"Better. The swelling's down."

"That fight was *horrible*!"

"I've been in worse."

I knew this to be true. Morelli'd had some wild years.

I sat up and hugged the quilt to my chest. "I was afraid you were going to kill each other."

"I was trying," Morelli said, sitting in my chair, pulling on socks. "Remember, you're talking to Berger this morning. And don't mess with him. He can make trouble for you if he wants." He came to the bedside and gave me a fast kiss. "I'll try to get away earlier tonight."

"I might have plans with Lula."

He took his gun off the nightstand and clipped it to his belt. "Don't mess with me, either. I'm running with a short fuse these days."

Jeez Louise.

I thrashed around in bed for a couple hours, trying to get back to sleep and having no luck. I finally rolled out of bed around eight and out of the apartment around nine. My plan was to stop in at the bonds bus before heading off to the FBI.

Traffic was slow on Hamilton, and I saw the reason for the gridlock when I was half a block from the bus. The bus was no more. A couple orange traffic cones marked the area of destruction. Beyond the cones lay the smoldering, blackened cadaver of twisted metal and stinking charred upholstery that used to be the bonds bus. I parked across the street, behind Vinnie's Cadillac, Lula's Firebird, and Connie's Hyundai. DeAngelo's Mercedes was noticeably missing. Vinnie, Lula, and Connie were on the sidewalk, eyes glazed, aimlessly staring at the mess.

"I'm thinkin' lightning," Lula said. "This here looks like a natural disaster. I'm thinkin' the lightning came in through the fan in the crapper and snaked around inside until it found the microwave, and then *BANG.*"

"There was no lightning last night," Connie said. "It hasn't rained in days."

"Well then, my next theory is terrorist," Lula said. "A suicide bomber."

"Why would a suicide bomber blow up the bonds bus?" Connie asked.

"They don't need a reason," Lula said. "They just be walking around with bombs stuck up their butt, and when they feel like pushin' the button—*KA-*

BOOM—there's terrorist guts everywhere. Maybe one of them walked by the bus and smelled doughnuts, so he went in, ate a doughnut, and blew himself up."

I was pretty sure it wasn't a terrorist who destroyed the bus. I was pretty sure it was DeAngelo, and I knew Connie was thinking the same thing. Neither of us was saying anything because we didn't want to set Vinnie off on a screaming rampage. Although it seemed unlikely, as he was currently one shade from comatose.

"Terrorist," Vinnie said. "Yeah, that makes sense."

"Lucille must have fed him a Valium smoothie this morning," I said to Connie.

Connie looked over at Vinnie. "He's been here since three this morning. He's as fried as the bus."

"Can we still operate?" I asked her.

"Yes. We lost the bus but not much else. I've been working off my laptop, and it travels with me. We lost a lot of files in the fire that took out the original office, but we didn't lose anything with *this* fire. It's all electronic now."

I glanced at Lula. She was dressed in black. Black faux lizard-skin cowboy boots, black jeans that looked like they were painted on her, black tank top with an acre of boob squishing out. Pink hair.

My curiosity was raised. "What's with the black?" I wanted to know. "You never wear all black."

"I told you yesterday, I'm gettin' serious. I'm not takin' this job lightly no more. I'm channeling my inner Ranger, and I'm wearing black like him. I figure he's on to something with the black deal."

"He wears black so he doesn't have to match socks in the morning."

"See, that's what I'm sayin'. It's about being efficient. Get the job done. *Wham.* That's gonna be my new motto. *Wham.* Now that I'm in black, I'm thinking I could catch Joyce Barnhardt. No problemo."

"It might not be that easy," I said. "There's a rumor going around that Barnhardt's been compacted."

"Darn," Lula said. "That would take all the fun out of capturing her."

"I heard the same rumor," Connie said.

"Too bad," Lula said. "I was ready to be all over Barnhardt. I was ready to *wham* her."

"I need to talk to a couple guys downtown this morning," I said to Lula. "It shouldn't take long. I'll pick you up when I'm done, and we'll go to the junkyard."

"Being that we don't have a bonds bus no more, I'll be at the coffee shop," Lula said. "I'm thinking about having one of them cinnamon rolls. What would Ranger eat?"

"He'd have half a bagel with a small amount of cream cheese and some smoked salmon."

Lula shook her head. "That man don't know much about eating."

SIX

I left the fire scene, drove down Hamilton, and spotted the tail when I turned onto Broad. Black Lincoln two cars back. Most likely they were with me when I left my apartment, and I hadn't been paying attention. The FBI had offices in a building in the center of the city. There was underground parking, but I chose not to use it. Even when security cameras were in play, I felt vulnerable in a parking garage. I found on-street parking half a block away, locked up, and walked to the FBI building. I waved at the Lincoln as it rolled past, but no one waved back or beeped the horn. Guess Lancer and Slasher were busy thinking up a new cover, since FBI was obviously out.

Berger's office was on the sixth floor. He had a small cubby with a desk and two chairs. I imagined Gooley had an identical cubby somewhere in the vast room filled with cubbies.

"Did you bring the photo?" Berger asked.

I sat in one of his chairs. "I don't have the photo."

Berger blew out a sigh. "Did you *ever* have the photo?"

"Yes. I discovered it when I got home. I had no idea how it got into my bag or what it was. There wasn't any writing on it. No name or address. I assumed I'd grabbed it by mistake when I bought magazines for the flight. So I threw it away."

"Any chance of retrieving it?"

"No, I tried. The garbage had already been picked up."

"Was it a man or a woman?" Berger asked.

"You don't know?"

He shook his head. "To my knowledge, only one person knew the identity of the person in the photo, and that person is dead."

"Would that dead person happen to be Richard Crick, the doctor who got stuffed into the trash can at LAX?"

"Bingo."

"It was a photo of a guy standing on a street corner," I told Berger. "Casual. Not posed. Completely unexceptional. No piercings or tattoos. Just a nice-looking guy. Somewhere around forty. Short brown hair. Fair-skinned. He was wearing a dark suit."

"Did you recognize the street corner?"

"No. It could have been anywhere. It looked like an office building in the background. No vegetation, so I don't know if it was Hawaii, Oregon, or New York."

"Would you recognize this guy if you saw him again?"

"Hard to say. Maybe. I didn't pay a lot of attention to the photo."

"I'd like to set you up with an artist,"

Berger said. "At this point, *anything* is better than nothing."

"Do I want to know why this photo is so important?"

"No. *I* don't even know. And I don't *want* to know. Something to do with national security."

"I'm being harassed by two men posing as FBI. Morelli ran them through the system, and they're not with the Bureau."

"American?"

"Yes."

"It's possible you'll also have some foreign nationals sniffing around," Berger said.

"Great. What am I supposed to do with these people?"

"Don't let them get too close. I imagine some of them are nasty buggers."

"Shouldn't you be protecting me?"

"Protection got cut from the budget. Come back tomorrow, same time. I'll have a forensic artist here. We'll see if you can give us anything useful."

I left the building and found Ranger lounging against my parked car, arms crossed over his chest, his expression unreadable, his posture relaxed. My messenger bag hung from his shoulder. He had a Band-Aid covering the stitches under his eye. The Band-Aid was a couple shades lighter than his skin. Ranger's heritage was Cuban and his look was Latino. He was multilingual, ambidextrous, and street-smart. He was formerly Special Forces. He was my age. He was more big jungle cat than golden retriever.

"You're driving without a license and probably no money or credit cards," Ranger said.

"It seemed like the lesser of two evils."

There was the hint of a twitch at the corner of his mouth, as if he might be thinking about smiling. "Are you saying I'm evil?"

Ranger was playing with me. Hard to tell if that was a good thing or a bad thing.

"I'm saying I don't know where I'm going with you," I told him.

"Would you like me to make some suggestions?"

“No! You made enough suggestions in Hawaii.”

“You made some of your own,” he said. His gaze dropped to my hand. “You’re still wearing my mark on your ring finger. Not as legal as a wedding band, but it would qualify you for a good time.”

“That ring mark got you seven stitches and a broken bone in your hand.”

“At least Morelli fights clean.”

“What’s that supposed to mean?”

“Babe, you stun-gunned me on the back of my neck.”

“Yeah, and it wasn’t easy with the two of you rolling around on the ground, whaling away at each other.”

Actually, I had stunned both of them, cuffed them while they were immobilized, and drove them to the emergency room. Then I changed out my plane ticket for an earlier flight, called Lula, and took off before they were finished getting stitched and patched. Not only did I want to put distance between us, but I thought it smart to leave the island before getting charged with illegal use of an illegal stun gun. Sometimes there's a fine line between a cowardly act and a brilliant decision, and my brilliant decision had been to get out of Honolulu and leave the stun gun behind.

Ranger transferred the messenger bag from his shoulder to mine, pulled me into him, and kissed me like he meant it. "Let me know if the guys following you in the Lincoln get too bothersome," he said, opening the door to my car.

No point asking how Ranger knew about the Lincoln. Ranger pretty much knows everything.

• • •

I slid behind the wheel of the RAV, cranked it over, and drove to the coffee shop. Lula and Connie were in the table area by the front window. Connie was working on her laptop, and Lula was drinking coffee, paging through a magazine.

"Is this the new office?" I asked Connie.

"Until I come up with something better. DeAngelo says the building will be done in three weeks. Hard to believe."

"Did he say that before or after he firebombed the bus?" I asked her.

"After. I just spoke to him."

Lula picked her head up. "You think DeAngelo did the bus?"

"It's a theory," I said.

I got a Frappuccino and a big cookie, and suggested to Lula that we head over to the junkyard to check out the rumor about Joyce.

"Hard to believe Joyce is dead," Lula said. "She's too mean to die. It'd be like killing the Devil. You see what I'm saying? I bet it's damn hard to kill the Devil."

We piled into the Firebird, and Lula cut through town and motored up Stark Street, past the mom-and-pop chop shops, groceries, bars, and pawnshops. The groceries and pawnshops gave way to crack houses, third-world sanitation, and hollow-eyed stoop sitters. The crack houses gave way to the burned-out, rat-riddled slums of no-man's-land, where only the crazies and the most desperate existed. And the junkyard rose fortress-like and defiant, a mountain of heavy metal and fiberglass discard, beyond no-man's-land.

Lula parked in the junkyard lot and tried to gauge her distance from the big electromagnet that swung the cars into the compactor.

"They better not get the wrong idea about my Firebird," she said.

"You're good," I told her. "You're in the visitor parking area."

"Yeah, but if these people were smart, they wouldn't be working in a junkyard at the end of the world."

No argument there. It wasn't so much the junkyard as it was the proximity to Hell. Connie's cousin Manny Rosolli owned the junkyard. I knew him in a remote sort of way, and he seemed like a nice man. And since 80 percent of Connie's family was mob, this gave Manny a certain amount of security in spite of the precarious location.

I found the trailer that served as an office and asked for Andy, the son of Grandma's friend Mrs. Kulicki. I was told he was stacking cars, and I was directed to the part of the lot where cars were stored when they came out of the compactor. Fortunately, the compactor wasn't currently in use, so I was spared the sound of cars getting crushed to death.

It was easy to find Andy since he was the only one there. Plus, he was wearing a bright orange jumpsuit with his name embroidered in black. He was a gangly tattooed guy with multiple piercings. I was guessing nineteen or twenty years old.

"You got a ankle bracelet on, too?" Lula asked him.

"This isn't prison clothes," Andy said. "It's so the crusher guy can see me, so I don't get a car dropped on me."

"I'm looking for Joyce Barnhardt," I told him.

"You might have a hard time finding her," he said. "She could have got compacted. I was cleaning up, and I found her driver's license on the ground, along with a smashed lady's high heel shoe and a lipstick. You'd be surprised what gets shook loose after the crusher. There's all kinds of stuff falling out of these cars when they get picked up and stacked."

"Where's the car now?"

"Dunno. No way to tell which car it came from."

"Did you tell the police?" I asked him.

"Nope. I told the office. But they said when it comes to suspecting bodies in the crusher, we have a 'Don't Ask, Don't Tell' policy."

"What happened to the license and the shoe?"

"Threw them away. The license was all torn and bent, and the shoe was a mess and it smelled real bad. Anyway, the office said no one ever comes to claim stuff that's been shook from the crusher."

"Probably, the junkyard's doing big disposal business since they put the surveillance cameras up at the landfill," Lula said. "I bet you could bring a cadaver dog here, and he wouldn't know where to go first."

SEVEN

"I'm hungry," Lula said, pulling out of the junkyard. "What would Ranger eat for lunch? I bet he'd be up for a bucket of fried chicken."

"He usually grabs a sandwich at Rangeman. Roast beef on multigrain. Or a turkey club."

"I could do that. What else does he eat?"

"An apple sometimes. And water."

"Say what? Is that it? How could he live on that? What about chips? What about a root beer float? And how many of those roast beef sandwiches does he eat for lunch?"

"One sandwich. No chips."

"That's un-American. He's not stimulating the economy like that. I'd feel it was my patriotic duty to at least have chips."

Lula stopped at a deli on the first block of Stark.

"This looks sketchy," I said. "The window is dirty, and I just saw a rat run out the front door."

"I've been here before," she said. "They give you a half-pound of meat on your sandwich, and they throw in pickles for free. If I'm only gonna have one sandwich, this is the place."

It looked to me like they threw in food poisoning for free, too. "I'll pass."

"You have no spirit of culinary adventure. You need to be more like that snarky guy on the Travel Channel. He goes all over the world eating kangaroo assholes and snail throw-up. He'd eat anything. He don't care how sick he gets. He's another one of my role models, except he needs ironing." She took her big silver Glock out of her purse and handed it over to me. "You wait here and don't let anyone take my car."

I hefted the Glock, aiming it out the window at an empty street corner. My own gun was smaller, a Smith & Wesson .45 revolver. I'd gotten it from Ranger when I first started doing bond enforcement and Connie had asked him to mentor me. He was scary tough and mysteriously complex back then. He isn't so different now. He's abandoned his Special Forces camo fatigues for Rangeman black, he's dropped the ghetto accent and lost the ponytail as his business needs changed, but he's still a tough guy with lots of secrets.

Lula hustled out of the deli with a large plastic food container in one hand, a massive wax paper–wrapped sandwich in the other, and a two-liter bottle of soda under her arm.

"He put all my free pickles right into the sandwich," she said, sliding behind the wheel. "And I got some homemade potato salad instead of chips. It was half price."

Oh boy. Bargain potato salad from

the Rats-R-Us. "The potato salad might not be a good idea," I said.

Lula opened the lid and sniffed. "Smells okay." She dug in with her plastic fork. "Tastes okay. Got a tang to it." She unwrapped her sandwich, ate half, and washed it down with some soda.

I tried not to grimace. I didn't want to ruin her eating experience, but I was getting queasy inhaling the meat and mayo fumes. I had my window down and my head halfway out when the Lincoln pulled up alongside.

Lancer made a gun with his hand, index finger pointed at me. "Bang," he said.

I still had Lula's Glock in my lap. I raised it and pointed it at Lancer, and he drove away.

"What was that about?" Lula asked.

"It's complicated."

"I'm getting real tired of hearing *it's complicated.* Would you say something like that to Ranger? I don't think so. I bet he calls you *Babe* and you tell him everything he wants to know."

I tell Ranger nothing. Ranger isn't a talker. Ranger reveals very little and doesn't encourage verbal spewing on the part of others.

"On the way home from Hawaii, I accidentally picked up a photograph of a man," I said to Lula. "I didn't know who he was or how I got the photograph, so I threw it away. Turns out it's one of a kind, it's tied to national security somehow, and now I'm the only one who knows what the guy looks like. The FBI is searching for the guy, and the two morons who just drove by are searching for the guy. And it's possible there are other people searching for the guy."

"And you say you're the only one who knows what he looks like?"

"Yeah."

"Do you know where this guy lives?"

"I don't know anything about him."

"This makes you real special," Lula said. "It's like you're a reality show, all by yourself."

Lula finished her sandwich and her tub of potato salad, and we looked over my list of skips.

"I'm just not excited about any of this," Lula said. "Now that I'm gonna be operating at Ranger level, I need more of a challenge. Where's the killers and the serial rapists? How come we don't have any of them? The best we got is Joyce, and she's not looking so difficult. If she's not dead, she's out there with only one shoe and no driver's license."

Joyce was weighing on me. She wasn't my favorite person, but I didn't like thinking she'd been crushed and discarded. *No one* should be crushed and discarded. I punched Morelli's number into my phone.

Morelli answered with a sigh.

"Is that you?" I asked him.

"Yup."

"Are you busy?"

"I'm up to my knees in blood and paperwork. I don't know which is worse. What did you have in mind?"

"Have you heard the rumor about Joyce Barnhardt getting compacted?"

Nothing for a beat. "No."

"Well, there's a rumor. It originated with Andy Kulicki. He works at the junkyard. I was just there, and Andy said the crusher shook loose a woman's high heel shoe, a lipstick, and Joyce's driver's license. You might want to go over there with a cadaver dog."

"Boy, I'm really happy to hear that, because I was hoping for another murder."

"I thought it was my civic duty to pass it on."

"You give me heartburn," Morelli said. And he disconnected.

"Well?" Lula's eyebrow raised.

"He said I gave him heartburn."

"That's not real romantic."

"He has a hard job."

"Me, too," Lula said. "I got heartburn, too."

"You have heartburn because you ate at the Rat Café."

"You could be right. It tasted okay, but it's not sitting so good in my stomach. Maybe I just need more soda." Lula drank more soda and burped. "Oh yeah," she said, "that's better."

"I'm going to take another shot at Lewis Bugkowski," I said. "This time, I'll use my stun gun and Flexi-Cuffs."

Actually, stun guns are illegal in New Jersey as well as Hawaii, but like carrying concealed, Trenton is pretty much unofficially exempt.

"WHAM!" Lula said. "Let's do it. Where's he live?"

"Pulling Street."

Lula turned onto Broad, cut across town, and started to sweat.

"Are you okay?" I asked her. "You're sweating, and your face isn't its usual color."

"What color is it?"

"Asparagus."

"I might be coming down with the flu."

"How about food poisoning?"

"I feel like my stomach's getting all swelled up," Lula said. "It's not fitting in my pants no more. And it's doing funny sounds. I might need a bathroom."

"Can you make it to the coffee shop?"

"Yeah, I just have to drive faster. You probably want to close your eyes."

Three minutes later, she slid to a stop in front of the coffee shop.

"I'm gonna make a run for it," Lula said. "Just stay out of my way, because when I stand up all hell's liable to break loose."

She kicked her door open and took off.

"Outta my way! Comin' through!" she yelled.

She disappeared into the restroom at the back of the coffee shop, and moments later two women ran out.

I bought a ham-and-cheese sandwich and joined Connie at the table in the window.

"Lula ate some green roast beef and half-price potato salad," I said to Connie.

"You play, you pay," Connie said. "How'd it go at the junkyard?"

"Andy found a shoe and Joyce's driver's license in the crusher area."

"Were you able to trace it back to a car?"

"No. Turns out your cousin Manny has a loosey-goosey policy about stuff that gets dumped out of the crusher."

"It's junkyard etiquette to never look in the trunk," Connie said.

The restroom door crashed open, and Lula staggered out. "I'm dying," she said. "Do I look like I'm dying?"

"You've looked better," I told her. "Do

you want me to drive you around the block to the emergency room?"

"Thanks for offering, but I'm taking myself home. And I'm never eating potato salad again. There should be a law against potato salad."

I finished my sandwich and stood. "Places to go. People to capture."

"If I'm not here, I'll be on my cell," Connie said. "I have some short-term offices to look at."

• • •

I left the coffee shop and drove to Buggy's house. I was better prepared today. I had plastic Flexi-Cuffs in my back pocket and my hand wrapped around my stun gun when I knocked on his front door.

"Boy, am I glad to see you," Buggy said, looking out at me. "I need to borrow your car. I need to go to the drugstore to get a box of Band-Aids."

He had a gash on his forehead and a cotton roll stuck up each nostril. I suspected this was damage from his run-in with my RAV4 yesterday.

"I have a better idea," I said. "I'll drive you."

"Nuh-ah. I like to drive."

I pressed the stun-gun prongs against his chest and pushed the go button. Nothing happened. Low battery.

Buggy snatched my bag from my shoulder. "Your keys are in here, right?"

"No! Give it back."

He rummaged around in the bag, found the keys, and dropped the bag on the ground.

"Thanks. I was wondering how I was gonna get a Band-Aid," he said, knocking me aside, muscling his way to the car and wedging himself behind the wheel.

I watched Buggy drive away, and I called Ranger. "You're not going to believe what just happened."

"Babe, it's getting so I'll believe just about anything."

"The big dopey guy took my car again."

Silence for a beat. "Maybe it'd be easier if I gave him a car of his own," Ranger finally said. "Does he have your bag?"

"No."

"I'll send Hal out to get your car. What about you? Is Lula rescuing you again?"

"No."

Another moment of silence. "Am I?"

"Would you like to?" I asked him.

EIGHT

The black 911 Porsche turbo eased to a stop in front of Buggy's house, and I angled into the car. Ranger was wearing the Rangeman uniform of black T-shirt and black cargo pants. He was armed, as usual. And also as usual, there was the subtle, lingering, tantalizing hint of his Bulgari shower gel.

"As long as we're together," I said to him, "would you have time to get me into a locked house in Hamilton Township?"

"I have a four o'clock meeting. Until then, I'm all yours."

I gave him the address and told him about Joyce. Twenty minutes later, Ranger parked next to an electrician's panel van in front of the Mercado Mews model home, and we walked a block and a half to Joyce's town house. Best not to have your car sitting in front of a house you're breaking into. We rang the bell and knocked on the front door. When no one answered, we circled to the back of the house, and Ranger stood hands on hips, looking at the bullet holes in the door to the privacy fence.

"It was locked," I said to Ranger.

"So you shot it?"

"Actually, Lula shot it."

Ranger pushed it open, and we went into Joyce's yard. I closed and locked the gate behind us, and Ranger tried the back door. Locked. He removed a slim case from one of the pockets in his cargo pants, selected a tool, opened the door, and Joyce's security alarm went off. He pulled me into the house and locked the door.

"Start working your way through the house while I watch for the police,"

Ranger said. "You probably have ten to fifteen minutes."

"Then what?"

"Then we hide and wait. There are no signs of forced entry into the house, so the police will walk around, look in windows, test the doors, and leave, probably."

I started in the kitchen, going through cupboards and drawers, snooping in the refrigerator, trying to ignore the alarm. I'd just finished the kitchen when Ranger signaled that the police were here. He pulled me into a broom closet and closed the door.

It was pitch-black in the closet. The alarm timed out, and the house went silent.

"How will we know when the police leave?" I asked Ranger.

"There was a Rangeman car in the area. I have them watching a couple blocks away, and they'll call when the police leave."

His arms were around me, holding me close against him. He was warm, and his breathing was even. Mine was more ragged.

"There's something hard poking into me," I said.

He shifted slightly. "It's my gun."

"Are you sure?"

"You could check it out."

Tempting, but I didn't want to encourage anything that might lead to nudity and compromising positions should the police decide to break into the house and open the door to the closet. Although, the longer I was pressed against him, the less I cared about the police.

Here's the thing about Ranger. He leads a dangerous lifestyle. He's scarred from past life choices, and he's dealing with serious issues. I have no idea what those issues are, because Ranger holds them private. I suspect no one will ever know what drives Ranger. What I know with certainty is that I'll never be more than a loving amusement for him. He'll care for me as best he can, but I'll never be his priority. I've come to believe his priority is to repair his karma. And I respect that. It's a noble priority. Problem is, while he's repairing his karma, I'm lusting after his body. Morelli is a wonderful lover. He's fun. He's satisfying. He's super sexy. Ranger is magic.

Ranger's phone rang, giving the all clear. I moved to open the closet door, and he tightened his hold on me. His mouth skimmed along my neck. His hand slid under my shirt to my breast. And he kissed me.

"That's not your gun, is it?" I asked him.

"No," he said. "It's not my gun."

When I finally tumbled out of the closet, I was missing some critical pieces of clothing, but I was feeling much more relaxed.

"Finish your search," Ranger said. "The Rangeman car will let us know if the police return."

We went through the rest of the house, and just before we left, I checked out the garage. No car.

"What does this mean?" I asked Ranger.

"No way to know, but the junkyard will have a log of cars taken in. Connie can probably get her cousin to go through the log. Did you report the found driver's license to the police?"

"Yes. I told Morelli."

"Then I'm sure he's there with a cadaver dog. He's an idiot, but he's a good cop."

"Why is he an idiot?"

"He lets me get close to you." Ranger glanced at his watch. "I have to go."

We set the alarm off again when we opened the door to leave. No problem. We'd be long gone by the time the police returned.

• • •

My car and Hal were waiting for me when Ranger dropped me off at the coffee shop.

"Your car was parked at Quaker Bridge Mall," Hal said. "The big guy was in the mall somewhere. We looked in the food court, but we couldn't find him, so we brought the car back here. Problem is, there's no key."

"I have an extra key at home."

"Great," Hal said. "Give me a minute, and I'll get the car running for you. You can take it from there."

I didn't see Connie in the coffee shop,

so I waited for Hal to roll the engine over, thanked him, and drove home. I was on Hamilton when my phone rang.

"Hi," Buggy said. "Boy, I'm real sorry, but someone stole your car. I parked it in a good spot where it wouldn't get any dings, and it's not there anymore. There's just a empty space. You should report it to the police or something."

"I have the car. A friend found it at the mall and brought it back to me. Where are you now?"

"I'm still at the mall."

"I thought you were going to the drugstore."

"I changed my mind," he said. "I needed new sneakers."

"Stay where you are, and I'll come pick you up and give you a ride home."

"Okay. I'll be at the food court entrance."

I raced back to my apartment, picked up my extra key, and took off for the mall. I cut over to Route 1 and made a plan. I couldn't stun him, so I probably wouldn't be able to cuff him. I'd just get him in the car and drive him to the police station. I'd pull into the back drop-off and let the police wrestle him out of the front seat. If he got unruly, I'd go to the nearest fast-food drive-thru and distract him with a bag of burgers.

I took the mall exit, cruised through the lot, and idled at the food court entrance. No Buggy. I hung there for five minutes. Still no Buggy. Probably got tired of waiting. I parked and ran inside to see if I could spot him in the food court. No luck. I got soft-serve ice cream, vanilla and chocolate swirl, and returned to the lot.

No car. My car was gone. I punched Buggy's number into my cell phone.

"Yuh," Buggy said.

"Did you take my car again?"

"Yeah, thanks."

"You need to bring it back. I have no way to get home."

"I'm going to the movies."

"This is really rotten of you," I said. "Out of the goodness of my heart, I volunteered to come get you, and now you've stolen my car."

"I didn't steal it. I only borrowed it."

"Bring it back!"

"What?" Buggy said. "I can't hear you. Must be bad reception."

The line went dead.

"Jeez Louise!" I yelled. "Stupid! Stupid! Stupid!" I thunked the heel of my hand against my forehead so hard I almost lost my ice cream. "I hate him," I said. "He should rot in hell."

An elderly woman walked out of the mall and cut a wide path around me, murmuring about drugs and young people.

"Sorry," I called after her. "Someone stole my car."

Get a grip, I told myself. It's just a car. It wasn't even a *good* car. That wasn't the issue, of course. The issue was that I got outsmarted by a moron.

I found a bench by the mall entrance and ate my ice cream. No way was I calling Ranger. It was too embarrassing. I couldn't call Lula. She was sick. Connie was busy looking for a temporary office. I didn't want to slow that process. If I called my mother, I'd get the *Why Don't You Have a Nice Job in a Bank* lecture. I could walk, but it would take me all day, and I'd probably get hit by a truck on the highway. A cab would be expensive.

I was sitting on the bench debating all this when Grandma and Annie Hart walked out of the mall.

"For goodness sakes," Grandma said, spotting me. "Are you sitting here waiting for a criminal?"

"More or less," I said. "What are you doing here?"

"Annie took me shopping to get bowling shoes, on account of I got my Social Security check."

Grandma drove with a lead foot and had lost her license several years back after racking up a bunch of speeding tickets. So Grandma was now dependent on other, more sane drivers for transportation.

"I'm having car problems," I said. "Can I hitch a ride with you?"

"Of course," Annie said. "I've been wanting to talk to you anyway."

"What's it this time?" Grandma asked me. "Did your car get blown up, smashed by a garbage truck, or stolen?"

I followed them into the parking lot. "Stolen. Don't tell my mother."

Annie's eyes widened. "Did you report it to the police?"

"Not yet," I told her. "I'll wait to see if it's returned."

"This happens to her a lot," Grandma said to Annie. "It's no big deal. We got a extra Buick in the garage she can use."

We all climbed into Annie's red Jetta, and Annie drove out of the parking lot onto Route 1.

"I'm going to be smokin' in these shoes," Grandma said, opening the box, looking at her new shoes. "Next month, I'm getting my own ball."

"It's important to have the proper equipment," Annie said.

"You should take up bowling," Grandma said to me. "There are some hot men at the bowling alley. It could be just what a young divorcée like you needs."

"I have enough hot men in my life already," I said. "In fact, I have one too many."

"You should make a decision," Annie

said. "I'm sure in your heart you know your true love. Just go with your heart."

It wasn't that easy. My heart was confused. My brain didn't want either of the men in my life. And my hooha wanted both of them!

"I could make a potion up for you that would simplify everything," Annie said.

"Thanks," I said, "but I'd rather not get involved with potions."

"They're perfectly safe," Annie said. "We're very high tech in our potion making now. I'm even a member of the APMA. American Potion Makers Association."

"Maybe I should take up making potions," Grandma said. "I've been thinking about coming out of retirement. Potions might be a good business to get into. How do you join that APMA?"

"You can join online," Annie said. "Just go to their website."

"Is it just love potions?" Grandma wanted to know. "Or can you make all kinds of potions?"

"I specialize in love potions," Annie

said. "But potions can solve a wide range of issues."

"I'll have to think about it," Grandma said. "I want to have a good specialty."

• • •

By the time Grandma and I got dropped off at my parents' house, it was after five o'clock, and I could smell chicken frying all the way out to the street. My original intention had been to zip into the house, get the key to the Buick, and track down Buggy. Now that I was smelling my mom's fried chicken, I was having second thoughts. I could stay for dinner and go after Buggy later. In fact, the heck with capturing Buggy today. Better to go after him tomorrow with a fully charged stun gun.

Grandma hustled into the house and went straight to the kitchen. "We found Stephanie at the mall," she said to my mother. "She's going to have dinner with us."

My mother was at the stove, turning pieces of chicken in her big fry pan. "I'm trying a new recipe. I found it in a magazine. And there's mashed potatoes and green beans. And before I forget, there were two men here looking for you. They said they were FBI."

My heart stopped beating for a moment. "Did they give their names?"

"One was named Lancer and the other was Slasher," my mother said. "They seemed nice. Very polite. I told them I didn't know where you were, and they went away."

"What's that about?" Grandma asked. "Are you tracking down some famous criminal? I bet it's someone on the Ten Most Wanted list."

"It's a misunderstanding," I said. "If there was someone in the area on the Ten Most Wanted list, Ranger would get that job, not me. I'll catch up with them tomorrow."

I set the table and wandered into the living room to say hello to my dad.

"Look at this," he said, gesturing to the television. "There's more on that guy who got stuffed into the garbage can. They're saying now they think he was drugged before he was snuffed and stuffed into the can. It's not official or anything, but that's what a security guard said. And I guess there's a woman involved."

"A woman?"

"They're referring to her as a person of interest. You know what that means. The kiss of death. The person of interest is always the killer."

I hated to think that was true, since I might be the person of interest.

My grandmother joined us. "Are you talking about the garbage can killer? I heard the dead guy was a doctor in the army, and he might have been a spy when he was over there in Afghanistan." She sucked on her dentures. "That spying catches up to you. One minute you're a spy, and next thing, you're dead in a garbage can. Unless you're James Bond. Nothing stops him. He's balls to the wall."

My father hunkered deeper into his chair and turned the volume up on the television.

"Shut the television off!" my mother yelled from the dining room. "It's too loud, and dinner's ready."

I took my seat at the table, and my phone rang.

"I'm at the junkyard," Morelli said. "The dog found a body, but we haven't been able to view it. We haven't got a big enough can opener."

"Only one body?"

"So far. The dog's still working. Where are you?"

"I'm having dinner at my parents' house. My mom made fried chicken."

"Oh man, that's cruel. I love your mom's fried chicken."

"I'll bring some back to my apartment for you."

"This could take a while," Morelli said.

"Whatever."

"Who was that?" Grandma asked when I hung up. "Was that Ranger?"

"No. It was Morelli."

"It's hard to keep up with it all," Grandma said. "I don't know how you do it. You're married, and then you're not married, and then you're saving chicken for Morelli."

I couldn't keep up with it, either. I didn't know what the heck I was doing.

"You need Annie to help you," Grandma said. "She's real smart. She's fixing up everyone at bowling. She even had a man in mind for me, but I told her he was too old. I don't want some flabby, wrinkled codger to take care of. I want a young stud with a nice firm behind."

My mother refilled her wineglass and my father put his fork down and hit his head on the table. *BANG, BANG, BANG, BANG.*

"Go for it," I said to Grandma.

"I'm not so old," Grandma said. "There's parts of me don't sit as high as they used to, but I've got some miles left."

My father pantomimed stabbing himself in the eye with his fork.

Okay, so my family's a little dysfunctional. It's not like they're dangerous. At least we all sit down and have dinner together. Plus, by Jersey standards, we're pretty much normal.

NINE

My father was settled in, watching sitcom reruns, when I left. My mother and grandmother were at the small kitchen table enjoying a ritual glass of port, celebrating the return of order and cleanliness in the kitchen. And I departed in the powder blue and white '53 Buick that was kept in the garage for emergencies. Sitting on the seat beside me was a doggy bag that included fried chicken, soft little dinner rolls from the bakery, a jar of pickled beets, half a homemade apple pie, and a bottle of red table wine. The wine had been sent along, I'm sure, with the hopes that I might have a romantic evening with Morelli and make a grandchild. So much the better if I got married first.

I drove past the Bugkowski house out of morbid curiosity to see if my car was there. Not only wasn't the car parked at the curb, but the house was dark. No one home. Probably, Big Buggy took his parents for a drive in his new RAV4.

Twenty minutes later, I rolled into the lot to my apartment building and did another car check. No RAV4. No black Lincoln Town Car. No green SUV that belonged to Morelli. No megabucks shiny black Ranger car. I found a space close to the building's back door, parked, and locked up. I took the elevator to the second floor, walked down the hall, and listened at my door. All was quiet. I let myself in, kicked the door closed, and a swarthy guy with lots of curly black hair jumped out of the kitchen at me. He was holding a huge knife, and his dark eyes were narrowed.

"I want photograph," he said. "Give it

to me, or I kill you big-time. I make you very painful."

I grabbed the bottle of wine from the doggy bag, hit the guy in the face with it as hard as I could, his eyes rolled back, and he crashed to the floor. I'd acted totally on instinct and was as surprised as he was that he got knocked out. I put a hand to the wall to steady myself and took a couple deep breaths. It felt icky to have the guy in my apartment, so I cuffed him and dragged him into the hall. I returned to my apartment and closed and locked the door in case there was a partner lurking somewhere.

I retrieved my Smith & Wesson from the cookie jar and walked through my apartment looking in closets and under the bed, finding dust bunnies but no more swarthy guys. I went back to the kitchen and called Bill Berger.

"There was a nasty-looking guy in my apartment when I came home just now," I told him. "He had a big knife, and he said he'd kill me if I didn't give him the photograph."

"And?" Berger asked.

"I hit him in the face with a bottle of table wine and knocked him out."

"Where is he now?"

"He's in the hall."

There was a beat of silence. "What's he doing in the hall?"

"I didn't want him in my apartment, so I dragged him into the hall."

More silence. Probably, Berger wasn't believing any of this.

"Did you check for ID?" he finally asked.

Damn! "No. Hold on, and I'll go look."

I opened the door, and the hall was empty. No swarthy guy.

"He's gone," I said to Berger.

"Problem solved," Berger said. And he hung up.

I closed and locked the door, plugged my stun gun into a wall socket, returned the Smith & Wesson to the cookie jar, and opened the bottle of wine. Thank God it hadn't broken, because I really needed a drink. A Cosmo or a Margarita or a water glass filled with whiskey would have been even better. I brought the bottle into the living room, settled in front of the television, tuned in to the Food Network, and tried to get my heart rate under control.

Some woman was making cupcakes. Cupcakes are good, I told myself. There's an innocence to a cupcake. A joy. I poured a second glass of wine, and I watched the woman frost the cupcakes.

Halfway through the bottle of wine, I flipped to the Travel Channel, and I don't remember much after that.

• • •

I woke up to the sun streaming into my bedroom. I was naked, tucked under the covers, and alone. I vaguely remembered half-waking to Morelli telling me the chicken was all he hoped it would be.

I rolled out of bed, wrapped myself in my robe, and padded into the kitchen. No Morelli. No chicken. No dinner rolls. No apple pie. A note was stuck to the counter by Rex's cage.

You were asleep on the couch, so I put you to bed and ate the chicken.

I dialed Morelli. "How'd I get naked?" I asked him.

"That was the way I found you. You were mumbling something about being hot, and God was just going to have to deal with it."

Good grief. "How'd it go at the junkyard?"

"We didn't find Joyce's body, but we found Frank Korda, the jeweler she supposedly stole the necklace from, and we found Joyce's other shoe."

"Was Korda dead?"

"Yeah, and then some."

"Do you think Joyce killed him?"

"Personally, I don't, but as a cop I'd have to consider it."

"Any leads?"

"The usual relatives and friends," Morelli said. "It looks like someone tried to break into Joyce's condo. I don't suppose you'd know anything about that?"

"Who, me?"

"If anyone does break in, they should be careful about withholding evidence."

"I have a feeling the condo would be clean. And let me take a wild guess that Frank Korda was found in Joyce's Mercedes."

"Your guess would be right. I have to run. We're taking the dog back to the junkyard."

"You should bring Bob. He could hang with the cadaver dog and get some exercise. Maybe Bob could help find another body."

"If Bob found a body, he'd eat it," Morelli said.

I disconnected, took a shower, and got dressed in my usual girly T-shirt, jeans, and sneakers. I fed Rex and gave him fresh water. He rushed out of his soup-can home, stuffed a bunch of hamster crunchies into his cheeks, and hustled back to his can. Maybe he was still creeped out by the guy with the knife last night. Understandable, because that would make two of us.

I tossed my fully charged stun gun into my bag and took off. First stop was the coffee shop. Connie, Lula, and Vinnie were sitting at a table in the window. I got a coffee and a cinnamon roll and joined them.

"They found Frank Korda at the junkyard," Connie said. "It came over the police channel."

I nodded. "Morelli told me. How's the office space search going?"

"I have it narrowed down," Connie said. "There's a vacant storefront a couple blocks from the police station. Or I can rent a Winnebago RV, which would be smaller than the bus, but we could park it in our usual location."

"We'd get more business by the police station," Vinnie said. "Let's go with the storefront."

"I'll pick the lease up this morning, and we can move in tomorrow," Connie said. "It's not pretty, but it's usable space."

"As long as it got good facilities," Lula said. "I might still have some potato salad left inside me."

"How about the fire investigation?" Vinnie asked. "Do they know what started it yet?"

Connie closed her laptop and stood. "They said it was suspicious, but they're still looking at all the little pieces they collected."

DeAngelo and his foreman walked into the coffee shop.

"Hey, what's doin' here?" DeAngelo said to Vinnie. "How come you're not at work in your office? Oh yeah, now I remember . . . it blew up."

Vinnie narrowed his eyes, said something in Italian, and flipped DeAngelo the bird.

"Better be careful," DeAngelo said. "Your house could blow up next."

Vinnie's lip curled back. "Are you threatening me?"

"I don't threaten," DeAngelo said. "I'm more a doer."

"Don't look to me like you do much of anything but flap your lips," Lula said. "If you were a *doer,* we'd be in our new office by now."

DeAngelo looked at Vinnie. "Who's the fat chick?"

Everyone sucked in air.

"Excuse me?" Lula said, leaning forward, hands on hips, eyes set in her *wild boar on the attack* squint. "Did you just say what I think you said? Because if you said that, you better say it was a mistake. I'm a reasonable person, but I don't stand for disrespecting and slandering. I'm a big, beautiful woman. I am *not* a fat chick. You don't apologize, and I'll squash you like a bug. I'll step on you until you're just a grease spot on the floor."

"I like it," DeAngelo said to Lula. "You want to spank me?"

"No, I don't want to spank you," Lula said. "That's disgusting. I don't know you good enough to want to spank you."

DeAngelo winked at her and went to pick up his coffee.

"He's giving me the runs," Lula said.

I pushed back from the table. "I have to talk to the FBI this morning."

"Then what?" Lula asked. "Who's up for today?"

"Big Buggy and my RAV4 for starters. I'll call when I'm done downtown."

TEN

Berger, the FBI artist, and Chuck Gooley were waiting for me in a conference room on the sixth floor. We started with face shapes, and from there we went to specifics like eyes and mouth and nose. By the time we were done, I was thoroughly confused and had no idea if the drawing even remotely resembled the guy in the photo.

"So is this the guy?" Berger asked me, pointing to the composite sketch.

"Sure," I said. "Maybe. So about the maniac in my kitchen who wanted to kill me . . ."

"What did he look like?"

"Middle Eastern complexion. Lots of unruly curly black hair. Crazy eyes. Six foot. Slim. Early forties. An accent I couldn't place. Tattoo of a rose on his knife hand."

"I'll feed it into the system and let you know if we get a match."

I left the sixth floor, exited the building, and stopped in the middle of the sidewalk because Lancer and Slasher were standing by the Buick, half a block away. Okay, here were my options. I could call Berger, but I wasn't sure what that would accomplish. Berger'd made it clear my safety wasn't his priority. I didn't want to drag Morelli away from his murders. If I asked Ranger for help, he'd have me under twenty-four-hour surveillance. Ranger tended to be overprotective.

I decided none of those options were going to work for me, so I transferred my stun gun from my bag to the pocket on my sweatshirt and approached Lancer and Slasher.

"Hey," I said. "What's new?"

Lancer was leaning against the

Buick's passenger-side door. "Looks like you're cozy with the FBI."

"They're interested in the photograph."

"No shit," Lancer said. "Did you give it to them?"

"I told them the same thing I told you. I don't have it."

"Yeah, but you saw it, right?"

"Wrong."

"You're lying," Lancer said. "I can tell."

"There's another guy after the photograph," I said. "Tall, curly black hair, looks Middle Eastern, rose tattoo on his hand."

Lancer and Slasher looked at each other and grimaced.

"Raz," Lancer said.

"Who's Raz?" I asked.

"No one knows his real name," Lancer said. "Raz is short for Razzle Dazzle. That's what he goes by. You don't want to deal with him. He has no scruples."

"I don't get it," I said to Lancer. "Why is everyone so interested in this photograph?"

"Don't know. Don't care," Lancer said. "We were hired to get it."

"Who hired you?"

"That's none of your business. If you don't have the photograph, I bet you know where it is. And I bet we could get you to tell us. We got ways of making girls talk."

Slasher smiled. "Yeah, we got good ways."

"I'll keep that in mind," I said, "but there's still nothing I can tell you about the photograph. And as much as I'd love to stay and chat, I'm afraid I have to go now."

"And I'm afraid we can't let you," Slasher said.

He reached out to grab me, I gave him a shot with my stun gun, and he crumpled to his knees.

"Hey," Lancer said to me. "Those things are illegal. You're not allowed to do that."

Zzzzt. I zapped Lancer, and he went down, too.

I looked around to see if anyone had noticed. No cars screeched to a stop. No concerned pedestrian rushed at me. Good deal. I relieved Lancer and Slasher of their wallets, scrambled into the Buick, and took off.

• • •

By the time I got to the coffee shop, my breathing had returned to normal and my heart had stopped skipping around in my chest. Lula was alone at the table in the window with four untouched cups of coffee in front of her, working at a crossword puzzle.

"What's with the coffee?" I asked her.

"I feel like I gotta buy something once in a while since I'm sitting here, but the only thing I'm drinking is Pepto-Bismol. Connie and Vinnie went to sign the rental agreement for the temporary office. And then after that, they were going across the street to bond out a guy who set all the birds loose in the pet store at the mall. He was singing that *Born Free* song and waving a double-barrel shotgun around, scaring the living daylights out of everyone."

"Was anyone hurt?"

"No, but a couple canaries lost some feathers in the overhead fan."

I put the two wallets on the table and went through the first. The guy's name was actually Mortimer Lancelot. Go figure that. It was almost as bad as Lance Lancer. I moved on to the second wallet. Sylvester Larder. Both guys had Long Branch, New Jersey, addresses. I took down the information on the two driver's licenses and called Berger.

"I have names for you," I said. "The two fake FBI guys are Mortimer Lancelot and Sylvester Larder. They have Long Branch addresses. The guy in my kitchen apparently is known as Razzle Dazzle. Any of these names mean anything to you?"

"Razzle Dazzle is a complete whack job. If you find him in your kitchen again, you might want to shoot him. Don't tell anyone I said that."

And Berger hung up.

I slouched in my chair, and sipped one of Lula's coffees.

"Looks to me like you caught some bad juju in Hawaii," Lula said. "I mean, you gotta look at the facts. You got naked skin where a ring used to be, and you don't want to talk about it, so I'm reaching the conclusion that your love life is in the crapper. And if that isn't bad enough, you're in the middle of some crazy whodunit shit that you didn't even go looking for. Not to mention we haven't caught any bad guys since you been back. You might want to do something about your juju."

"What did you have in mind?"

"I didn't have anything in mind. I'm just sayin'."

I wasn't exactly sure what constituted juju, but I had the general picture, and Lula had a point. Lately, my luck sucked. It had been excellent when I arrived in Hawaii, and somewhere mid-vacation it turned bad.

A flash of black caught my eye, and I looked out the big plate-glass window in time to see the Lincoln stop and double-park in front of the coffee shop. Lancer and Slasher lunged out of the car, stormed into the coffee shop, and stood over me, glaring.

"You stole our wallets," Lancer said.

I took the wallets off the table and

handed them to Lancer. "Identity check."

"You better not have put anything on my credit card," Slasher said.

"That's insulting," Lula said. "What does she look like, anyway? She's a successful businesswoman. She don't need your dumb-ass credit card. She got her own credit card. You need to learn some manners. Who the heck are you?"

"Sylvester Larder, also known as Sly Slasher," I said.

He took his wallet from Lancer. "Everyone calls me Slasher."

"Is that a work-related nickname?" Lula asked. "On account of you don't look like a slasher. You look more like a insurance salesman. Or one of those guys who sets out the grapefruits in the supermarket."

Lancer gave a bark of laughter.

"Real funny," Slasher said. "Why don't you ask her if you look like a Lancelot?"

I stood up from my seat. "Gotta go," I said. "Sorry about your wallets and rearranging your neurons."

"You better play ball with us before we have to get rough," Lancer said. "We need results. Our boss doesn't like being disappointed."

• • •

Lula and I left the coffee shop, piled into the Buick, and headed for Buggy's house.

"They could be in big trouble if their boss doesn't like being disappointed," Lula said. "And I don't think they believe you about not having that photograph. You really don't have it, right?"

"Right."

"How come everyone thinks you have it, if you don't have it?"

"Because I used to have it."

"Like you used to have a ring on your finger," Lula said.

I felt my blood pressure edge up a notch. "Give it a rest, okay?"

"Hunh," Lula said.

I turned onto Pulling Street and saw my RAV4 at the curb in front of Buggy's house.

"I guess he borrowed your car," Lula said.

"Something like that."

"We gonna do our bounty hunter thing on him?"

"Yeah. I'll use my stun gun, we'll cuff him when he goes down, and we'll drag him into the Buick. It has a bigger backseat."

"Let's do it. I'm there," Lula said. "If you notice, I'm wearing black again today. I'm in the Ranger zone. WHAM!"

I was glad Lula had such a positive attitude, because I was experiencing some self-doubt. And I appreciated that Lula was in the zone, although I suspected her outfit was from her S&M 'ho collection, since she was wearing over-the-knee black leather boots with four-inch heels, a black leather miniskirt, and a skintight black leather bustier.

I parked, and Lula and I went to the door. I had the Flexi-Cuffs ready, and I was holding the stun gun.

"You distract him," I said to Lula. "When he looks over at you, I'll stun him."

"Sure," Lula said. "I'll distract the hell out of him."

I rang the bell and Buggy answered.

"Howdy," he said, opening the door, looking out at me. "What's up?"

"I came to get my car."

"I'm thinking about keeping it. I like it a lot."

"You can't just go around keeping cars," Lula said to him.

"Yu-huh, I can," he said, glancing at her but turning back to me.

"Tell him why he can't do that," I said to Lula.

"Because," she said.

"That's it?" I said to her. "That's all you got?"

"Because it's not right," she said to Buggy. "You gotta buy a car. You can't take other people's."

Buggy wasn't paying attention to Lula. Buggy was looking at me, his brow drawn together, his mouth tight. "I *want* it," he said.

"He's not paying attention to you," I said to Lula.

"Don't I know it," she said. "What's

this boy's problem?" She leaned forward and yelled at him. "Hey! You!"

"Yuh," Buggy said.

Lula popped one of her giant boobs out of her black leather bustier. "What do you think of this?"

"It's big," Buggy said.

"You bet your ass," Lula told him.

I whipped the stun gun out, pressed it against Buggy's arm, and hit the go button.

"Ow," Buggy said.

His eyes didn't roll back into his head. He didn't crash to the ground. He didn't go down to his knees.

I blasted him again.

"That stings," Buggy said. "Stop it."

"Must be about body weight," Lula said. "You need the shit they make for elephants."

Buggy grabbed the stun gun out of my hand and threw it into the bushes bordering the house. "Go away," Buggy said. "And you better not take my car, or that would make me mad."

No point getting goofy over this, I told myself. Just very calmly take the RAV, go home, and make a reassessment. Surely there's a way to capture this man. A big net, maybe. A rhinoceros tranquilizer dart. Get him to follow a trail of cheeseburgers leading to the police station.

I scrounged through the bushes, found my stun gun, handed Lula the key to the Buick, and smiled pleasantly at Buggy. I turned, walked to the RAV, plugged my key in, and opened the driver's side door. Buggy grabbed me from behind, and tossed me into the street.

"Hey, idiot," Lula said to Buggy. "You can't do that to her. That's friggin' rude."

"I'll do whatever I want," Buggy said. "It's my car now."

Lula hauled her Glock out of her purse and aimed it at Buggy. "At the risk of gettin' too personal, I got a delicate intestinal condition today, and you're not making it any better. And I already explained to you about how car ownership works. Now, you need to get your lard butt outta here, or I'll put another hole in it."

"You don't scare me," Buggy said. "You can't shoot an unarmed man."

"Says who?" Lula said. "I shoot unarmed men all the time."

I scrambled to my feet, came up behind Buggy, pressed the stun gun prongs to his neck, and held the button down. Buggy went dead still, sank to his knees, and wet his pants.

"Third time's a charm," Lula said.

I slipped the plastic Flexi-Cuffs around his wrists and secured them behind his back. Buggy was still on his knees, his eyes were glazed, and he was drooling.

"How are we gonna get him in the car?" Lula stared at him. "He must weigh three hundred pounds, and he got wet pants. We need a forklift to move him. Maybe one of them skyhooks."

"Maybe now that he's cuffed, he'll be reasonable," I said.

Buggy's eyes snapped into focus. "Grrrrr," he said.

Lula looked down at him. "He don't look reasonable."

Buggy struggled to free his hands. *"GRRRRR!"* He came off one knee and then the other. He shook his head as if to clear it, stood, and swayed a little getting his balance.

"You know that movie where they bring the Frankenstein monster back to life?" Lula said. "This is like that movie. You know what happened when Frankenstein first woke up? *He wasn't happy.*"

"We need to go downtown and get you rebonded," I said to Buggy. "It won't take long."

Buggy lunged at me. His hands were bound behind his back, and his gait was awkward. He lunged at me a second time, but I jumped away. He stumbled, went down to the ground, and rolled onto his back. That's where he stayed, kicking his feet, unable to right himself.

"He's like a big giant turtle," Lula said. "What are we gonna do with him?"

I didn't know. We couldn't lift him. I wasn't even sure we could drag him. When we got near, he kicked out at us. His face was red and sweating, and veins were popped out in his forehead and corded on his neck.

"You need to calm yourself," Lula

said to Buggy. "You're gonna give yourself a stroke. And you're not a real attractive man to begin with, so you don't want to make it worse with the whole bulging vein thing. It's not a good look for you."

He was rocking side to side and grunting. "Unh, unh, *UNH*!" And on the last *UNH,* he broke out of the Flexi-Cuffs, rolled to hands and knees, then stood beady-eyed, arms out, mouth open. Killer grizzly.

"YOW!" Lula said. "Every man for himself."

She ran for the Buick, and I ran for the RAV4. I jumped in, pulled the door closed, and took off with Lula following.

I drove to my parents' house, parked at the curb, and sat for a couple beats, getting it together. Lula rapped on the driver's side window, and I got out.

"You see, that's what I'm talking about," Lula said. "You got a juju issue. That wasn't a wonderful experience. You ever see anyone break out of those plastic handcuffs before? I don't think so."

ELEVEN

Grandma was at the front door, waving at us. "You're just in time for lunch," she said.

Lula's face brightened. "Lunch! That's what I need after my traumatic experience."

Grandma led the way to the kitchen. "What happened?"

"We almost got torn limb from limb by a idiot," Lula said. "Only we avoided it and came here."

My mother was putting food on the kitchen table, trying not to rant over the thought of me getting my limbs torn off.

"Ham, olive loaf, Swiss cheese, some macaroni salad," she said. "Help yourself."

I sat down and Grandma gave me a small glass bottle.

"Annie dropped this off for you this morning. She said you should drink it next time you see your true love, and it'll take care of your indigestion."

Lula looked across at me. "Does this mean you decided on your true love? Not that I especially care, but I was wondering for the sake of conversation if it has something to do with the ring that used to be on your finger."

My mother and grandmother stopped eating and leaned forward a little, waiting for my answer.

"Oh, for goodness' sakes," I said. "Why is everyone making such a big deal about this stupid tan line? It's just a tan line!"

"Yeah," Lula said, "but you've been real secret about it, and all this talk about true love and indigestion has me putting it together, and I finally got it figured out. You're preggers!"

My mother clapped a hand over her

mouth, made a strangled sound, and went facedown into the olive loaf. For a brief moment, I thought she'd had a heart attack, and I was responsible.

"She just fainted," Grandma said. "She used to faint all the time when she was a little girl. A real drama queen."

We stretched my mom out on the floor, and Grandma got a wet towel. My mom finally opened her eyes and looked up at me. "Who? What?"

"I'm not pregnant," I said.

"Are you sure?"

I had to think about it for a minute. "Pretty sure." I'd be more sure in a week.

We sat my mom back in her chair, I got the whiskey from the cupboard, and we all chugged some.

"I can't take it anymore," Lula said to me. "I want to know about the ring. I want to know who you married. What the heck happened in Hawaii anyhow?"

"Yeah," Grandma said. "I want to know, too."

"Ditto," my mom said, taking another hit from the whiskey bottle.

I'd been avoiding this. There were

parts to my vacation that were spectacular, but there were also parts I'd just as soon forget . . . like the ending. Not only didn't I *want* to talk about it, I had no idea what to say. It was all too awkward. Unfortunately, I owed Lula and my family an explanation. I just wouldn't tell them *all* of it.

"It was nothing. It was business. I'll tell you what happened, but you have to swear not to repeat it."

Everyone made the sign of the cross, drew zippers across their mouths, and threw the keys away.

"I offered the second free plane ticket to Morelli," I said, "but he couldn't get away from work. He *never* gets away from work. So I went by myself. I got off the plane in Honolulu, and as I was walking through the terminal, I spotted Tootie Ruguzzi."

"Get the heck out," Lula said. "The Rug's wife?"

"Yeah."

"Those two disappeared off the face of the earth," Grandma said. "We all thought they got planted."

Simon Ruguzzi, better known as The

Rug, is a local celebrity hit man. He's part of the Colichio crime family, but he's also been known to do freelance. Three years ago, he executed seven members of a Hispanic gang that was trying to muscle in on Colichio territory. Two other gang members witnessed the massacre but escaped and fingered The Rug. He was arrested and charged and somehow managed to get released on a ridiculously high bail bond. That was the last anyone ever saw The Rug or Tootie. Vinnie had written the bond, and Ranger and I have been looking for The Rug ever since.

"Was The Rug with her?" Lula asked.

"Not in the terminal. She was alone. I followed her outside and watched her get on a shuttle to a resort. I picked up my rental car and drove to the address on the side of the shuttle. It was one of those really expensive beachfront, view-of-Diamond-Head resorts that cater to special-events packages. I tried to get in, but it was married-couples-only re-treat month. High-security, exclusive, strictly enforced privacy."

"They weren't even letting bounty hunters in?" Lula asked.

"My name wasn't on the guest list. End of story."

"How about if you were a guest?"

"I had to be married."

"I'm getting a picture," Lula said.

"It was more complicated than that," I told her. "Even if I captured The Rug, I don't have the authority to return him to Jersey. Vinnie and Ranger handle the high stakes bonds and extradition."

"So you called Ranger," Lula said.

"Yes. He caught the next flight, and we checked into the resort as Mr. and Mrs. Manoso."

Lula fanned herself with her napkin. "Lordy, lordy."

My mother had her hands over her ears. "I'm not listening."

"I'm listening," Grandma said. "This is getting good."

Grandma had no idea *how* good. And I wasn't going into details, but Ranger arranged for a beachfront cottage with total privacy for enjoying the spa au naturel and a king-sized bed for après spa.

"So the whole marriage thing was fake to get into the resort," Lula said.

"Yep."

"Did you get The Rug?"

"No, but he was there. They were in a cottage on the other side of the property. Unfortunately, they checked out and disappeared before we were able to make contact."

Okay, truth is, we probably didn't try as hard as we might have. The spa that went with our cottage was pretty darn fantastic, and I'm not sure Ranger was totally motivated to make an apprehension and leave the island.

Lula took seconds on the macaroni salad. "So why'd you keep saying things were complicated? And why all the secrecy?"

"We haven't given up on capturing The Rug," I said. "I don't want it passed around that I spotted him in Hawaii, and I don't want him spooked."

Not to mention that Morelli had felt bad because I was vacationing alone and showed up as a surprise. Fortunately, I was fully clothed and not in the spa when he badged his way past the front desk and appeared on my doorstep. Unfortunately, Morelli's temper kicked in the minute he saw Ranger, and Morelli coldcocked him with a fist in the face. The result of all this was the hospital drop-off and my early departure.

"I was hoping for a better story than that," Lula said. "But I guess you could still be pregnant."

"It's not likely," I told her.

"Yeah, but you never know. There could be a chance," Lula said.

I cut my eyes to my mother to see if she was going to faint again. She had her hand wrapped around the almost-empty whiskey bottle, she was smiling, and her eyes were unfocused.

"She's shit-faced," Grandma said. "You should take the bottle away from her before she takes another header into the olive loaf."

I pried the bottle out of my mother's hand and returned it to the cupboard.

"Did you by any chance tell Morelli where I was staying in Hawaii?" I asked Grandma.

"Yeah, he called just before you came

home. I guess he thought you were in a different hotel, so we told him about the new one. He said he was going to surprise you, and we figured you were spending the last couple days together."

Okay, so that mystery was solved. I finished my sandwich, dropped Annie's bottle into my bag, and stood.

"I have to keep moving," I said to Grandma. "Let me know if you hear anything about anything. I've got my RAV back, so I'm leaving the Buick here."

• • •

Lula and I buckled ourselves into the RAV, and Lula looked through my files.

"We need a capture to break the cycle," Lula said. "We gotta get the juju turned around. Especially if you're pregnant."

"I'm *not pregnant.*"

"Yeah, but you said that about being married."

"And I wasn't married."

Lula held fast. "You were sort of married."

Good grief.

"Anyways, I'm voting we go looking for Magpie," Lula said, "because we could snag him for sure if we could just find him."

Donald Grezbek, better known as Magpie, was wanted for burglary. He'd been caught on tape breaking into a flea-market stall at the fairgrounds and making off with about $700 worth of gold chains. It wasn't his first arrest. Usually, it was shoplifting. Magpie took things that caught his eye. He loved things that were glittery or shiny. After he got his treasures, he had no clue what to do with them. Mostly, he wore them until someone found him and confiscated the loot.

Magpie lived hand to mouth out of a beat-up Crown Vic. And that was the problem. He had no job, no permanent address, no relatives, no friends. No favorite parking place. He preferred to squat on seldom-used roads. Once in a while, he was known to set up housekeeping in a cemetery.

"He could be anywhere," I said. "I wouldn't know where to begin looking."

"We could rent a helicopter and try to spot him from the air," Lula said.

"The helicopter would cost more than I'd make from the capture."

"It's not always about money," Lula said.

"It is if you don't have any."

My cell phone rang, and the display showed an unfamiliar Jersey number.

"I'm looking for Stephanie Plum," a woman said. "I need to talk to her about Richard Crick."

"You're not another FBI agent, are you?" I said. "I'm up to my armpits in FBI agents."

"I was Ritchy's fiancée."

"Jeez," I said. "I'm sorry for your loss. I didn't know he had a fiancée."

"I need to talk to you. You must have been one of the last people to see him."

"I was sitting next to him on the plane, but I slept through most of the flight."

"You're in Trenton, right? I am, too. I'd really appreciate it if I could meet you someplace."

"There's a coffee shop on Hamilton, next to the hospital," I said.

"Thanks. I'm not far from there."

"What was that about?" Lula looked over at me when I disconnected.

"That was Richard Crick's fiancée. How does everyone find me? The real FBI guys I get, because they have resources. But what about everyone else? They know I was sitting next to Crick. They know where I live. They know my cell phone number."

"It's the electronic age," Lula said. "We aren't the only ones got search programs. And then there's the whole social network. 'Course, you wouldn't know about that since you're in the Stone Age. You don't even tweet."

I put the RAV in gear. "Do you tweet?" I asked Lula.

"Hell, yeah. I'm a big tweeter."

• • •

I drove to the coffee shop and parked. Connie was back in the window. No Vinnie. Lula and I went inside and pulled chairs up to Connie's table.

"Do we have an office?" I asked Connie.

"Yeah, Vinnie signed the papers. He wanted to come back here and punch out DeAngelo, but I told him he had to stay and wait for the furniture-rental truck. With any luck, by the time the furniture's delivered, DeAngelo will have gone home for the day."

"What all furniture did you rent?" Lula asked. "You got a big ol' comfy couch, right? And one of them flat-screen televisions."

"I got two cheap desks and six folding chairs. I'm counting on this being short-term."

A woman walked into the coffee shop, looked around, and came over to the table.

"Is one of you Stephanie Plum?" she asked.

I raised my hand.

"I'm Brenda Schwartz, Ritchy's fiancée. I just talked to you on the phone. Could we go outside?"

She was about 5'5" and excessively curvy. She had a lot of overprocessed blond hair piled on top of her head in a messy upsweep. Her makeup was close to drag queen. She was wearing platform heels, a tight black skirt, and a red scoop-neck sweater that showed a lot of boob enhanced with spray-on tan. Hard to tell exactly what was under the makeup, but I was guessing she was in her forties.

I followed her out, and she immediately lit up. She sucked the smoke in all the way down to her toes and blew it out her nose.

"This cigarette tastes like ass," she said.

I wasn't sure what ass tasted like, but she looked like she would know, so I was willing to take her word for it.

She took another hit. "I'm trying to get off menthol, and it's a real bitch. I swear, I'm just inches away from trying one of those electronic things."

"You wanted to see me about Richard Crick?"

"Yeah. Poor Ritchy. It's so sad." She squinted at me through the smoke haze. "The worst part is he was bringing me a picture. He said it was a special present for me, but they didn't find it when they dug him out of the garbage can. So I was wondering if you knew anything about it, because it would be real sentimental for me. It would help with the pain of losing Ritchy."

"What kind of picture are we talking about?"

"A picture of a person."

"Man or woman?"

"This is sort of embarrassing, but poor Ritchy didn't say."

"And it's important, why?"

"Because Ritchy took the photo. And it was, like, his last wish that I have it. And now he's dead." She sniffed and contorted her face like she might cry. "I just want something to remember Ritchy. Something he did for me, you know?"

"Ritchy must have been a sweet guy."

"Yeah, and he liked photography. He was always taking pictures."

"I'd love to help you out," I said, "but I don't have the photograph."

"Maybe you have it stuffed somewhere, and you don't even know it. Like, have you emptied all your suitcases and bags?"

"Yes. I don't have it."

"Okay, here's the thing. Ritchy called me from LAX, and he said he might have misplaced the photo, and he was sitting next to you, and he was pretty sure he might have accidentally put it in your bag."

"Why didn't Ritchy just get back on the plane?"

"He wasn't feeling good. And then he was . . . you know, dead."

"Jeez."

"Shit happens," Brenda said. "So where's the photograph?"

"Don't know. Don't have it."

Her lips compressed. "You want money, right? How much?"

"I don't want money. I don't have the stupid photograph."

Brenda stuck her hand into her hobo bag and pulled out a little silver gun. "I want the photograph. We all know you have it. So get smart and hand it over."

I looked down at the gun. "Is that real?"

"You bet it's real. It's pretty, right? And it's light. I bet you carry some piece of shit like a Glock or a Smith and Wesson. Those guns ruin your whole look. You get a neck spasm, right?"

"Yeah, I have a Smith and Wesson."

"They're dinosaurs."

"Who *are* you?"

"Boy, you don't listen. I already told you. I'm Brenda Schwartz. And I want the photograph."

"Shooting me isn't going to get it."

"I could shoot you in the knee for starters. Just so you know I'm serious. It hurts a lot to get shot in the knee."

Lula swung through the coffee shop door and came over to us. "Is that a gun?"

"Oh, for Crissake, who's this?" Brenda said.

"I'm Lula. Who the heck are you?"

"This is a private conversation," Brenda said.

"Yeah, but I want to take a look at your little peashooter. It's kinda cute."

"It's a *gun,*" Brenda said.

Lula pulled her Glock out of her bag and aimed it at Brenda. "Bitch, *this* is a gun. It could put a hole in you big enough to drive a truck through."

"Honestly," Brenda said, "this is just

so boring." And she huffed off to her car and drove away.

"She was kinda snippy, being I just wanted to see her gun," Lula said.

Snippy was the least of it. She was a perfect addition to my growing collection of homicidal misfits.

"She's in mourning," I told Lula. "Thanks for stepping in."

"She didn't look like she was in mourning," Lula said. "And she didn't look like no doctor's fiancée."

Lula and I returned to Connie, and I called Bill Berger.

"I've got a third party interested in the photograph," I told him. "Do you care?"

"Who've you got?" Berger asked.

"Brenda Schwartz. Says she was Crick's fiancée. Blond, five foot five, in her forties. Carries a little bitty gun."

"As far as we know, Crick didn't have a fiancée."

I ended the call with Berger and turned to Connie. "Can you find her?"

"Brenda Schwartz is a fairly common name," Connie said. "Do you have an address? Did you get her license plate number?"

"The first part was 'POP,' and I didn't get the rest. She was driving one of those cars that looks like a toaster."

"It was a Scion," Lula said.

Connie plugged the information into a search program and started working her way through it. I got a black-and-white cookie and a Frappuccino, and came back to the table.

"I think I've got her," Connie said. "Brenda Schwartz. Age forty-four. Hairdresser, working at The Hair Barn in Princeton. Divorced from Bernard Schwartz, Harry Zimmer, Herbert Luckert. One child. Jason. Looks like he's twenty-one now. Most current address is West Windsor. Renting. No litigation against her. Picked up for possession of a controlled substance five years ago. Got a slap on the wrist. There's more personal information. I'll print it for you later. I haven't got a printer here."

I wrote down Brenda's address, ate my cookie, and sipped my drink, wondering what I should do about the photograph mess. Probably, I should tell Ranger, but he might kill everyone, and that wouldn't help his karma issue. I glanced out the big front window and realized my car was gone.

"Damn! Shit! Sonovabitch!" I said.

"That's a lot of swearin'," Lula said.

"He took my car again."

Everyone turned and looked out the window.

"Yep, it sure looks gone," Lula said.

I called the Rangeman control room. "Where's my car?" I asked the tech who answered.

"It's on Hamilton. Looks like it just parked at Cluck-in-a-Bucket."

I stood at my seat. "Let's roll," I said to Lula. "He's at Cluck-in-a-Bucket."

"WHAM!" Lula said. "Turn me loose on him."

"I have two guys I'd like you to run through the system for me," I said to Connie. "Mortimer Lancelot and Sylvester Larder." I wrote the Town Car's license plate number on a napkin. "And I'd love to know who owns the car."

Five minutes later, we were in the Cluck-in-a-Bucket lot, and Lula was idling behind my RAV. We could see Buggy inside, standing in line at the counter.

"Now what?" Lula said. "You got any ideas how we're gonna do this? Maybe we should go to the packing plant and borrow a cattle prod."

"I just want my car. At this point, I don't care if Buggy stays in the wind forever."

"Yeah, but how are you gonna keep him from taking it again if you don't get him locked up?"

"I'll trade the RAV in. I give up. I can't get the key away from him, so I'll get another car."

"Wow, that's smart thinking."

"I'm probably done working for the day," I said to Lula. "I'll call if anything changes."

TWELVE

It was late afternoon by the time I swapped out the RAV for a four-door Chevy Colorado pickup. I don't usually buy trucks, but the price was right, and I didn't have a lot of choices. Apparently, a couple kids had been driving it, smoking weed, and the seat had caught fire. There wasn't much mechanical damage, but the interior was trashed. New seats had been installed, but the smell of seriously smoked cannabis remained.

I'd removed the Rangeman tracking device from the RAV undercarriage, slipped it into the Chevy's glove box, and called the vehicle change in to the control room. I called Morelli to tell him about the change, but he wasn't picking up his cell. Probably, the electromagnet at the junkyard was interfering. Or maybe he saw the call was from me, and he threw his phone into the Delaware River.

I was in a bad place with Morelli. Technically, I hadn't done anything wrong, since I wasn't in a committed relationship with him. That fact didn't stop my stomach from frequently turning queasy, because I had an ongoing relationship with two men I really cared about. And it was obvious Morelli was the more vulnerable of the two. Ranger accepted the limitations, took full advantage when he had the opportunity, and rolled with the rest. Morelli was capable of none of that. Morelli's temper and libido ran in the red zone. And the truth is, while Morelli was sometimes more difficult to live with, I preferred the transparency of his emotions.

My dilemma was that I wanted Morelli to know Ranger had come to Hawaii on legitimate business, but I was afraid the conversation would lead to an ugly discussion about sleeping arrangements. And it was becoming obvious Morelli didn't want to have that discussion any more than I did.

I drove my truck off the lot and headed for Hamilton Township. If there was anything that could partially push thoughts of Morelli aside, it was thoughts of Joyce Barnhardt.

• • •

Barnhardt was unfinished business. I'd hated her in grade school and high school, and I'd found her naked and woman-on-top on my brand-new husband on my brand-new dining room table. In the end, it had turned out she'd done me a favor, because the man was a philandering jerk. Still, her behavior hadn't gotten better after that, so I really shouldn't care if she was dead or alive, but it turns out I did care. Go figure.

I cruised through Joyce's neighborhood, which was empty as usual. I idled in front of her town house. No sign of life inside. I left Mercado Mews and returned to the Burg.

The Barnhardts live on Liberty Street. Joyce's mom teaches third grade, and her father installs air-conditioning units for Ruger Air. The Barnhardts keep their house and lawn tidy, and their lives private. Grandma says Joyce's father is an odd duck, but I wouldn't know personally. I've never had any interactions with Joyce's father, and I learned early on to avoid Joyce's mother. Her mother turned a blind eye to Joyce's many shortcomings. Pleasant for Joyce, I suppose, but difficult for the kid who got Joyce boogers on her sandwich.

I checked out the Barnhardts' house, made a U-turn, and crept past a second time. The house felt benign. At least as benign as was possible, considering Joyce had lived there. If circumstances had been different, I might have knocked on the door and questioned the Barnhardts.

Because I was in the neighborhood, I stopped to see if my mother was sober and making dinner.

"She's sleeping it off," Grandma said,

meeting me at the door. "I ordered pizza. You're welcome to stay. I got three extra-large pies from Pino's, and they just got delivered."

My father was in the living room watching television, one of the pizza boxes on his lap, a beer bottle stuck between his legs. I sat in the kitchen with Grandma and pulled off a piece with pepperoni, extra cheese.

"What's the word on Joyce Barnhardt?" I asked.

"No one's seen her. Grace Rizzo thinks Joyce was having an affair with the jeweler. Grace's daughter works across the street at the nail salon, and she said Joyce would go into the jewelry store and wouldn't come out for a long time. And once the closed sign got put up on the front door when Joyce was there."

"Frank Korda was married. Hard to believe he'd press charges against Joyce and create controversy if he was sleeping with her."

"I don't know. Anyway, they released his body already," Grandma said. "There's a viewing scheduled at the funeral parlor for tomorrow night. It's gonna be a full house. Not everyone gets compacted at the junkyard. I heard the TV people might even be there."

I felt a twitch run the length of my spine. I didn't share Grandma's enthusiasm for viewings.

"I got an appointment to get my hair and nails done tomorrow morning, so I look good," Grandma said.

• • •

I sat in the parking lot to my apartment building with half a pizza on the seat next to me and my motor running. I didn't see any Scions or Town Cars, so I felt safe from two-thirds of the people who wanted to kill me. I didn't know what kind of car Razzle Dazzle drove, and that worried me. I had a stun gun that was low on juice, and a full can of hair spray. That was pretty much my whole bag of tricks for self-defense.

I dialed Morelli, and this time he answered.

"Are you hungry?" I asked him. "I have half an extra-large Pino's pizza."

"Do I have to talk to you?"

"No."

"Good, because I'm not ready to talk to you."

"Understood. Are you still working?"

"I'm home," Morelli said. "I had to walk Bob and give him dinner."

"So can you come over now?"

"Yeah."

I was going to rot in hell. Did I love Morelli? Yes. Did I miss him? Yes. Was that why I was inviting him over for pizza? No. I was inviting him over because I was afraid to go into my apartment alone. Morelli was big and strong and carried a gun that actually had bullets in it. Jeez, I was such a loser!

I cut the engine and made my way across the lot with the pizza box. I waited in the foyer until I saw Morelli's SUV. I took the stairs and waited in the hall in front of my door. The elevator doors opened, Morelli walked out, and I smiled at him.

"Did you just get here?" he asked.

I bit into my lower lip. I couldn't do it.

"No," I said. "I've been waiting for

you. I was afraid to go into my apartment."

"So you lured me here with pizza?"

"No. I brought the pizza home for you. I just had a sort of panic attack when I drove into the lot."

"Should I go in with gun drawn?"

"Your choice, but it might not be a bad idea."

Morelli looked at me. "Who do you think is in there?"

"Could be most anyone, the way things are going. Could be Razzle Dazzle."

"What's a razzle dazzle?"

"According to Berger, he's a killer nutcase."

Morelli pulled his gun out, unlocked my door, and pushed it open. He did a walk-through and came back to me. "No Razzle Dazzle." He pulled me into the apartment, closed and locked the door behind me, and holstered his gun.

"What kind of pizza is that?" he asked.

"Pepperoni with extra cheese." I put the box on the counter and flipped the lid. "Sorry, I don't have any beer."

"Just as well," Morelli said, folding a piece and biting in. "There's a chance I'll have to go back to work tonight."

"You're always working."

"If people would stop shooting, stabbing, and compacting each other, my hours would cut back."

"Speaking of compacting . . ."

"No other bodies at the junkyard. Connie's relatives make sure there's a fast turnover of cars. Smash 'em, and ship 'em out."

"There's a rumor that Joyce was doing the jeweler."

"Joyce did everyone."

"Did Joyce ever do you?" I asked Morelli.

"No," he said. "She's scary. Just so you know, you aren't the only one looking for her. She's wanted for questioning regarding the Korda murder."

"Any leads?"

"No. How about you?"

"Nothing."

Morelli took a second piece of pizza, and the doorbell rang. He moved to the door and looked out the peephole.

"It's a woman," Morelli said. "She's holding a cake box."

I sidled up next to him and looked out. It was Brenda Schwartz.

"You remember the guy who got killed and stuffed into a garbage can at LAX?"

"Richard Crick."

"Yeah. And you know about the photograph?"

"Un-hunh."

"And you know how there are fake FBI guys and real FBI guys and Razzle Dazzle, who all want the photograph?"

Morelli didn't say anything, but the line of his mouth tightened ever so slightly.

"Well, this is Brenda Schwartz," I said. "She says she's Crick's fiancée, and she's another photograph hunter."

"So she brought you a cake?"

"Possibly. There could be a bomb in the box. She seems a little unstable."

"Anything else I should know?" Morelli asked.

"She carries a gun, but it's not very big."

"This is why I have acid reflux," Morelli said. And he opened the door.

"Oh cripes," Brenda said, looking at Morelli. "Do I have the wrong apartment? I was looking for Stephanie Plum."

I peeked around Morelli. "You have the right apartment. This is my boyfriend."

"Maybe," Morelli said. "Maybe not."

"I figured we got off on the wrong foot earlier," Brenda said to me. "What with threatening to shoot you and everything. Anyhoo, I got you a cake. I thought we could have a girl-to-girl over it."

"That's nice of you, but I don't have the photograph," I told her.

"Yeah, but you know where it is."

"No, I don't know where it is."

She pinched her lips together for a second. "Then why do certain people think you got the photograph?"

"Misinformation," I said. "Probably originating from your fiancé."

"Richard Crick didn't give out misinformation," she said. "He was a *doctor.* May he rest in peace."

"Why do you want the photograph?" Morelli asked her.

"None of your beeswax," she said. "I just do. It's sentimental. I was his fiancée."

"You're not wearing an engagement ring," Morelli said.

"Honestly," Brenda said, rolling her eyes. "He's dead. You don't expect me to pine away forever, do you?" She looked back at me. "So are you going to give me the photograph, or what?"

I felt a vein start to throb in my temple. "I *don't* have the photograph."

"Fine. Have it your way," Brenda said. "But I'm giving you warning. I'm going to get that photograph. And you're not getting any of this cake, either." And she turned and sashayed down the hall to the elevator.

Morelli and I retreated into my apartment and closed and locked the door.

"Tell me the truth," he said. "Do you have the photograph?"

I smacked the heel of my hand against my forehead so hard I almost knocked myself out. *"Unh!"*

"Does that mean *no* or *yes*?" Morelli asked.

"It means *NO*! No, no, no, no, no."

"Don't get your panties in a bunch. I'm not exactly in the loop here."

"You're too busy to be in the loop."

"No one could stay in the loop with you. You're a disaster magnet. You suck it in. I used to think it was because of your job. But that's too simple an explanation. You can't even go on vacation without attracting killers. Not just one killer, either. You have a whole gaggle of killers after you. Is Berger any help with this?"

"They've had budget cuts."

He went to my brown bear cookie jar, removed the lid, and took my gun out.

"It's not loaded," he said.

"You don't really want me going around with a loaded gun, do you?"

He returned the gun to the cookie jar. "Good point. I can't believe I'm asking this, but is Ranger watching your back?"

"He monitors my car. Beyond that, it's hard to tell what Ranger's doing."

Morelli's phone buzzed with a text message. He read the message and gave up a sigh. "I have to go. I'd like to help you, but I have no idea, short of handcuffing you to my furnace and locking the cellar door, how to keep you safe. It's not like you're good at accepting advice."

"Jeez, it's not that bad."

"Cupcake, you gotta be careful." He pulled me to him and kissed me. He broke from the kiss and cut his eyes to the pizza box. "Are you going to want that last piece of pizza?"

"It's yours."

He dropped a piece of crust into Rex's cage and took the pizza, box and all. "Lock your door when I leave and don't let anyone in."

I watched Morelli walk down the hall and disappear into the elevator. This is unsettling, I thought. I had no clue where I actually stood with him. In some ways, he'd traded places with Ranger as the man of mystery.

I closed and locked my door and slouched in front of the television. After an hour, I was restless. There's a limit to how many sitcom reruns you can watch, and I was tired of *Cupcake Wars* on the Food Network. I was sleeping through a documentary on fire ants when my cell phone rang. It was nine o'clock, and I assumed it was Morelli.

Turned out it was Joyce Barnhardt.

"I need help," Joyce said.

"There's a rumor going around that you're dead."

"Not yet."

This was only marginally better than the fire ants. "What's going on?" I asked her. "Why the big disappearance?"

"People are looking for me."

"And?"

"And I figure you can help me. If you help me out, I let you bring me in. You get your capture money. Vinnie's happy. It's all good."

"What do I have to do?"

"For starters, I need something from my town house."

"Your town house is locked, and you have an alarm system."

"I'm sure you can get around it."

"Only if you give me a key and your code."

"There's a house key hidden in a fake rock to the right of the front door. The code is 6213."

"What do you need?"

"I need a key. It looks like a little padlock key. It should be in my top dresser drawer in my bedroom."

"What do I do with this key if I get it?"

"Hang on to it, and call me. You've got my number in your cell now."

"Where are you?"

She disconnected.

Here was a problem. I was dying to go out this very second and get the key. I'd totally had it with the fire ants, and I could use the money Joyce's capture would bring me. Problem was getting back into my apartment. I'd already played my Morelli card, and he'd be drinking Pepto by the gallon if I asked him to help me again, much less told him I was in league with Barnhardt. If I asked Ranger for help, I'd end up naked. It had some appeal, but truth is, I was beginning to not like myself so much. The honest confusion of loving two men was giving way to something that felt a little like unhealthy self-indulgence.

I'm not an especially introspective person. Mostly, I go day by day putting one foot in front of the other, hoping I'm moving forward. If I think weighty thoughts about life, death, and cellulite, it's usually in the shower. And these thoughts are usually cut short by lack of hot water in my decrepit apartment building. Anyway, like it or not, I was presently caught in the throes of self-examination, and I was coming up short. And there was a voice, sounding a lot like Lula's, in the back of my head, telling me I'd been loosey-goosey with my morals in Hawaii, and that's what had messed up my juju.

THIRTEEN

I went to bed early, and I got up early. I showered, got dressed, and pulled my hair back into a ponytail. I swiped on mascara and laced up my Chucks. This is a new day, I told myself. I was going to start out right. I was going to have a healthy breakfast, and I was going to charge ahead with a new, positive attitude. No more boinking in closets with Ranger. No more hiding behind Morelli's muscle. I was a woman in charge this morning.

I was low on breakfast food and fruity things, so I made myself a sandwich and headed out. I stopped short in the parking lot, momentarily confused when I didn't see the RAV. After a couple fast heartbeats, it all came back to me. I was driving a truck now. Appropriate, I thought. Empowering. I'd practically grown testicles.

I drove to Mercado Mews, parked in Joyce's driveway, and went in search of the fake rock. I found the rock, got the key to the front door, opened the door, and decoded the alarm. I went straight to Joyce's bedroom and rifled the top drawer to her dresser. I found the small padlock key, slipped it into my jeans pocket, and left. I reset the alarm for her, locked her door, put the key back in the fake rock, and drove off. I pulled into the parking area for the model home and called Joyce. No answer. No way to leave a message.

Forty minutes later, I eased the truck to the curb in front of the new office. A makeshift sign in the window advertised Vincent Plum Bail Bonds. Connie was at one of the two desks, and Lula was looking uncomfortable in a folding chair.

"Who designs these things anyways?" Lula said when I walked in. "My ass don't fit. They think everybody got some bony ass? What about us big-and-beautiful-ass people? Where are we supposed to sit? I'm gonna have an ass crease from hangin' off this thing. And it don't got arms or nothin'. Couldn't you get a chair with arms? Where am I supposed to set my chicken bucket?"

"You haven't got a chicken bucket," Connie said.

"Yeah, but I'm gonna," Lula told her. "And where am I gonna set it?"

The office was beyond bare bones. Voices echoed in the empty room. The walls were army-surplus khaki. The floor was liquidation linoleum. It was lit by light from the storefront window and an overhead forty-watt bulb.

"This is sort of depressing," I said to Connie.

"This is nothing," Connie said. "Wait until it rains. You'll want to eat a bullet."

I saw Vinnie's Caddy angle in behind my truck. Vinnie literally sprang out and skipped into the office.

"I don't know what he's on, but I want some," Lula said.

Vinnie stopped in the middle of the room, stuffed his hands into his pants pockets, and rocked back on his heels. He was grinning and snorting with happiness. "I did it," he said. "I fixed DeAngelo good. You don't mess with Vincent Plum. No way. You pay the price." And Vinnie did one of those spike-the-ball things you see football players do when they make a touchdown. "Yeah, baby," he said. *"Yeah!"*

"What did you do?" Lula asked.

"I filled his Mercedes with horse shit," Vinnie said. "I know this guy who has horses, and I got him to take his dung pile and dump it into DeAngelo's Mercedes last night. Filled that Mercedes from the floor to the roof. Had to break a window to get it all in. DeAngelo blew up my bus, so I filled his car with shit. Genius, right?"

"DeAngelo didn't blow up the bus," Connie said. "I just got the report from the fire marshal. The coffeemaker shorted out and started the fire."

Some of the color left Vinnie's face. "Say what?"

"Oh man," Lula said. "DeAngelo is gonna be pissed. Least he won't know who did it."

"I left a note," Vinnie said.

Lula gave a hoot of laughter and fell off her chair.

"But we all thought he did it," Vinnie said.

"This could be bad," Connie said. "DeAngelo is connected. And I don't think he has a sense of humor."

I caught a flash of black on the street and saw an Escalade double-park.

"Uh-oh," I said. "I think this is DeAngelo."

Vinnie dove for cover under Connie's desk.

The front door banged open, and DeAngelo stormed in, red-faced and crazy-eyed.

"Where is he? I know he's here," DeAngelo said. "Perverted, slimy little weasel."

Lula stood. "Hey, look who's here. It's Spanky."

DeAngelo looked over at Lula. "Your asshole boss filled my car with horse shit."

Lula brushed herself off and adjusted her girls. "That car was all wrong for you anyways," Lula said. "You should be driving something hot, like a Ferrari or one of them Lamborghinis. Or maybe some big ol' muscle car. You just don't belong in that plain-ass Mercedes. He did you a favor. You'd get a lot more complimentary BJs if you was driving a Ferrari."

"You're right," DeAngelo said. "Tell your boss if he delivers on a Ferrari, I won't kill him."

DeAngelo turned on his heel, left the office, and was whisked away in the Escalade.

"That went pretty good," Lula said.

Vinnie crawled out from under the desk. "Where am I going to get a Ferrari? Do you have any idea what a Ferrari costs? It costs more than my house."

• • •

"That was fun," Lula said. "What are we gonna do next? I'm in a mood to *wham* somebody."

"We need to pay another visit to Lahonka Goudge," I said.

Lula hiked her bag onto her shoulder. "I'm up for that."

We took my truck, and I drove into the projects and crept past Lahonka's unit.

"We gonna be sneaky, or we just gonna bust in?" Lula asked.

"We're going to ring her doorbell and politely but firmly reason with her."

"Oh yeah," Lula said. "That always works. How about I just wait in the truck."

"Fine," I said. "Wait in the truck. This won't take long, because I have a positive attitude this morning, and I'm going to get the job done. I'm changing my juju."

"Good for you," Lula said. "Only you'd change your juju faster if you sneak up on her, put a pillowcase over her head, and hit her with a big stick. *WHAM*!"

I parked, and we both got out of the truck.

"I thought you were staying behind," I said.

"I don't want to miss the juju-changing moment," Lula said.

"Scoff all you want, but you'll see. I'm turning this around."

"I'm not scoffin'," Lula said. "Do I look like I'm scoffin'?"

"Yes."

"Well, okay, maybe I'm scoffin' a little."

We threaded our way through the kids' toys littering the sidewalk, and I rang Lahonka's doorbell.

"Go away!" Lahonka yelled through the door.

"I want to talk."

"I'm busy. Come back next year."

"How about this," Lula said. "How about you open this door, or I'll shoot it full of holes."

"You can't do that," Lahonka said. "This here's public housing. That's a taxpayer door. Us taxpayers put in good money for that door."

"You pay taxes?" Lula asked.

"Not me personally," she said. "I

don't *give* money. I just *get* money. I'm on the good side of that coin."

"Stand back," Lula said. "I'm shooting."

"No! No shooting." Lahonka opened the door. "Do you have any idea how long it takes to get a new door in public housing? And all kinds of vermin could climb in through those holes. Last time someone shot a hole in my door, I got a vampire bat in here."

Lula looked through the open door. "You do pretty good for not paying taxes. You got a big flat-screen television and nice furniture. And is that your Mercedes at the curb?"

"I'm a entrepreneur," Lahonka said. "I'm the American dream."

"More like the American nightmare," Lula said.

"Back to business," I said to Lahonka. "We need to take you downtown to get rebonded. You missed your court date."

"I know I missed my court date. You already told me that. I'm electing not to participate in the judicial system."

"You don't want your kids growing

up thinking you're a scofflaw, do you?" Lula said.

"I don't know what the heck scofflaw means. Is that Russian?" Lahonka pulled some credit cards out of her pocket. "I can see you two ladies are no dummies. So I'll make a deal with you. You can each have your pick of all these credit cards if you forget this whole thing."

"Are you tryin' to bribe us?" Lula asked. "Because we don't take no bribes. We got honor. We got integrity coming out our ass." She looked down at the cards. "Holy smoke. Is that a platinum American Express card? And a Tiffany card? Where'd you get a Tiffany card?"

"Is that the one you want?" Lahonka asked. "You want the Tiffany? That's a real good choice."

"I guess I could use a Tiffany card," Lula said. "Don't see no harm in taking a Tiffany card. It's not like I'd have to use it, but it would class up my wallet."

"She doesn't want the Tiffany card," I said to Lahonka. "You're going to have to come downtown with us."

She stepped back, slammed the door shut, and locked it. "Bite me!" she yelled through the door.

"Shoot the door," I said to Lula.

"What about the politely reasoning shit?" Lula asked.

"Just shoot the damn door."

"You can't shoot it," Lahonka yelled. "I'm standing right here behind it, and if you shoot the door, you'll shoot me. And I'm a unarmed woman."

"No problem," Lula said, hauling her Glock out of her purse. "I'll shoot low." And Lula squeezed one off.

"YOW!" Lahonka shrieked. "You shot me. You sonovabitch, you shot me in my foot. I'm gonna die. I'm gonna bleed to death. I don't got no insurance, either. And what about my kids? Who's gonna take care of my kids when I'm dead? I'm willin' them to you. You deserve them, you sonovabitch. Let's see *you* buy new sneakers every time their goddamn feet grow."

"Do you think she's really shot?" I asked Lula.

Lula shrugged. "I didn't think the bullet would go through the door, but looks like that's one of them cheapskate hollow jobs. There should be a law against those doors."

Lahonka ripped the door open. "Of course I'm shot, you moron. What the hell's wrong with you, shooting a unarmed woman? I'm feelin' faint. Everything's goin' black."

And Lahonka crashed to the floor.

Lula looked down at Lahonka's foot. "Yep, she's shot all right."

"This is going to mean a lot of paperwork," I said to Lula.

"You told me to shoot her. Wasn't my idea," Lula said. "I was just following orders. Hell, I'm not even a real bounty hunter. You're the bounty hunter in charge, and I'm just a bounty hunter helper."

I had a twitch in my left eye. I put my finger to it and took a couple deep breaths. "We need to take her to the emergency room. Help me drag her out to the truck."

"Good thinking that you got a truck," Lula said. "We can lay her out in the back, and you don't even have to worry about her bleeding all over the place."

Fifteen minutes later, I pulled into the hospital emergency drive-thru. I stopped in front of the entrance, and Lula and I ran around to get Lahonka.

"Uh-oh," Lula said. "There's no Lahonka here. She must have jumped out at a light or something."

We retraced our steps to make sure Lahonka wasn't roadkill, toes cocked in the gutter.

• • •

"I didn't even see no blood trails," Lula said when I parked in front of the office. "I thought I shot her good enough to at least draw blood."

"You've got to stop shooting people," I said. "It's against the law."

"That wasn't my fault," Lula said, pushing through the front door to the office. "That was your fault. It's your juju. It sucks. It's getting frightening just being next to you."

"Oh God, now what?" Connie said.

"No big deal," Lula said. "We just can't catch anyone."

"As long as you didn't shoot anyone,"

Connie said. “You didn’t shoot anyone, did you?”

Lula’s eyes got big. “Why do you ask? Did you hear something?”

Connie put her hands over her ears. “I don’t want to know. Don’t tell me.”

“Fine by me,” Lula said. “I don’t want to talk about it, either. Wasn’t exactly a gratifying experience. Not that it was my fault.”

“Anything new come in?” I asked Connie.

“No. It’s been slow,” Connie said. “Moving the office around isn’t helping business.”

I stepped outside and tried Joyce again, but she still wasn’t picking up. While I was standing on the sidewalk a gray Camry parked behind my truck and Berger and Gooley got out.

“I liked the last office location,” Gooley said. “One-stop shopping. You could get bonded out and buy a black-and-white cookie all at the same time.”

“We have the finished sketch,” Berger said to me. “We wanted you to take a last look at it before we send it up the line.” He pulled the sketch out of a folder and handed it to me. "Is this the guy in the photograph?"

"I can barely remember the photograph," I told him, "but this guy looks familiar."

Lula swung out of the office and looked over my shoulder. "I know this guy," she said. "It's Tom Cruise."

I looked back at the photograph. Lula was right. It was Tom Cruise. No wonder he looked familiar.

Connie wandered out. "What's going on?"

Lula showed the sketch to Connie. "Who is this?"

"Tom Cruise," Connie said.

Gooley gave a snort of laughter, and Berger closed his eyes and pinched his nose between thumb and index finger, indicating an approaching migraine. They turned on their heels, retreated to the Camry, and drove off.

"What were they doing with a picture of Tom Cruise?" Lula was excited. "Is he in the area? Is he making a movie here? I wouldn't mind seeing Tom Cruise. I hear he's short, but I wouldn't hold that against him."

"It was supposed to be a sketch of the guy in the photograph," I said, "but I guess I was thinking of Tom Cruise when I gave the description to the FBI artist."

"Or maybe the guy in the photograph *was* Tom Cruise," Lula said.

I shook my head. "He wasn't Tom Cruise, but I think there were similarities. His hair and the shape of his face."

"I say we go proactive," Lula said. "What we gotta do is root out the bad guys. We gotta get to the bottom of this. This is like one of them intrigue things. If we just knew what this story was, I bet it could be a television show. They're always looking for good shit like this."

"I don't want to be a television show," I said.

"Okay, but you don't want to be dead, either. I don't see those FBI idiots doing anything for you. I say we take charge and figure out what's going on. WHAM! And then if you don't want to sell it to television, we could sell it to one of them book publishers. We could even write the book ourself. How hard could it be?"

I had mixed feelings about going proactive. On the one hand, I was in my take-charge mode, and Lula was right about the FBI not doing a lot for me. On the *other* hand, I hated to get more involved. I was really hoping that if I just stuck to my story, eventually everyone would leave me alone. And from a purely practical point of view, I wasn't making money when I chased down the people looking for the photograph.

"We could start by checking out Brenda," Lula said. "She works at one of them strip malls before you get to Princeton. And we could look for Magpie on the way."

Good compromise, I thought. There were two cemeteries off Route 1. He'd been known to hunker down in both of them. And on the way back to Trenton, I could take an early exit and head for the farmer's market and flea market. There were acres of woods around the markets, and the woods were laced with single-lane dirt roads used for romance, and drugs, and, in Magpie's case, camping. Magpie drove and lived in an ancient Crown Vic. In its glory years, the Crown Vic had been a black-and-white police car, but it had been sold at auction, and eventually found its way to Magpie. Magpie had hand-painted black over the white, but the car was still a bashed-in, rusted-out, retired cop car.

I drove one exit on Route 1 and turned off into the newer and smaller of the two cemeteries. For the most part, it was all flat ground, broken by an occasional tree. All grave markers were the same. Small granite slabs sunk into the grass. Easy maintenance. You could probably get the tractor up to about 40 mph and be done with the whole deal in an hour.

I took the loop around the cemetery, circled the little chapel and crematorium, and headed out, finding no indicators that Magpie had recently squatted here. No blackened splotch from a campfire. No stains from leaking transmission oil. No bag of discarded garbage. No ribbons of toilet tissue floating across the landscape.

The second cemetery was ten miles down the highway. It was a real monster, with rolling hills, lush landscaping, and elaborate tombstones. I methodically worked my way through the maze of feeder roads curling over and around hill and dale. Again, no sign of Magpie, so I returned to Route 1.

Lula had The Hair Barn plugged into the GPS app on her cell phone. "It's on the left," she said. "Take the next light."

The Hair Barn was located in a complex that included some light industrial businesses, a budget hotel, two fairly large office buildings, and an outdoor shopping mall. The shopping mall was anchored at one end by a Kohl's and a Target at the other. The Hair Barn was in the middle of the mall. The Scion was parked at the outer perimeter of the lot with what I assumed were a few other employee cars.

I found a space close to Kohl's, and Lula and I walked to the cluster of stucco-faced buildings. We stood outside The Hair Barn and watched Brenda fiddle with an older woman's hair, teasing it up and smoothing it out.

"That's not good," Lula said. "That woman looks like Donald Trump on a bad day. And he don't look all that good on a good day."

Brenda finished, the woman tottered to the desk, and Brenda took a moment to clean up her station. Lula stayed outside, and I went in to talk to Brenda.

Brenda got steely-eyed when she saw me. "What are you doing here?" she asked. "Did you wise up and bring me the photograph?"

"No. I want some answers."

She looked through the front window at Lula. "I see you left your muscle outside. Isn't that risky?"

"Lula isn't my muscle."

"Well then, what is she?"

Good question. I didn't know the answer. "She's just Lula," I said. "Okay, yeah, I guess she's my muscle."

Brenda dropped her brush and comb into a drawer. "So what did you come here for? You want a haircut? I could do a lot better than what you got. You got no style."

"It's a ponytail."

"Yeah, but it's boring. You should add a piece. We got a bunch on the wall. Or you could put some color in it. Like gold streaks. Pull some of the hair out and rat it. You know, mess it up like mine. You see how much better my hair looks?"

I glanced at her hair and bit my lip. She looked like an exploded canary. "Maybe next time," I said. "I want to know about the photograph. Why does everyone want it?"

"I told you why I want it. Poor dead Ritchy wanted me to have it." She stiffened a little. "Wait a minute. What do you mean *everyone*?"

"You. And everyone."

"There's others?" she asked.

"You didn't know?"

Brenda's lips curled back and her eyes got squinty. "That sonovabitch. He's trying to cut me out. I should have guessed."

"Who?" I asked her. "Who's the sonovabitch?"

"Boy, this really steams me."

"Who? Who?"

"Never mind *who.* And you better not

be dealing with him. He's a snake in the grass. And he hasn't got any money, either. Don't believe him if he tells you he's got money."

"Give me a clue. What does he look like? Old, young, fat?"

"I can't chat anymore," Brenda said. "I got a client."

"Well?" Lula said when I left the shop. "How'd that go?"

"It didn't go anywhere."

"You must have learned something."

"Nope," I said. "Nothing useful." I felt my ponytail. "Do you think my hair is boring?"

"Compared to what? It's not as good as my hair, for instance. But it's better than lots of other white folks' hair."

We climbed into the truck, and I stuck the key in the ignition.

"I think we should take a look at Brenda's apartment," I said to Lula. "Connie has it in West Windsor."

Why not? I thought. If for no reason other than grim curiosity.

Lula tapped the address into her cell phone GPS. "I got it. It's not all that far from here."

I drove one exit on Route 1, turned off, and followed Lula's directions.

"She's renting, but not an apartment," Lula said. "Looks to me like she's renting a house."

We were winding our way through a neighborhood of small, single-story homes in varying stages of disrepair. Several were empty with FOR SALE signs planted in their small front yards. Most had curtains hanging in windows. Many had swing sets in the backyards.

I found Brenda's house and sat at idle, taking it in. Driveway leading to single-car attached garage. The house had been painted pale green with bright yellow trim. The yard was bare but neat.

"Let's take a look," Lula said.

"We can't just walk around and look in windows. There are cars parked in some of the driveways. Probably, there are people at home in some of the houses. We'll be noticed."

"Yeah, but we do that all the time," Lula said.

"We do it when we're looking for a felon and they've waived their rights. Brenda isn't a felon."

I returned to the highway, and Berger called.

"We'd like you to work with an artist again," he said.

"I don't think that's going to accomplish anything," I told him. "I can barely remember the photograph. And now I've got Tom Cruise stuck in my head."

"Just try, okay? There's a lot riding on this . . . like my pension."

If I hadn't been doing eighty, I would have banged my head against the steering wheel. "When do you want me to come in?"

"Now."

FOURTEEN

I dropped Lula at the office and swung around into town. It was midday and the roads were clogged with cars. Lots were filled, street parking was nonexistent, and after ten minutes of circling several blocks, I gave up and drove into the FBI building's underground garage. It was public parking, but there was a designated FBI area.

I took the elevator to the sixth floor and went directly to the conference room. Berger, Gooley, and the artist were already there.

"We thought maybe it was the last

artist who was thinking about Tom Cruise," Berger said. "So we're starting over with Fred."

I took a seat and nodded at Fred. "Good luck."

Fred managed a tight smile that was a shade away from being a grimace. An hour later, we had a new sketch.

"How do you feel about this?" Berger asked me. "Is this the guy?"

I did palms up. I didn't know. "Maybe," I said.

"At least it's not Tom Cruise," Berger said.

Gooley studied it. "It's Ashton Kutcher."

We crowded in to see the sketch.

"Shit! He's right," Berger said. "It's freaking Ashton Kutcher."

I took another look at it, and I had to admit it did look a lot like Ashton Kutcher.

"Well, they both have brown hair, so we can be pretty sure he has brown hair," I said. "Do you guys validate parking?"

"Not anymore," Berger said. "Budget cuts."

• • •

I took the elevator to the second parking level and walked to my truck. It seemed to me Ashton Kutcher and Tom Cruise weren't so far apart. Brown hair, nice-looking, angular face, potential for *Top Gun* attitude. Maybe it was the attitude that was the common denominator. A quality in their faces that projected a boyishly endearing wiseass personality.

I pressed the unlock button on my car key, reached for the door handle, and got yanked off my feet from behind. In a matter of seconds, I was dragged across the garage and slammed against a panel van. I was so caught by surprise that I barely reacted, ineffectively flailing my arms and yelling, the yelling getting lost in the cavernous garage.

I caught a flash of light from a knife blade and felt the tip of the knife bite into my neck. I went dead still, and Raz's face swam into focus inches from mine.

"You will be stopping moving," he said. "You are understanding?"

I nodded.

"Into the van," he said. "Facedown, or I kill you good. I carve you into pieces and eat you for snack."

I was too scared to totally focus, but I knew getting into the van wasn't a step in the right direction. I pulled back, opened my mouth to scream, and he hit me in the face with the butt end of the knife. I tasted blood, a switch got flipped on in my brain, and I went into killer survival mode, kicking, screaming, scratching, gouging. The knife got knocked out of his hand, we scrambled for it, and I got there first. I lunged at him, catching him in the thigh, digging the blade in deep, opening a long gash that gushed blood. He shrieked and grabbed his leg. It was a panicky blur after that. I kicked at him, and he tried to roll away. He was bleeding and cursing, and I kept kicking. I slipped on the blood-slick garage floor, and he took the opportunity to dive into the van and ram the door closed. The motor caught, and his wheels spun and screeched on the cement as he sped away.

I bent at the waist and sucked in air. I looked down at the ground and realized I was dripping blood. I wasn't sure where it was coming from. I walked on wobbly legs to the elevator and pushed the sixth-floor button. The doors opened, and I stepped out and stood still for a beat, not sure what to do because I was tracking blood on the tile floor.

Several people rushed over to me. One of them was Berger.

"Jeez, I'm sorry about the blood," I said.

I saw his eyes go to my right hand, and I realized I was still holding the bloody knife. I dropped the knife and went down to one knee.

"I don't feel good," I said. And it was lights out.

• • •

I had a paramedic bending over me when I opened my eyes.

"Am I dead?" I asked him.

"Nope."

"Will I be dead anytime soon?"

"Not from these injuries, but the consensus is you're a train wreck."

"You're not the first person to tell me that."

"I bet. You have a cut lip. I don't think it needs stitches. I put a butterfly bandage on it. I'm going to get you up and give you an ice pack. You might also have a slightly broken nose. I'm giving you an ice pack for that, too. The nose looks okay, but you should see a doctor. You were gushing blood out of it."

"Anything else?"

"Some superficial cuts on your arms and legs. And you'll probably have some monster bruises on your face. Do you think you can sit?"

"Yeah, I'm good. Get me up."

He helped me up, and I sat until my head cleared and my lips weren't numb. I got to my feet and did some deep breathing, trying to calm myself. My clothes were soaked in blood, and there was blood all over the floor.

"Is this all from me?" I asked.

"The stuff on the floor is from you,"

Berger said. "I imagine some of the blood you're wearing is from the other guy, since you were the one who ended up with the knife."

"Razzle Dazzle," I said.

"I have someone down in the garage securing the scene," Berger said. "If you parked in the FBI area, we'll have the attack recorded."

"He came out of nowhere," I told him. "I was unlocking my car, and he was on me, trying to get me into a van."

Gooley elbowed his way through the crowd around me. "They have the tape up in the conference room," he said. "I haven't had a chance to preview it."

I thanked the paramedic, took my ice packs and towels, and followed Gooley and Berger down the hall to the conference room. We sat around the table, and Gooley pulled the tape up on the flat screen at the end of the room.

"Are you sure you want to watch this?" Berger asked me.

"Absolutely." Mostly because I couldn't remember anything. It was a total blur after Razzle said he was going to cut me up and eat me.

The image was grainy black-and-white.

"Not in color?" I asked.

"Budget cuts," Berger said. "We got discontinued stock from Radio Shack."

For thirty seconds, there was only the still image of the parking area. My truck could be seen at the edge of the picture. Finally I appeared and walked across the traffic lane. I approached my truck, pressed the remote, and a man rushed in behind me. He was wearing jeans and a windbreaker. He had a knife that looked like something out of *Arabian Nights*. It had a big curved blade and a thick handle. He grabbed me by my ponytail and yanked me back, pulling me across the garage to a van. He held the knife to my neck, and got up into my face.

"What is he saying?" Berger asked.

"He said he was going to kill me good. And then he was going to cut me up in little pieces and eat me."

"Sick," Gooley said. "I like it."

The tape continued, and I watched myself try to pull away from Raz, watched Raz hit me in the face with the butt of the knife, snapping my head back.

The three of us sucked in air when I got hit. There was a moment of suspended animation where Raz stepped back and I gathered myself together. What followed was pure instinct on my part. I brought my heel down on his instep as hard as I could, catching him by surprise. He bent slightly to look at his foot, and I kicked him in the face.

"Whoa!" Gooley said. "Ow."

Raz tackled me at knee level, we went down, and it turned into a catfight. He was trying to punch me, and I was scratching and biting. I grabbed his hair and kneed him in the nuts.

"Cripes," Berger said. "That had to hurt."

I saw myself reach for the knife, wrap my hand around it, and slash at Raz, catching him in the leg, opening a twelve-inch gash in his thigh.

"Holy shit," Berger and Gooley said in unison.

Raz reached for his injured leg, and I scrambled to my feet. He was in a semi-fetal position, trying to protect his nuts and the knife wound, and I kicked him as hard as I could in the kidneys a bunch of times.

Gooley and Berger leaned forward, eyes wide.

"Fuck," Gooley said.

Raz rolled away, managed to get to his feet, catapulted himself into the van, and slammed the door shut. I was waving the knife and yelling when he drove away.

"I need to go home and change out of these clothes," I said. "Is there anything else?"

"I'm good," Berger said.

"Yeah, me, too," Gooley said. "I got nothing. I might need some air. I'm lucky I didn't lose my lunch when you kicked him that last time."

"I felt threatened," I said by way of explanation.

• • •

There were no scary cars in my parking lot. No black Town Car, no van, no Scion. I limped into my building and let myself into my apartment. I stood in the kitchen, stripped down naked, stuffed all my clothes into a big plastic garbage bag, and set the bag by the door. The clothes were beyond washing. They were going down the trash chute.

I limped into my bathroom and stood under a hot shower until all the blood was washed away and I stopped sobbing. I had no idea why I was crying. I mean, it wasn't like I lost the fight, right? I shampooed my hair and lathered up one last time. I got out of the shower, avoided looking at myself in the mirror, and wrapped myself in a towel.

I stepped into my bedroom and came face-to-face with Ranger.

He did a slow, full-body scan. "Babe."

"Do *not* tell me I'm a train wreck."

"Have you seen yourself?"

"No."

He handed me a fresh ice pack. "You need to keep this on your face. Has a doctor looked at your nose?"

"No. Do you think I should get it X-rayed or something?"

"Can you breathe?" Ranger asked. "Are you in pain?"

"Yes, I can breathe. And it hurts about as much as the rest of me."

"You have some minor swelling. Other than that, it looks okay. If things change, you should get it checked out."

"How did you know I was attacked?"

"We have a friend on the sixth floor."

Ranger wasn't a man who showed much emotion, but I could swear I detected some steam curling off the roots of his hair. "Are you angry about something?" I asked him.

"Anger isn't a productive emotion. Let's just say I'm not happy."

"Should I ask why?"

"I expect you already know. You're caught up in the middle of something bad, and you're not being careful. Get dressed and come out to the dining room. I have a show-and-tell for you."

Oh boy. Ranger didn't stay to watch me get dressed. He didn't rip the towel off me. He didn't get naked. I must really look bad. I went into the bathroom and looked in the mirror. EEK! This was worse than I thought. Huge black bruise developing and swelling under my right eye. Still small amount of blood seeping from my nose. Swollen lip with ugly cut and huge bruise. Then there was the rest of me, with assorted bruises and scrapes. Not exactly a sex goddess.

I pulled on jeans and a T-shirt and half dried my hair. I plastered the ice pack to my face and went out to see Ranger.

"Here's your Smith and Wesson," he said. "I took it out of the cookie jar. From what I can see, you haven't any ammo. I took the stun gun out of your bag. It's dead. Needs recharging. And it looks to me like you're out of pepper spray and using hair spray."

I adjusted the ice pack. "Hair spray works surprisingly well."

"Don't push it," Ranger said. "I'm not in a good place." He took a gun off the table and handed it to me. "This is a semi-automatic baby Glock. It's smaller and lighter than the one I carry. It's ready to go. Do you know how to use it?"

"Yes."

"Do you know how to load it?"

"Yes."

"The only time I want to see the clip empty is immediately after you've dumped every round into a warm body."

"Jeez," I said.

"Humor me. Next up is the stun gun. This is larger than the one you're currently carrying. It'll drop a 1,500-pound cow. If you don't keep it charged, it won't drop anything."

I nodded. "Yes sir."

"Is that snark?" he asked.

"It might be."

Ranger almost smiled.

"The truth is, I'm kind of proud of the way I've defended myself so far. I'm still alive, and I only cried once. And as bad as I look, I'm in a lot better shape than the other guy."

"You work well with panic and rage," Ranger said.

I looked down at the table. "What's with the watch?"

"It works as a watch, but it's also a tracking system. As long as it's on your wrist, I can find you. There are three little buttons on the side. If you push the red button, we come get you."

"What's the blue button?"

"It sets the time."

Duh.

I removed the watch I was wearing and strapped the new watch to my wrist. "It should have diamonds," I said to Ranger.

"Maybe if you're a very good girl."

"How good would I have to be?" I asked him.

"You have a black eye, a cut lip, a broken nose, and you're flirting with me?"

"That's not the worst of it," I told him. "I've decided I'm off men."

"All things considered, that's not a bad plan," Ranger said. "I have to go. Call if you need help, or anything else."

"Now *you're* flirting," I told him.

"That wasn't flirting," Ranger said. "That was an open invitation."

I locked the door when he left. I slid the chain into place and flipped the dead bolt. None of those locks ever prevented Ranger from entering, and I'd long ago stopped wondering how he did it.

• • •

I made myself a sandwich and took it to the dining room table. Chewing was painful, but I managed to get the whole thing down. I pulled up a search program on my computer and started working my way through Brenda's husbands.

Brenda married Herbert Luckert right out of high school. The marriage lasted ten years and ended in divorce. A year later, she married Harry Zimmer. That marriage lasted seven months and ended in divorce. She was unmarried for nine years after that, eventually marrying Bernard Schwartz. The Schwartz marriage ended after three years when Schwartz emptied his medicine chest into the blender along with half a pint of vodka and drank himself into a blissful final slumber.

When Brenda married Schwartz, he owned thirty-five car washes spread throughout the state. When he killed himself, he owned four, and they were in foreclosure. He'd lost his house a couple months before. I had no idea if or how this related to the photograph, but it seemed like something to file away.

I got out of the search program and checked my email. Mostly spam. I gingerly touched my lip and my nose. Tender. I went to the bathroom and took another look. Not good, but at least I didn't have a foot-long, inch-deep gash in my thigh. I hoped Razzle Dazzle was in a lot of pain. And I really wouldn't mind if the cut got infected and his leg fell off.

My cell phone rang, and I was hoping for Joyce so I could tell her I had the key, but it was my parents' number that came up on the display.

"The Korda viewing is at seven o'clock tonight," Grandma said. "I figure you want to go and snoop around, and I was hoping I could have a ride."

"Sure."

"Are you coming for dinner? Your mother's making chicken and rice."

My mother would have a coronary incident if she saw my face. "I'm going to skip dinner," I said.

"Okay, but make sure you're not late. There's gonna be a crowd tonight, and

I don't want to get muscled to the back of the room. All the action's gonna be up by the casket."

I said good-bye to Grandma, and I went to get ice. Lots of ice, I thought. The more the better.

By six-thirty, it was clear there was only so much improvement I could expect from ice. I got dressed in a black pencil skirt, black heels, a cream sweater with a low scoop neck and matching cardigan. I wore my hair down and fluffed out, hoping it would distract from my monster bruise and cut lip. I smeared on a lot of concealer, tried to balance out the black eye with extra blush, and I was wearing my push-up bra for maximum cleavage. I took one last look in the mirror and thought this was as good as it was going to get.

I dropped my new Glock into my purse, along with the stun gun on steroids. I was wearing the GPS watch, pearl earrings, a Band-Aid where the knife had knicked my neck, and a huge Band-Aid on my skinned knee. I was the All-American Girl.

FIFTEEN

Grandma was at the door, waiting for me. I pulled to the curb, and she hustled over to the truck. She was wearing chunky black heels, a lavender suit with a white blouse, and she was carrying the black leather purse that I knew was big enough to hold her .45 long barrel.

She hoisted herself up and into the truck, buckled her seat belt, and looked over at me.

"Don't you look pretty," Grandma said. "That's such a nice sweater set."

No comment on my face or the various Band-Aids.

"Anything else?" I asked her.

"I like your hair down like that. I hardly ever see it down anymore." Grandma looked at her watch. "We gotta get a move on."

"What about my face?"

"What about it?"

"For starters, I have a black eye."

"Yeah, it's a pip," Grandma said, "but I've seen you with worse. Remember that explosion that burned your eyebrows off?"

Good lord, this is what it's come to, I thought. My own grandmother isn't shocked to see me with a black eye. I might as well admit it. I'm a train wreck.

"Is there a good story that goes with the shiner?" Grandma asked.

"I slipped in a parking garage."

"Too bad," Grandma said. "I could use something juicy for conversational material. Do you mind if I make something up?"

"Yes, I mind!"

I drove the short distance to the funeral home, off-loaded Grandma at the entrance, and trolled for a parking place. The small funeral home lot was full, but I found parking on the street a block away. Grandma had been right about the viewing. The building was packed. At three minutes after seven, the people were already spilling out the door onto the large wraparound front porch.

I kept my head down as I inched my way through the crowd, hoping not to attract attention. I was in the lobby, about to enter Slumber Room #1, and I got a call on my cell phone.

"I knew you would go to the viewing," Joyce said.

"Where are you?"

"I'm outside. And don't come out looking for me. You'll never find me. I'm dying to come in and check it all out, but it's too risky."

"Yeah, I'd capture you."

"You're the least of my worries," Joyce said. "Did you get the key?"

"Yes. Now what?"

"Hang on to it. Did you get up to the casket yet? Did you see the grieving widow?"

"No. It took me twenty minutes to cross the lobby. It's jammed in here."

"I want a report on the widow," Joyce said. "I want to know what jewelry she's wearing. It's a closed casket, right?"

"I don't know for sure, but the guy was compacted and aged for a couple days. I'm guessing he's not real attractive at this point."

"He wasn't real attractive before. How about the people there? Anyone stand out?"

"In what way?"

"Remember David Niven in the *Pink Panther* movies?"

I looked around. I didn't see David Niven. "No David Nivens here," I told her.

I hung up with Joyce, and I bumped into Morelli.

"What are you doing here?" I asked him. "Is this official business or did you come for the cookies?"

"Official business. The captain wanted police presence, and I'm supposed to be looking for Joyce."

"Do you think you'll find her?"

"Not here. She'd be crazy to show up here. Although it's hard to assess the extent of Joyce's craziness."

"My exact thoughts."

Morelli was wearing his show-no-emotion cop face. "Berger let me see the tape."

"And?" I asked.

"And I'm glad I tangled with Ranger and not you. You're an animal. You kicked the crap out of that poor bastard."

"I felt threatened."

"No doubt." His gaze traveled from my face to my enhanced cleavage, and his expression softened. "I like this sweater."

Now this is the Morelli I know and love. "Does this sweater fixation mean things are returning to normal?"

"No, this means I'm trying not to focus on your face. You look worse than I do, and I have a broken nose." He very gently touched a fingertip to my nose and the corner of my mouth. "Does it hurt?"

"Not a lot, but you could kiss it and make it better."

He brushed a whisper of a kiss across my nose and my mouth. "I'm so sorry this happened to you."

"You like me?" I asked him.

"No, but I'm working on it."

I guess I could live with that. "I was attacked by Razzle Dazzle. Did you recognize him on the tape?"

Morelli shook his head. "No. But Berger seemed to know him."

"I talked to Brenda earlier today. Not much came of it. I still have no idea why everyone's interested in the photograph."

"Berger's briefed me on the major players, and he called me in to see the tape, but he isn't talking beyond that. I don't think he knows the whole story. Someone above him wants that photograph. This isn't trivial."

"Why is Berger playing nice with you?"

"You're the only one who's seen the photograph, and I'm a connection to you."

"But I don't have the photograph, and I don't know anything. I described Tom Cruise and Ashton Kutcher to the FBI sketch artists."

Morelli did a palms up. "No one believes you."

"Do you?"

"Yes. You have nothing to gain by lying. And you look really sexy tonight from your neck down."

"I thought you didn't like me."

"Cupcake, that sweater transcends *like* or *not like.*"

I punched him in the chest. "I'm going to find Grandma."

Grandma had scored a folding chair in the third row and had saved the one next to her for me.

"This here's a real disappointing viewing," Grandma said. "I expected better, what with Frank Korda being packed off to the junkyard. I don't think there's even a reporter for the paper. And so far I haven't seen any killers pass by. Only Connie's Uncle Gino, and he's pretty much retired. He's just here for the refreshments. I was hoping to see Joyce Barnhardt. Now, that would be something." Grandma stared at the casket for a long moment. "Do you think they got him dressed up in there?" she asked. "What kind of tie do you suppose he's wearing? I bet it's hard to dress someone after they've been compacted. He probably looks like a waffle." She sighed with longing. "I sure would like to take a look."

I didn't want to look. Not even a little. Like Morelli, I'd come here on the odd chance Barnhardt would show. Now that I'd made contact with her, I was anxious to leave.

"How long do you want to stay?" I asked Grandma. "Are you ready to go?"

"Maybe another ten minutes," Grandma said. "I'm waiting to see if the widow Korda's gonna cry."

I thought chances of that were zero to nothing. The widow Korda was tight-lipped and dry-eyed, looking like she'd rather be home watching *Cheers* reruns. It was hard to see jewelry details from the third row, but it looked to me like she was wearing small gold hoop earrings and a simple gold necklace.

"I'm going to wander around," I told Grandma. "I'll meet you by the refreshments."

I reached the table with cookies and coffee set out just as my mom called me.

"What happened to you? Are you all right?"

"I'm fine."

"You're not fine. Eighteen people have called me so far asking if you were in a car crash. I've been calling you for a half hour and you haven't been answering."

"I couldn't hear the phone ringing when I was in the viewing room. Too much noise."

"Myra Kruger said you had a black eye. And Cindy Beryl said you had a broken knee. How can you drive with a broken knee?"

"I don't have a broken knee. I have a scrape on my knee, and a bruise under my eye. I slipped in a parking garage and banged my face into a parked car. It's not serious."

"Did you get shot?"

"No!"

I disconnected and stared at the tray of cookies. Nothing soft enough for me to eat with a split lip. I looked around the room and wondered who else had ratted me out to my mother. My phone rang again. Joyce.

"Well?" Joyce asked. "What was she wearing?"

"Small gold hoops and a gold necklace. It didn't look especially expensive, but what do I know."

"Were there diamonds in the hoops or the necklace?"

"No."

"Interesting," Joyce said. And she hung up.

It was close to nine o'clock when Grandma found her way to the cookie table. She ate three cookies, wrapped four more in a napkin, put them in her purse, and she was ready to head for home.

"It got better after you left," she said. "Melvin Shupe came through the line and cut the cheese right when he got up to the casket. He said he was sorry, but the widow made a big fuss over it. And then the funeral director came with air freshener, and when he sprayed it around, Louisa Belman got a asthma attack and they had to cart her out the back door to get some air. Earl Krizinski was sitting behind me, and he said he saw Louisa's underpants when they picked her up, and he said he got a stiffy."

"Louisa Belman is ninety-three years old."

"Well, I guess to Earl underpants are underpants."

We walked the block to the truck without incident. We got in and Grandma got a text.

"It's from Annie," Grandma said. "She wants to know if you found your true love."

"Tell her I'm not looking, but if he happens along, she'll be one of the first to know."

"That's a lot to write," Grandma said. "I'll just say *not yet.*" She tapped out the message and sat back in the seat. "It was so much easier when I was young. You got a boyfriend, and you married him. You had some kids, you got older, one of you died, and that was it."

"Jeez. No true love?"

"There's always been true love, but in my day, you either talked yourself into thinking you had it, or you talked yourself into thinking you didn't need it."

• • •

I took Grandma home, but I didn't go in. It had been a long day, and I was looking forward to my quiet apartment. I did the usual bad guy car search in my lot, parked the truck, and crossed to the apartment building's back door with one hand wrapped around the Glock. I took the elevator to my floor and walked down the hall thinking I should probably learn how to shoot. I knew the basics. Lula, Morelli, and Ranger all carried semiautomatics. So I had a lot of exposure, but my actual use was limited.

I let myself into my apartment, still holding the Glock. I stepped into the small foyer and realized the television was on. I was thinking Ranger or Morelli, but it turned out to be Joyce Barnhardt.

"Hey, girlfriend," Joyce said.

"What the heck are you doing here? And I'm not your girlfriend. I've *never* been your friend. I will never *want* to be your friend."

"Gee, that hurts."

"How did you get in?"

"I climbed up the fire escape and jimmied your window."

I raised the Glock. "I guess I should be thanking you. This makes everything easy for me."

"Don't be silly. I'm not going anywhere, especially not to jail."

"I have an arrest agreement, and I have a gun aimed at you."

"Honestly," Joyce said, "put the gun down. You're not going to shoot me. For one thing, I'd bleed all over your carpet. Not that it's all that great. And I'm unarmed. Just think of the paperwork, not to mention you'd probably get charged with assault with a deadly weapon. That carries a decent amount of time in an orange jumpsuit."

"I hate you."

"Blah, blah, blah," Joyce said. "Get over it. Besides, I'm an entirely new person."

"You don't lie?"

"Well, of course I lie. Everyone lies."

"You don't steal husbands?"

"Okay, once in a while I steal a husband. I don't see what the big deal is. They all turn out to be losers anyway."

"So how are you new?"

"For one thing, I have blond streaks in my hair. What do you think?"

Joyce dyed her hair flame red, so the blond streaks were icing on the cake. Some of the hair was real, and some of it was fake, and when you put it all together there was a lot of it. She wore it teased up, exploding out into big curls and waves, like Farrah Fawcett's hair on steroids.

I looked more closely at the color. "I like it. It's flattering to your skin tone." Good grief, I thought, now I was complimenting her hair. This was absolutely wrong.

"It wouldn't be a bad idea for you to do some sprucing up," Joyce said. "You don't ever look wonderful, but you look worse than usual. You get into a fight with Morelli?"

"I slipped and fell in a parking garage."

"Yeah, right. That's how you got the

busted-up face. What, do I look stupid today?"

"Why are you here?"

"I was going to come get my key, and then I realized this was the perfect place to hide out. No one would ever think to look for me here."

"Hide out? Here?" I vigorously shook my head. "No. No, no, no. No way."

"Deal with it," Joyce said. "I'm not leaving."

Keep your eye on the prize, I told myself. Go with a capture plan. Let her stay here, and when she falls asleep, sneak up on her, zap her with the monster stun gun, and cuff her. Then drag her ass back to jail and collect the money.

"Did you kill Frank Korda?" I asked her.

"No, but if he wasn't already dead, I'd consider it. The asshole lied to me."

"Despicable."

"No shit." Joyce was on the couch surfing television channels. "I can't believe you've just got the basic package. You don't get anything on this crappy television. It's going to be a real hardship for me to live here."

Eye on the prize, I repeated to myself. Don't go goofy and shoot her just for the fun of it. She's right about the bloodstain on the rug. Blood is a bitch to get out.

"I usually watch the Cooking Channel," I said.

"Jesus, that's friggin' domestic. Can you cook?"

"No. I like watching other people cook."

"Kinky."

I took the key out of my purse and gave it to Joyce. "What's the key all about?"

"It's the key to the treasure chest."

Oh boy, the treasure chest. Best not to ask, I decided. I probably didn't want to know.

"I looked all through your apartment," Joyce said. "I couldn't find any wine. For that matter, I couldn't find much of anything. It looks to me like you're one step away from making hamster stew. I don't know how you tolerate this spartan existence."

After I zap her and cuff her, I might shave her head, I thought. That would be fun. I could shave her eyebrows off, too.

"Gosh, I'm sure enjoying all this girl talk," I said, "but I'm beat. I'm going to turn in."

"I suppose I have to sleep on the couch," Joyce said.

"Yeah, the Queen of England is using my guest suite."

I brought Rex and my laptop into the bedroom with me. I wasn't leaving them out there with the spawn of Satan. I threw a pillow and an extra quilt out to Joyce, and locked my bedroom door. I laid my cuffs, stun gun, and Glock out on my bureau. *Mise en place*. I learned that from the Cooking Channel. Everything in its place for efficiency of use.

I changed from my dressy funeral home skirt and sweater to T-shirt and sweatpants. I turned my lights down and brought my laptop to bed with me. It was still early, and like most rodents, Joyce was nocturnal. So my plan was to do some research on my computer and check on Joyce after midnight.

At midnight, I dragged myself out of bed, carefully opened my door, and peeked out. Joyce was watching a movie.

"What's up?" she said.

"Not much. Everything okay out here?"

"As good as it could be, considering I'm in deprivation central."

I closed and locked my door again. Damn. I couldn't keep my eyes open. Especially the one that was black-and-blue and swollen. I set my alarm on low for four o'clock, turned my light out, and crawled under the covers.

SIXTEEN

It was dark when I woke up. The alarm hadn't gone off. I had to pee. I stumbled out of bed, unlocked my door, and squinted out into the black apartment. Joyce had finally gone to sleep. Good deal. I could quietly pee, and then I could zap Joyce.

I tiptoed into the bathroom, where I'd left a dim night-light burning. I felt my foot brush against something furry, and I jumped away. I ran back to my bedroom with my heart racing, got the Glock, and ran back to the bathroom door.

I saw the animal backed into the corner. Too big for Rex. Rat, I thought. *Big* rat! I could see its tail and hideous fat body. I drilled about ten holes into it. It wasn't moving. I flipped the light on and looked at the carnage. It took a couple beats for me to figure it out. It was Joyce's hairpiece.

"What the hell?" Joyce said, standing behind me. "You just killed my piece."

"I thought it was a rat."

"You ever see a redheaded rat? I paid big bucks for that piece. It was real hair."

"I'm sorry. It was dark."

"I don't know why I'm living with you," Joyce said. "You're such a loser."

"Be careful," I told her. "I've still got the gun in my hand. And I'm caring less about my rug."

I looked at Joyce and realized she was naked.

"You're naked," I said. "What's with that?"

"That's how I sleep."

"That's disgusting. I don't want to see you naked. And I don't want you naked on my couch. I'm going to have to fumigate it."

"What, I suppose you haven't got an STD?"

"Eeeeuw. No!"

I scurried into the bathroom, wiped the toilet seat down with rubbing alcohol, took care of business, and went back to my bedroom. I locked my door and moved my chest of drawers in front of it.

• • •

When I ventured out of my bedroom a few hours later, Joyce was dressed and watching television. Her hair was without enhancement, looking freaking scary, and she hadn't removed last night's makeup. The overall effect was Bride of Frankenstein.

I slipped into my bathroom and looked at the floor. The dead hair had been removed, but there were ten rounds embedded into the tile. The good news is that I obviously know how to shoot the Glock. One less thing to worry about.

I studied my face in the mirror. The swelling had gone down, but the bruising would stop traffic. I took a fast shower, got dressed, and hustled to the kitchen.

"Coffee!" Joyce yelled at me. "I need coffee."

"Coming up. Why didn't you make it for yourself?"

"I couldn't find any Kona. Where do you keep your good coffee?"

"The same place I keep my crappy, cheap coffee. Oh wait a minute, I only have one kind of coffee."

If she stayed here long enough, I would for sure kill her. I needed a new plan. Something that didn't involve hair pulling and bitch slapping, because I'd lose that one. I'd missed my chance to zap her last night. I had to think of something better today. Maybe I could tag team with Lula. One of us could distract her and one of us could zap her.

I made coffee, but beyond that, there wasn't much. My mom's leftovers were gone. I had half a box of crackers, half a box of Froot Loops, and hamster crunchies. No milk, no juice, no fruit, no bread. The peanut butter jar was empty. I ate a handful of Froot Loops and brought the rest of the box to Joyce with her coffee.

"This is all I've got," I said. "I have to go shopping."

"Froot Loops?"

"They're almost like fruit," I told her.

"I need cream for my coffee. And I like a croissant for breakfast."

"Turns out I'm all out of cream and croissants, but I'll bring something good back for lunch."

Plus, I would bring Lula and the stun gun.

"I want chicken salad from Giovichinni's," Joyce said. "And get a bottle of chardonnay."

"You bet."

What I was going to get her was enough volts to light up a small city.

I chugged my coffee, shoved my computer between my mattress and box spring, put the tools of my trade back into my messenger bag, and grabbed a sweatshirt.

"There are a bunch of people trying

to kill me," I said to Joyce. "So keep the door locked and don't let anyone in."

"Bring them on," Joyce said.

I checked my peephole before I opened the door. No one in the hall. Yay. Also, no one in the elevator or parking lot. I drove through town, parked in front of the office, and spotted the Lincoln across the street. I waved to Slasher and Lancer, and joined Connie and Lula inside.

"Whoa," Connie said. "What happened to you?"

I felt my cut lip for swelling and decided it was almost back to normal. "Parking garage incident."

"Are you okay?"

"Yep," I said. "I'm good to go."

"Anyone we know do this?" Lula asked.

"Razzle Dazzle. He's one of the idiots after the photograph I don't have."

"Talk about idiots," Lula said. "Those two clowns been sitting across the street for an hour. They're real dummies. They didn't shoot at you just now or try to snatch you. They probably don't even got a Taser. I'm starting to feel sorry for them. It's like they're amateurs."

Connie handed me a file. "I plugged them into one of the search programs for you. They look to me like rent-a-thug. They were both employed as security for one of the casinos in Atlantic City and were terminated six months ago when the casino budget was trimmed. No work record since. Lancelot is married with two kids. Larder is divorced and living with his mother. His last wife got the condo."

"How many wives has he had?"

"Four," Connie said. "No kids."

"And the Lincoln?"

"The Lincoln is hot. It was stolen off a lot in Newark. Do you want me to turn them in?"

"No. The Lincoln is easy to spot. I'd rather know where they are."

"How's your stomach?" I asked Lula.

"It was good when I got up, but it's not so good now," Lula said.

"Maybe it was the two double-sausage, extra-grease breakfast sandwiches you ate," Connie said. "Followed by a dozen doughnuts."

"I didn't eat the whole dozen," Lula said. "There's two left in the box. And I wouldn't have eaten so many if they weren't all different. I hate when I miss a culinary experience."

"I have a new stun gun," I said. "I thought I'd test-drive it on Buggy."

"Wham!" Lula said. "Let's do it."

Lula and I walked out of the office, and Lula climbed into my truck while I crossed the street and went to the Lincoln to talk to Lancer.

"You look like you got run over by a truck," Lancer said.

"I took a meeting with Razzle Dazzle."

"Did you give him the photograph?"

"I don't have the photograph to give."

"You're lucky you're alive. He's a real freak."

Not what I wanted to hear.

"Lula and I are going after an FTA. In case you want to catch some breakfast, I'll be back in an hour or two."

"No way. We're sticking to you like

glue," Lancer said. "We go where you go."

"Then why weren't you in my apartment building parking lot this morning?"

"We got chased out by some old guy. He said it was a private lot, and we weren't allowed to park there. And besides, we were in his parking space."

"Was he driving a big burgundy Cadillac?"

"Yeah. And he was yelling at us, threatening to call the police."

Mr. Kolakowski, from 5A, God bless him. Crankiest man to ever walk the earth.

"In case you lose me, I'm going to Orchard Street," I said to Lancer.

"That's north Trenton, right?"

"Yeah."

I jogged across the street, hoisted myself up behind the wheel, and drove off. I wasn't going anywhere near Orchard Street. Buggy was on the other side of town. I pulled away from the curb, drove a block, and hooked a left. Lancer was behind me. I took a right turn and sailed through the light at the next intersection. Lancer was stopped on the red. I took a left at the next block, left again, and Lancer was good-bye.

I cut across Hamilton and turned onto Pulling.

"I don't feel so good," Lula said. "It was that last doughnut. There was something wrong with it. It was one of them cream-filled, and I think they used old cream."

"You ate ten!"

"Yeah, and none of the others bothered me. I'm telling you, it was that last doughnut. I'd feel better if I could burp."

I parked and sat looking at the Bugkowski house for a couple minutes. No activity. I was betting Buggy was holed up inside, wishing he had a way to get food. I should have brought the last two doughnuts. I put the truck in gear, made a U-turn, and drove to Pino's. Twenty minutes later, I was in front of the Bugkowski house with a steaming hot pizza.

"Here's how it's going down," I said to Lula. "You're going to get into the back of the truck with the pizza box. Then I'm going to ring his bell and tell him we want to rebond him. He's going to say no, but he'll smell the pizza, and he'll go after it. As soon as he gets himself up into the back of the truck, I'll zap him and cuff him."

"You tried to zap him before, and it didn't work."

"I have a bigger zapper now."

I lowered the tailgate and got Lula up into the truck bed. I stuffed the key into my pocket, so Buggy couldn't grab it, and I went to his door.

Buggy opened the door and looked past me. "Nice truck."

Lula waved a piece of pizza at him. "Yoohoo, Buggy honey."

"She got pizza," Buggy said. He pushed past me and went straight to the truck. "You got more?" he asked Lula.

"I got almost a whole pie," Lula said. "You want some?"

"Yuh," Buggy said, climbing over the tailgate.

I scrambled after him, and when he reached for a piece of pizza I pressed the stun gun to the back of his neck and hit the go button. He went dead still for a beat, and I swear his hair lit up, and then he crumpled face-first into Lula's lap.

"He got his nose in my lady parts," Lula said, holding the pizza box to the side. "Not that I haven't been in this predicament before, but there's a time and place for everything, you see what I'm sayin'?"

I looked at the pizza box. There were two pieces missing.

"Did you eat two slices of pizza?" I asked Lula.

"I thought it might settle my stomach, but I was wrong."

I wrapped the Flexi-Cuffs around Buggy's wrists, shackled his ankles, and rolled him off Lula.

"We don't want a repeat of Lahonka," I said. "Take the stun gun and stay in back with Buggy. If he comes around and gets unruly, give him a shot."

"I don't know if I'm gonna make it to the police station," Lula said. "You got antacids? You got Pepto?"

I searched my bag.

"What's that pink stuff in there?" Lula said. "It looks like Pepto."

"It's the stuff Annie Hart gave me."

Lula reached in and took the bottle. "Whatever." She chugged it down and burped. "Oh yeah, that's better."

My eyes were wide and my mouth was open.

"What?" Lula asked.

"You drank the stuff Annie gave me. I have no idea what was in it. The woman is a kook. She makes love potions. For all I know, you just drank yak eyes and buffalo piss."

"It didn't look like buffalo piss," Lula said. "It was a pretty pink color. How do those love potions work?"

"I don't know."

"Like, do they make you have love at first sight? Because I like that idea. There's not enough romance in the world. I always said that when I was a 'ho. I always threw in some romance for free if the customer wanted. And some of those customers didn't inspire romance, if you know what I mean. Like take Buggy, for instance. He's kinda cute."

Buggy's eyes were half open, he was drooling, and he farted.

"He's a bridge troll," I said.

"Yeah, but I just drank a love potion, so I could be excused for havin' bad taste. And besides, bridge trolls are in now. What about Shrek? Everybody loves Shrek. Remember when he blew bubbles in the bathtub? He was adorable."

"He was a cartoon."

"I'm feeling warm," Lula said. "It might be on account of I sort of had a romantic experience just now with Mr. Cutie Pie here. And much as I hate to admit this, my love life has been a barren wasteland for at least a week."

I was going to pretend I didn't hear that. I was going with the assumption there was grain alcohol in the pink stuff. I jumped down, closed the tailgate, and got behind the wheel. I had no confidence that I could drag Mr. Cutie Pie across the street and into the municipal building if I parked in the lot, so I drove to the police station drop-off and asked for help.

• • •

Vinnie was in the office when Lula and I returned.

"I just brought Lewis Bugkowski in," I said to Vinnie.

"He already called," Vinnie said. "He wants to get bonded out again, but he has no one to post the bond. His parents won't put up any more money. They said it's bad enough they have to feed him."

Lula's hand shot up. "I'll do it. I'll post the bond. Let me do it."

"That's a shame," Connie said. "She was clean for so long."

"It's not drugs," I said. "She's developed this weird attachment to Buggy."

"He's adorable," Lula said. "Like Shrek. I could just love him to pieces."

"That's wrong," Connie said. "That's very, very wrong."

"I'm all excited," Lula said. "I'm getting my first bondee. It's like going to the animal shelter and adopting a kitten."

"This isn't a good idea," Connie said. "Buggy isn't a kitten. Buggy is a . . ."

"Dullard?" I suggested. "Slackard, village idiot, leach on society, clod, brute, oaf, dumb ox, not to mention purse snatcher and car thief?"

"You be careful what you say about my honey," Lula said. "And makin' him my bondee is a perfectly good idea. I got a right to adopt a felon. I'm gonna take care of him, too."

"How are you going to post bond?" Vinnie asked. "Where are you going to come up with the money? What are you going to put up as collateral?"

"I got my Firebird," Lula said.

We all gasped. Lula *loved* her Firebird.

"This is serious," Connie said. "You need to take her to the clinic and get a blood test. Or maybe she just needs to go home and lay down for a while. She could be having some sort of reaction from all the sugar in the doughnuts."

"I just got a big heart," Lula said. "I got a heart of gold, and I recognize goodness in places it don't seem to be. Like, you look at Lewis and you see apple-cider vinegar, and I see a big apple dumpling."

"You never saw apple dumplings before," Connie said.

"Well, I got my eyes open now," Lula said. "Hallelujah. And on top of that, I'm takin' love at first sight for a test-drive. I might have drinked a love potion."

"I like it," Vinnie said. "If Buggy goes AWOL, I get the Firebird. I could give it to DeAngelo, and he might not kill me." Vinnie passed papers over to Lula. "Sign where I made a mark."

Lula was on her feet. "I want to go with you when you get my sweet patooti released," she said to Vinnie. "I want to take him home."

"I need you to help me capture Joyce," I said to Lula.

"No problem," Lula said. "This won't take long. Soon as I get my honeybee out of jail, I'll help you with Joyce."

I was gagging on the sweet-patooti, honeybee, adorable-apple-dumpling stuff, but I needed to get Joyce out of my apartment, and I needed the money from her capture.

"Excellent," I said. "We'll follow Vinnie to the police station, we'll spring Buggy, take him home, and go get Joyce."

"WHAM!" Lula said.

I stepped outside and waved at Slasher and Lancer. They were parked across the street again.

"You lied to me!" Lancer yelled. "You're not going to heaven if you keep fibbing to people."

Vinnie took off in his Cadillac, Lula and I followed, and Lancer and Slasher brought up the rear. Vinnie went straight, I turned right, and Lancer followed me. I drove two blocks, turned left, and zipped through a traffic light. Lancer wasn't going to make the same mistake twice. He ran the light and got T-boned by a Jeep. I pulled to the side to see if anyone was hurt.

"They all look okay," Lula said, "but they don't look happy."

SEVENTEEN

I dropped Lula off at the municipal building and waited for her in the truck. I checked my mail on my phone and listened to some music. I was afraid to nap. With my luck, Raz would stumble on me. I'd been sitting there for almost an hour when Connie called.

"Your friends are back across the street," she said. "And their car is all bashed in. Are you okay?"

"I'm fine. They tried to run a light and got T-boned. Have a pizza delivered to them and put it on my tab."

Minutes later, Lula, Vinnie and Buggy

walked out of the building. Vinnie jumped into his Caddy and sped away. Lula and Buggy got into my truck. Lula took the front seat, and Buggy wedged himself into the small jump seat behind us.

"I don't fit here," he said. "I want to drive."

"Here are your options," I told him. "You can stay where you are, or you can walk."

"I want to drive!"

"Isn't he the cutest thing," Lula said. "You should let him drive. He's a real good driver."

"How do you know?" I asked her.

"I could tell. And all the times he stole your car, he never wrecked it."

"He's not driving," I said. "End of discussion."

"I'll hold my breath," Buggy said.

I cranked the engine over and looked at him in the rear-view mirror. "Fine by me. I don't care if you turn blue and die."

"I always pee my pants when I hold my breath," Buggy said.

"That's endearin'," Lula said. "I bet Shrek pees his pants, too."

I cut my eyes to Lula. "He's going to have to get out and ride in the back."

"Sweetums, you want to ride in the back?" Lula asked.

"No. I want to drive."

Lula rooted through her purse and found a Snickers bar. She got out of the truck and threw the Snickers bar into the back. "Go fetch," she said.

Buggy rolled out of the cab, ran around, climbed over the tailgate, and I stepped on the gas just as he wrapped his hand around the Snickers.

I took Broad to Hamilton, turned onto Pulling, and stopped in front of the Bugkowski house. I stuck my head out my window and yelled at Buggy. "You're home. You can get out now."

"Nuh-ah," Buggy said.

"Isn't that special," Lula said. "He doesn't want to leave me. We bonded real good."

"And now you're going to have to unbond because we need to bring Joyce in."

"It's just so sad to have to leave him," Lula said.

She pulled another Snickers bar out of her purse and threw it out the window onto the Bugkowski front lawn. Buggy bounded out of the truck bed, snatched up the Snickers, and I put my foot to the floor. Adios, muchacho.

• • •

Joyce was still watching television when we walked in.

"You're late," she said. "I'm starving. Where's my chicken salad? Where's my wine?"

"It's in the fridge," I said. "Help yourself."

"Are you sure this is Joyce?" Lula said. "She don't look like tramp. She look more like bag lady."

"Get out of my way, fatso," Joyce said to Lula, brushing her aside to get to the fridge.

Lula glared at her. "Say what?"

Joyce opened the fridge door and I stepped behind her. *Zzzzzzzt.* Joyce crashed to the floor.

"You don't mind if I kick her, do you?" Lula said.

"Yes, I mind. I don't want to deliver her with unexplainable bruises."

I was about to cuff Joyce, and Connie called.

"I don't know if this is good news or bad news," Connie said, "but the charges have been dropped against Joyce. The court's returning the bond."

"I just stun-gunned her."

"Good for you," Connie said.

I disconnected the phone and passed the message on to Lula.

"Does this mean I can kick her since we're not bringing her in?" Lula asked.

"No!"

"What are we gonna do with her?"

"We're going to get her out of my apartment."

We dragged Joyce and her belongings into the hall, I locked my door, and Lula and I went back to the truck.

"I feel much better," I said to Lula. "It would have been satisfying to take her to jail, but at least she's out of my space."

"Yeah, now all you gotta do is get rid

of her cooties. You want to buy some bleach today, and maybe you can get some of that holy water to sprinkle around."

"I'll add it to my shopping list."

"She had a good idea with the chicken salad," Lula said. "We should stop at Giovichinni's and get some. I'm gonna eat healthier and set a good example now that I got my honey pot."

I motored down Hamilton and slowed when I passed the bonds office construction site.

"They're making good progress," Lula said. "They got windows in now, and they're putting on the brick front. Too bad Vinnie gonna be dead when they finally finish."

There was room for me to pull the truck to the curb in front of Giovichinni's. Lula and I got out and went straight to the deli counter. I got a chicken club sandwich, and Lula got a large-size tub of chicken salad, a large-size tub of coleslaw, and a large-size tub of rice pudding.

Gina Giovichinni was at the register when we checked out.

"Omigod," she said, looking at my black-and-green eye. "I heard Morelli beat you, but I didn't believe it until now."

"He didn't beat me," I said. "I fell in a parking garage."

"He pushed you, right?" Gina said.

"No!"

I grabbed my sandwich, went through the store's front door, and stopped short. Buggy was sitting in the back of my truck.

"It's my apple dumpling!" Lula said. "Are you hungry?" she asked him.

Buggy eyed the bag. "Yuh," Buggy said.

Lula handed him her food and ran back to Giovichinni's to get more. I got behind the wheel, locked the doors, and ate my sandwich. I unlocked the doors when Lula returned and relocked them as soon as she was settled. I was afraid the apple dumpling would yank me out of my truck and drive away.

"Now what?" Lula clicked her seat belt in place.

"I think our luck has changed. We captured Buggy. We got Joyce out of my apartment. I say we go get Lahonka."

"Wham," Lula said. "And double wham!" She turned and looked out the back window at Buggy. "We should take him with us."

"What?"

"If you take him back to that empty house, there's no telling what could go on. He's such a bad boy."

I checked the bad boy out in the mirror. He had a glob of rice pudding on his shirt. "I thought he was an apple dumpling."

"You could be a apple dumpling and a bad boy all at the same time," Lula said. "They could go together. That's what makes him so appealing. He looks like a acorn squash, but he's real complex. I like that in a man. And besides, I don't have any more Snickers bars. I don't know how we're gonna get him out of the truck."

Good point. I put the truck in gear and drove to Lahonka's apartment. Lula and I got out, and Lula told the acorn squash to wait in the truck.

"Nuh-ah," Buggy said, throwing a leg over the side.

"He's your responsibility," I said to Lula. "I don't want him taking my keys, my messenger bag, or my truck."

I marched up to Lahonka's door and banged on it. Lula and Buggy were right behind me.

"That door has a Band-Aid on it," Buggy said.

"It's covering the hole I made when I shot it," Lula said.

"Go away," Lahonka yelled from inside. "I hate you."

"She's not nice," Buggy said.

"She's a felon," Lula told him. "We need to arrest her."

Buggy pushed us aside, gave the door a head butt, and the door came off its hinges.

"What the hell?" Lahonka said.

She had her foot wrapped in a big bandage, and she was standing on crutches.

"What's wrong with her foot?" Buggy wanted to know.

"I shot it," Lula said.

"Har!" Buggy said. "Good one." He

looked at Lula. "Do you want her in the truck?"

"Yeah," Lula said. "We have to take her to the police station."

"The police station isn't so bad," Buggy said. "They gave me a cheeseburger."

He grabbed Lahonka and tucked her under his arm like she was a rag doll, while I scrambled to get her crutches.

"I'm just about gonna faint on account of my honey pie is so strong," Lula said. "I'd never say anyone was fat due to that bein' hurtful, but let's face it, Lahonka's a sandbag. I carry a certain amount of weight, but mine's perfectly distributed. My big beautiful bubble butt balances out my oversized boobs. Lahonka here got all her weight sunk into one of them low-slung behinds. It gotta be hard to get someone like Lahonka off the ground."

"You got a lot of nerve sayin' those things about me!" Lahonka yelled at Lula. "You're not nothin' but a big 'ho."

"Am not," Lula said, hands on hips. "I gave up bein' a 'ho."

"I like 'hos," Buggy said. "It's like

goin' to Cluck-in-a-Bucket. You order something and that's what you get."

"Sugar, it's like that with a girlfriend, too," Lula said.

"Hunh," Lahonka said. "Not with me. You get what I want to give you, and then you better say *thank you.*"

Not with me, either, I thought. My new policy was nobody gets *anything*!

Buggy carted Lahonka to the truck and dumped her into the back.

"We need to cuff her, Sweetums," Lula said, handing Buggy cuffs.

Lahonka was spitting and clawing and swearing, and Buggy was having a hard time catching a wrist.

"You don't hold still for me, and I'm going to kick you in your foot," Buggy said.

Lahonka went still for a beat, digesting the threat, and Buggy sat on her and cuffed her.

"Good job," Lula said to Buggy. "Don't let her escape. She's sneaky."

Buggy looked at Lula. "Do you have any more of them Snickers?"

"No," Lula said, "but we'll get more as soon as we drop Lahonka off."

"You aren't gonna leave me back here with King Kong, are you?" Lahonka said. "He got his fat ass on me, and I can't breathe. Isn't it enough you shot up my foot? I'm just a poor workin' woman. I got kids to support."

I drove to the municipal building and parked in the lot. I didn't need police assistance. I could get Buggy to cart Lahonka across the street if she refused to walk. Lula and I got out and went to the back of the truck.

No Lahonka.

"I could have sworn Lahonka was here when we took off," Lula said.

Buggy was sitting with his back against the rear window. "She got out at the last light."

"You were supposed to make sure she didn't escape," I said to him.

"Yeah, but she said she was a mama, and she was cryin'. So I let her go."

"That's so sweet," Lula said to Buggy. "You're a man with a good heart."

"It's not sweet!" I said. "Lahonka Goudge is a con artist and a felon. She steals people's identities. And Mr. Potato Head here just let her go."

"Do I get my Snickers now?" Buggy asked.

"You get nothing," I said. *"NOTHING."*

Buggy squinched his face up. "You promised."

"The deal was you'd get Snickers after we delivered Lahonka. Did we deliver Lahonka?" I asked him. "No, we did not. So you get nothing. There are consequences to all actions."

"Nuh-ah. I do lots of things without them consequences."

"Not in my truck," I told him. "There are consequences in my truck."

"That's a good policy," Lula said. "Just think where we'd be if we didn't pay attention to consequences. Like, there's consequences if you don't got bullets in your gun. And there's consequences if you eat bad potato salad. And there's consequences if you're not taking precautions with your sweetie pie."

I had a flash of panic recalling a small inadvertent lapse in my birth-control program in Hawaii.

"Are you okay?" Lula asked me. "You

got real pale just now, and you're sort of sweating."

"I was thinking about consequences."

"Yeah, they freak me out, too," Lula said.

EIGHTEEN

I off-loaded Lula and Buggy at the bonds office so Lula could get her car. Slasher and Lancer were still parked there, both of them sound asleep. Vinnie's car and Connie's car were gone, and the office was closed. Everyone left early on Saturday.

"I'm going to take you home in my Firebird," Lula said to Buggy.

Buggy's eyes got wide. "I want to drive."

"Of course you do," Lula said, "but this here's a finely tuned machine."

"Yuh."

"Well, okay, since you're so adorable," Lula said. And she handed him her key.

"Get in fast, before he takes off without you," I said to Lula.

"He wouldn't do that," Lula said. "He's my big honey."

The big honey rammed himself behind the wheel and took off.

"Hey!" Lula said. "Wait for me."

"Get in the truck," I told her. "I'll catch him."

Three blocks later, Buggy was stopped in traffic. Lula jumped out, ran to the Firebird, wrenched the passenger-side door open, and got in. Mission accomplished, as far as I was concerned.

I stopped at the supermarket and got a couple bags of groceries. Bread, milk, juice, peanut butter, olives, bag of chips, a frozen pizza, Vienna Fingers cookies, a bucket of assorted fried chicken parts, strawberry Pop-Tarts. I made one more stop and got a six-pack of beer and a bottle of red wine. I was going to have a feast tonight. I was going to have fried chicken, beer, and Vienna

Fingers. Tomorrow, I'd have pizza and wine. No men. No Joyce. No Apple Dumpling. Just me and Rex and the TV.

I lugged the bags up to my apartment, set them on the kitchen counter, and a chill ran down my spine. The television was on. I grabbed the Glock and peeked into the living room. It was Joyce. "What the heck?"

"That was really shitty," Joyce said. "You dumped me out in the hall. If I had any other place to go, I'd be there."

"How did you get back into my apartment?"

"I had to climb up the stupid fire escape again. It's getting old." She came into the kitchen and looked at the food I was unpacking. "Where's my chicken salad and wine?"

"I didn't get chicken salad. I didn't think you'd be here. But here's the good news. The charges have been dropped against you."

"Big deal. The charges were bogus. I was never worried about the charges."

"What *are* you worried about?"

"There's nothing green here," Joyce said.

"Olives."

"Olives are a fruit. Look at this mess. You haven't got a single vegetable."

"There's tomato sauce on the pizza."

"Another fruit."

As if my life wasn't enough in the toilet, Joyce Barnhardt was now smarter and obviously ate better than me.

"You didn't answer my question," I said. "What are you worried about?"

Joyce selected a mystery piece from the fried chicken bucket. "You ever hear of the Pink Panthers?"

"The movies?"

"No, the organization. Interpol has assigned the name Pink Panthers to an international jewel thief network. Interpol took the name from the movies."

"The movies are great."

"Focus," Joyce said. "We're talking about the network. Frank Korda was part of the network. I know it's hard to believe that there's this nebbish guy in Trenton associated with the Pink Panthers. I mean, the Pink Panthers are *big*. They're *HUGE*! They stole a $27 million diamond necklace one time from a store in Tokyo. Anyway, somehow Korda connected with these guys."

"What's the advantage?"

"According to Korda, the Panthers have the ability to fence the stolen jewelry. Korda said it's not hard to steal jewelry, but it's risky to try to sell it."

"Korda was stealing jewelry?"

"Big-time. He'd get the real thing into his store, sell it at a profit, and send the customer home with a knockoff. Plus, he'd shop around and lift and replace."

"And what's your role in this?"

"He wanted to go bigger. He saw a couple pieces in New York. One was at Harry Winston. There was another at Chopard. He said it was a four-man operation. There were two other Pink Panthers who were going to help out, and he was going to use me as a distraction. He said if I did a good job, the Panthers would let me into the network."

"You wanted to be a Pink Panther?"

"I'd give my right nut to be a Pink Panther."

"You have a nut?"

"No, but if I *had* one, I'd *give* it."

"Do you know who killed Korda?"

"It was the Panthers. I used to come to the store to help Frank plan his capers, and . . ."

I inadvertently giggled.

"What's so funny?" Joyce asked.

"You said capers."

"Grow up. That's what we call the jobs in the trade."

I cracked open a beer and chugged half. No laughing, I told myself. If you laugh at Joyce, she won't tell you the whole story, and you want to hear the whole story, no matter how ridiculous.

"Okay," I said. "Sorry. You were helping Frank plan his capers."

"Yeah, and we were fooling around a little. And he promised me this necklace he stole, but he couldn't give it to me because it was too hot. And next thing I know, his wife is walking down the street wearing my necklace. So I went to the store to find out what the fuck's going on, and we had a big fight. He said everything was off. He said the Pink Panthers didn't want me, and he was getting out of the network anyway.

He said something went sour. So I said what about the necklace? And he said his wife saw it and wanted it. So I told him he owed me, and I took a necklace out of the case. And the shithead came out after me, yelling that I stole a necklace. Can you believe it?"

"So you got arrested, and Vinnie bonded you out."

"Exactly. I put my Mercedes up."

"The one that got crushed?"

"Yeah. There's something sort of good about that part, right? Anyway, next thing, I get a text message from Frank, and he wants to talk to me. So I go park in the lot behind the store, just like always. And Frank comes out, and he's got the necklace. And he's real sorry. And one thing leads to another, and I sort of have my face buried in his lap, so my vision is limited, right?"

Eeeuw.

"But I catch a flash of pink," Joyce said. "And everything instantly goes limp on Frank. *Everything.* And next thing, I get stunned. And when I come around I'm stuffed into the trunk of a car with Frank. And Frank's dead. I don't know how he got dead. He wasn't shot. There was no blood. For all I know, he could have had a heart attack. By the time I was able to get out from under Frank and get to the inside trunk latch, it was dark, and turned out the car was parked at the junkyard. I barely got out of the trunk, and the dog came at me and I ran for my life. Good thing the car was parked close to the fence. I went up the chain-link like a ninja."

"And you think it was the Pink Panthers?"

"Who else would it be? I saw the flash of pink material when they zapped Frank."

"And you're afraid to go back to your condo."

"They could be watching," Joyce said. "They tried to kill me once. I figure they'll keep trying if they see I'm alive."

I gnawed on a piece of chicken and chugged the rest of my beer. "It doesn't add up. Why would they want to kill you?"

"I guess I know too much. Frank told me the names of some of the thieves.

And I saw pictures of the two people we were going to be working with in New York."

I didn't know how the Pink Panthers operated, but if I wanted someone dead, I wouldn't just abandon them in the junkyard. I'd make sure they were totally and completely dead before I walked away.

"Why don't you go to the police?" I asked her.

"Even if they believe my story, what are they going to do to help me?"

Here was the question I dreaded asking. "Why are you here? What do you expect *me* to do to help you?"

"I need the treasure chest. Everything is in there. All the Pink Panther contact information. I figure if I could get in touch with the Panthers, I could negotiate."

"Where is this treasure chest?"

"Frank used to keep it at the store."

"You know what it looks like, right?"

"It looks like a miniature pirate chest. Frank said you hide things in obvious places because that's never where anyone looks. He kept the chest on the shelf behind the register. There are some picture frames, and small glass vases, and the chest is in the middle."

I finished my piece of chicken and washed my hands. I wanted a cookie, but I wasn't going to open the package of Vienna Fingers in front of Joyce. I didn't want to share.

"I'm not breaking into the store," I said.

"It's not a big deal. I know the code. I watched Frank punch it in."

"Then why don't *you* do it?"

"The Panthers could be watching."

"I think there's a real good chance they've all gone back to Pink Panther land."

"No way. The Panthers are tenacious." She eyeballed the Vienna Fingers sitting on the counter. "I guess I'll just have to stay here forever."

"Don't even think about eating those Vienna Fingers," I told her.

"Better on your hips than mine. Obviously, you don't care how big your ass gets."

Here are my options, I thought. I

could stun her when she goes to sleep, drag her into the hall again, and have bars installed on my bedroom window. I could get the treasure chest. Or I could kill her.

"How am I going to get into the store?" I asked her.

"I assumed you had skills."

"You assumed wrong. I have no skills." That wasn't even an understatement. What I had was luck, friends, and tenacity born of desperation.

"You know people who *do* have skills," Joyce said.

"Fine," I said, "I'll get the stupid treasure chest." I grabbed the Vienna Fingers and shoved them into my messenger bag. "Do not eat my frozen pizza. Do not drink my wine."

Joyce tore a scrap off one of the grocery bags and wrote the code on it. "Say hello to Ranger for me. Tell him if he ever wants to trade up, I might give him a tug."

For a moment I considered option number three. Someone really needed to kill Joyce. My fear was that I'd bungle it. Then what? She could be a living vegetable in my apartment for the rest of her life while I spooned soup into her and rubbed her feet.

I hiked my bag up onto my shoulder and left my apartment. I took the elevator and called Ranger when I got to the foyer.

"I need help," I said. "I need to break into a jewelry store."

There was a beat of silence. "Looking to accessorize?"

"I need to get into Frank Korda's store. Can you get me in? I know the security code."

"No problem."

"I'm leaving my apartment now. I'll meet you behind the store in about twenty minutes."

I still had the Glock in my bag. I wrapped my hand around it, left the building, and walked to my truck with my eyes sweeping the lot, looking for Razzle Dazzle. I made it to the truck, got up behind the wheel, and locked the doors.

The drive to Korda's store was uneventful, and Ranger's Porsche 911 Turbo was already parked in the lot when I got there. I pulled in beside him and got out.

"Babe," Ranger said. "You're supposed to dress in black for a nighttime jewel heist."

Ranger was in black, of course.

"It's not a jewel heist," I told him. "I'm looking for a little pirate chest."

He handed over infrared goggles. "Use these. It's dark in there and a penlight will give you away."

Ranger went to the door and looked at the lock. He removed a slim tool from his pocket, inserted the tool into the lock, and in seconds we were inside.

I punched the code into the security system, put the goggles on, and went directly to the shelf behind the register. There were picture frames and vases, but no chest. I methodically went through the room. No chest. I moved to the back storeroom and worked my way around. Nothing.

"I'm getting the impression this isn't going well," Ranger said.

"Joyce said the chest would be on the shelf behind the register, but it isn't there. I've looked all through the store, and I can't find it."

"Joyce?"

"Barnhardt. She's moved into my apartment, and I can't get her out. I stun-gun her, drag her into the hall, and she comes back."

"How does she get in?" Ranger asked.

"Fire escape."

"I could have it electrified."

"I thought of that, but Mrs. Delgado's cat would get fried."

Ranger removed my goggles. "Would you like to come home with me?"

I stepped away from him. "Thank you for the offer, but *no.* I'm done with men."

Ranger smiled. "Forever?"

"Until I figure some things out."

"And if you don't figure them out?"

"If I can't figure them out on my own, I'll ask you to help me."

"Babe, that's like the blind leading the blind."

• • •

I sat in the parking lot to my apartment building and ate half a package of Vienna Fingers. Lights were on in my apartment. Joyce was all cozy up there, watching television, probably drinking my wine. Ranger was no doubt back in his penthouse on the seventh floor of Rangeman. Morelli was most likely at home, watching a ball game with Bob. And here I was hiding out in my truck. It was pathetic. I slipped the uneaten Vienna Fingers into my bag and grabbed the Glock. I left the truck and crossed the lot to the back door. I was ten feet from the building, and Raz jumped out of the shadows, knife in hand.

"You bitch lady," he said. "Now we talk. We deal, eh?"

He lunged at me with the knife, and I shot him in his good leg. We both stood dead still for a long moment in shock.

He looked down at his leg and made a strangled sound deep in his throat. "Motherfucking shit," he said.

"What's this about?" I asked him. "Why do you want the photograph, which by the way I don't have?"

"Boss say to get it, and I get it. I don't get it, and I get shot again. This time in the eye, hanging upside down with heavy rocks tied to my testicles."

He turned and limped into the lot.

"Hey," I said. "I'm not done. Stop or I'll shoot."

"Crazy American bitch," he said. "Shoot me. You think I care? Shoot me again. I live for pain."

He dragged himself into a silver Sentra and drove away.

Mr. Daly stuck his head out of his second-floor window. "What was that? Did I hear a gunshot?"

"I didn't hear anything," I said, looking up at Mr. Daly, dropping my gun into my bag. "Must have been someone's t-t-television."

I was hyperventilating and my hands were shaking when I got to my apartment, and I had to two-fist the key to unlock my door. I got inside, did some deep breathing, and went straight to the kitchen for the wine. Half a bottle left. Good enough. I poured some into a water glass and took it into the living room, where Joyce was waiting.

"The chest wasn't in the store," I said to her. "It wasn't on the shelf. It wasn't anywhere."

"That's impossible. It was always on the shelf."

"When was the last time you saw it?"

"The day I was arrested. Frank said we were out of the Pink Panther business, and he wanted his key. And I told him I didn't have it on me, not to mention he could kiss the key good-bye. I remember looking up at the chest when I said it. That was the last I was in the store. I didn't go into the store when I came back later in the day."

"I bet the Pink Panthers broke into the store and took the chest after they dropped you off at the junkyard."

"That would be a real bitch," Joyce said. "I needed that chest to bargain. At least I have the key. There are numbers on the key that go with the chest. Problem is, I don't know how to get in touch with the Panthers without the chest."

I looked at my wineglass. It was empty. "You could put the key up on Craigslist and see if you get any takers.

And did you look to see if there's a Pink Panthers Facebook page? Everyone has a Facebook page. Not me, of course, but everyone else."

"Somehow I don't think the Pink Panthers are going to have a Facebook page."

"Did anyone come looking for me tonight?"

"Yeah, some Russian Gypsy who looked like he got run over by a front loader. I didn't catch his name, but he was limping. He didn't impress me as much of a good time, so I didn't invite him in. Did he catch up with you?"

"Yeah. He was waiting downstairs."

"And?"

"I shot him, and he left."

"Nice. I was thinking we should put the frozen pizza in the oven. Is there any more wine?"

NINETEEN

Ordinarily, I wake up Sunday morning feeling glorious. I apologize to God for not attending Mass, and then I roll over and go back to sleep. This morning, I woke up worrying about the guy I'd shot. It hadn't looked like a life-threatening wound, but he still would have to get the bullet dug out and make sure it didn't get infected. The good news was he'd probably already gotten a tetanus shot from when I knifed him. And truth is, I'd be much better off if the infection killed him. He wasn't a nice man.

Thoughts of Raz got pushed aside

when I remembered Joyce Barnhardt was in my living room. I had to find a way to get her out, once and for all, the sooner the better. I pulled on sweatpants and a T-shirt and trudged into the kitchen. Joyce was already there, searching the cabinets, undoubtedly looking for smoked salmon and caviar and croissants.

"You went shopping, but I can't find any food," she said.

"Au contraire, I got all my favorite staples, plus my Sunday morning special treat. Strawberry Pop-Tarts."

I got the coffee brewing, and I took a Pop-Tart out of the box.

"I've been thinking," I said to Joyce. "You need to leave. You should go home. I'm sure the Pink Panthers have moved on to bigger and better projects. And besides, you have a gun, right? If they get irritating, just shoot them."

"These guys are professionals," Joyce said. "It's not like they're Burg stumblebums. And by the way, you look like crap. What have you got on?"

"Sweatpants. They're comfy. And since we're on the topic, have you looked in a mirror recently? You're Fright Night in the orangutan house at the zoo."

"In case you haven't noticed, I've been on the run. I hocked the necklace I was wearing and bought a few things, but it's not like I have access to my closet."

"How about combing your hair for starters."

"My hair would look just fine if you hadn't shot my piece. And you should talk about hair. Has yours *ever* looked good?"

"Morelli likes my hair. He says it has energy."

"If he's so in love with your hair, why isn't he here? As far as I can tell, you never even *see* him."

"He's busy."

"Yeah, he's busy with Marianne Mikulski."

I filled a mug with coffee and added milk. "He's busy with his job."

"Sure he is. You keep on believing that."

"Marianne Mikulski is married."

"Marianne Mikulski is separated from

her loser husband, and she's on the hunt. Rumor has it she's bagged your ex-boyfriend."

"Getting back to your departure from my apartment."

"I need the chest. I don't want to believe the Panthers have it. The only other possible place it could be is in Frank's house."

"Why would it be in his house?"

"Maybe he brought it home for safekeeping after I got arrested. Or his wife could have taken it after he disappeared."

"Why would his wife take it?"

"I don't know. He could have told her about the Panthers. Or it could hold sentimental value for her."

"I can't break into the house. The store was empty, and you knew the code. The house is too risky."

"Go in when no one's home."

"When is that?"

"Tomorrow. When they bury Frank."

"I'll do it if you move out today," I said.

"I'll move out when you find the chest."

I was back to the same three options. It was Sunday and highly unlikely I could get bars instantly installed on my windows. Though killing Joyce was by far the most appealing option, I knew I wasn't capable of carrying it out. So I was stuck with getting the chest.

I finished my Pop-Tart and coffee, took a shower, got dressed, and left the apartment to Joyce. I drove out of the building's parking lot and passed the Town Car parked on a side street. Lancer fell in line behind me and followed me to Morelli's house.

I parked and had a moment of craziness, wondering if I should call before going to the door. What if Marianne Mikulski's in there? What if I interrupt something I don't want to know about?

I was sitting there debating what to do next when Morelli called on my cell phone.

"Are you just going to hang there or are you coming in?" he asked.

"Are you alone?"

"Does Bob count?"

I disconnected and went to the door. Bob came thundering across the living room and threw himself at me, almost knocking me over. I scratched his neck and made dog sounds at him.

"Here's my boy," I said. "Here's my big boy. Is he good? Has he been a good boy?" Bob was a big, shaggy red dog that on a decent hair day might resemble a golden retriever.

"You have an escort," Morelli said, looking out at the Lincoln.

"Lancer and Slasher. The fake FBI guys. They're low on the threat level."

"Who's high?"

"Razzle Dazzle. The guy in the parking garage. And Marianne Mikulski."

"Why is Marianne a threat?"

"Rumor has it you've been seen with her."

"So?"

Morelli was barefoot, wearing faded jeans and a navy T-shirt. His hair was still damp from a shower, and he smelled like fresh-baked cinnamon rolls. I was torn between wanting to rip his clothes off and wanting to lick his neck. Fortunately, I didn't have to make a choice since I was off men.

"Just checking," I said.

Morelli headed for the kitchen. "Marianne is a neighbor. She lives two doors down, and she brings her dog over to play with Bob. Who's spreading rumors?"

"Joyce Barnhardt."

Morelli poured out two mugs of coffee and handed one to me. "My mother dropped cinnamon rolls off this morning when she was on her way to church with my grandmother. They both asked about you. Conjecture out there is that I punched you in the nose."

I took a roll and leaned against the counter. "I got that one, too. People seem genuinely disappointed when I deny it."

"It's nice to have you back in my kitchen, and I hate to ruin the moment, but I wouldn't mind knowing when you had a chance to gossip with Joyce."

"She's squatting in my apartment. I can't get rid of her."

Morelli choked on his coffee. He wiped coffee off his chin with the back of his hand.

"You want to run that by me again?"

"Have you heard of the Pink Panthers?"

"Are you talking about the movies or the network of jewel thieves?"

"Jewel thieves. Joyce thinks they're after her."

"Keep going," Morelli said.

"According to Joyce, Frank Korda was a Pink Panther. She was playing footsie with Korda, and she was helping him plan a big New York job with the Panthers. And then something went wrong, and the Panthers tried to kill them, but Joyce managed to escape."

"And she's living with you, why?"

"She doesn't seem to have any money, and she's afraid to go back to her condo."

"Because the Panthers still want to kill her?"

"That's the fear. And there's a little chest she needs to find."

"And she wants you to find it for her?"

"Yeah."

"Let's start at the beginning," Morelli said. "Korda wasn't a Pink Panther. In fact, there's no actual organization called the Pink Panthers. Interpol assigned that name to cover a group of diamond thieves loosely associated with one another. For the most part, they're hardened criminals from what was once part of Yugoslavia and is now Montenegro."

I finished my cinnamon roll and sipped my coffee. I wasn't completely shocked to hear this. It had all seemed pretty far-fetched.

"Moving on," Morelli said. "We collected enough forensic evidence from Frank Korda and the crushed Mercedes to build a case. I can't tell you more than that because we're still waiting on some of the tests, but I can guarantee you the killer wasn't from Montenegro."

"Joyce?"

"Unlikely, but she's not ruled out."

"I know she's a primo liar, but she seemed to believe the Pink Panther thing."

"Maybe Korda was conning her," Morelli said.

"For what reason?"

Morelli shrugged. "Not for sex. You

could buy Joyce with beads from the Dollar Store."

I didn't want to get into the treasure chest thing. In light of the information Morelli just gave me, the treasure chest story made no sense. Still, on the very slim chance I would go after the chest and break into the Korda home, I didn't want to involve Morelli in the crime. Mostly because I was afraid he'd choose the law over me and turn me in.

Morelli ran a finger along the neckline of my T-shirt. "Speaking of sex, I have some beads upstairs, if you're interested."

"Are you equating me with Joyce?"

"No. I wouldn't offer my beads to Joyce."

"It's an attractive offer, but I'm off men."

"All men?" Morelli asked.

"Yes."

"As long as it's *all* men, I guess I can deal. Let me know when the policy changes."

I hiked my bag onto my shoulder. "Places to go. Things to do."

Morelli grabbed me and dragged me

up against him. He kissed me with enough tongue to make me reconsider the beads, and I felt the heat curl through my stomach.

"Mmmmm," I said.

"Too bad you can't stay. I could sweeten the bead deal by throwing in another cinnamon roll."

"It was a really great cinnamon roll."

An hour later, I was back at Morelli's front door. "I can't believe I did that," I said to Morelli.

"Does this count as our make-up sex? Or do we still have make-up sex coming to us?"

"I was supposed to be off men. And I didn't get any beads."

"Yeah, I lied about the beads, but you can have another cinnamon roll if you want."

"I'll take a rain check," I told him.

"Do you need help getting Joyce out of your apartment? I could physically remove her."

"I've done that. She comes back in through the fire escape."

"I can put better locks on your windows. I can install an alarm. I can arrange to have security screening or bars."

"It might come to that, but for now I'm going home to talk to her."

I had the door open, and I looked across the street at the Lincoln.

"Do you want me to get rid of them?" Morelli asked.

"No. I'm sort of getting used to them following me around. I think they're mostly harmless."

Morelli kissed me on the forehead. "You know where to find me."

"More or less."

• • •

I climbed into the truck, and before going back to Joyce, I decided to have one last go at Lahonka. I parked in front of her apartment and stared at the empty yard. No toys. I walked to the door and knocked, and the door swung open on jerry-rigged hinges. The apartment was empty. No furniture. No big-screen television. No Lahonka.

Lancer and Slasher had parked behind me. They were sitting quietly, taking it all in. I knocked on the door to the apartment next to Lahonka, and an older man answered.

"I'm looking for Lahonka," I told him.

"She's gone. She took off early this morning. Backed a truck up to her door, loaded everything into it, and took off."

"Do you know where she went?"

"South is all she said. She has a sister in New Orleans and one in Tampa, Florida. She might have gone to one of them."

I thanked him and returned to my truck. Once someone flees the area, the file gets moved to the back burner for me. If the bond is high enough, Connie takes over the search electronically. If she locates the skip, she can use an out-of-state bounty hunter, or she can send Vinnie or Ranger. Lahonka's bond was marginal.

I cut across town with the Lincoln half a car length behind me. I stopped at Tasty Pastry Bakery on Hamilton and got a bag of croissants for Joyce. I would have gotten something for Lancer and Slasher, but I'd already treated them to a pizza, and it wasn't like I was rolling in money. They followed me to the edge of my apartment building lot and parked on the side street. I backed up until I was parallel with them, and I powered my window down.

"What's the plan?" I asked Slasher.

"We're following you," Slasher said. "We're waiting for you to lead us to the photo, and then we're gonna pounce."

"How do you know the photo isn't in my apartment?"

"You said you didn't have it."

"You believed me?"

Slasher got some color in his cheeks. "Maybe."

I powered my window up and drove into my lot. I didn't see Raz lurking anywhere. Even though he liked pain, I expected getting shot had slowed him down a tad.

Joyce was watching cartoons when I let myself into my apartment. I gave her the bag of croissants and shut the television off.

"News flash," I said. "I talked to Morelli. Frank Korda wasn't a Pink Panther. The Panthers are diamond thieves operating in Europe, and it's not even a real organization."

"Maybe he belonged to a different Pink Panthers," Joyce said. "Who's to say there's only one?"

I had no way to argue that. "It doesn't matter," I told her. "You have to go. You can't live here anymore. I don't care if someone's trying to kill you. If you stay here any longer, *I'm* going to kill you."

Joyce stood with her bag of croissants. "I can't take it anymore, either. I'd rather be dead than spend any more time in your bathroom. And your television sucks. I'll make a deal. I'll leave, but you have to promise to look for the chest tomorrow."

"No way."

"Promise, or I won't go. If you can put up with that bathroom and this television, I can, too."

Jeez Louise. "I'll make an effort," I said, "but I can't promise."

Five minutes later, Joyce and the croissants were out the door, almost out of my life. I carted Rex and his cage back into the kitchen and put him on the counter. I gave him fresh water and a chunk of Pop-Tart, and I ate the rest. I pulled my laptop out from under the mattress, put it on my dining room table, and plugged it in. I was making progress.

TWENTY

Frank Korda and his wife, Pat, lived in a white colonial house with black shutters, a mahogany front door, and a two-car garage. It was at the end of a cul-de-sac in a middle-class residential neighborhood in Hamilton Township. Korda's memorial service was scheduled for nine in the morning, burial was to follow, and friends and relatives were invited back to the house for refreshments. I'd driven past the house at sunrise to check it out. Everything had been quiet. No lights on. The widow wasn't an early riser.

I wasn't an early riser, either, but I was on a mission today. I wanted to keep Joyce out of my apartment, and I had developed a curiosity about the chest. I wanted to see the contents.

I'd called Lula and told her I needed her to stand watch for me. We were to meet at the coffee shop at eight-thirty. I suggested she dress funeral appropriate, so we didn't look out of place should neighbors see us sneaking around. I had no idea how I was going to get into the house. Break a back window maybe. If a security alarm went off, I was out of there in a flash, and Joyce would have to live without the chest.

I was wearing my standard black funeral suit and heels, carrying a big slouchy black leather bag that would easily contain a small pirate chest.

I parked in front of the coffee shop, and Lula's Firebird pulled in behind me. Lula got out and walked over.

"I thought you might want to take my Firebird," she said. "It might blend in better than your truck."

I looked back at her car. "I don't

know. It's a toss-up. The Firebird's really red."

"Yeah, but my sweetie don't fit inside your truck, and he gonna look obvious sittin' in the back in his suit."

"Your sweetie?"

"I thought we might need muscle, so I brought him along. I got him dressed up in a suit and everything. And I met his mama last night. She didn't say much, but I think she liked me."

"He can't come," I said to Lula. "We're breaking into a house. It's illegal."

"That's okay. He does illegal shit all the time."

"That's not the problem. I don't want a witness."

"I see what you're saying, but I don't know how we'll get him out of my car."

"Leave him in your car. We'll take my truck. Tell him we'll come back for him in an hour."

Lula trotted to the Firebird, had a short conversation with Buggy, trotted back to my truck, and got in.

"It's all set," she said.

I pulled into traffic and Buggy followed.

"Hunh, he must have misunderstood," Lula said, looking in the side mirror.

I wove around a few streets, but Buggy stayed close on my bumper.

"I'm losing time trying to get rid of him," I said to Lula. "Call him on his cell phone and tell him to go away."

"He don't have a cell phone," Lula said. "His mama won't give him money for one. And he don't make enough stealin' purses to get one on his own. People got a misconception about purse snatchers. It's a real hard way to make a living."

"Then why doesn't he get a job?"

"I guess you gotta do what you love," Lula said. "He's a man who follows his heart."

I turned onto Korda's street and the black mortuary limo glided past me going in the opposite direction. It was carrying Pat Korda to the memorial service, and that meant her house might be empty. I parked and sat watching the house for a few minutes. There were no other cars parked outside, and I didn't see signs of activity. I'd stopped at Giovichinni's and picked up a noodle casserole to use as cover. My story, if I needed one, was that I had misunderstood the time and arrived at the wake early.

I carried the casserole to the door and rang the bell. No answer. I listened carefully for sounds inside the house. The house was silent.

Lula and Buggy were close behind me. Lancer and Slasher were parked behind the Firebird. Lula was wearing a black spandex miniskirt, a black silky spandex wrap shirt, and a fake leopard jacket that had been designed for a much smaller woman. She was in black four-inch spike-heeled shoes, and her hair was sunflower yellow for the occasion. Buggy looked like Shamu in a Russian-made secondhand suit.

"You want my sweetie to kick the door in now?" Lula asked.

"No!"

"How about we go around back and break a window?"

"No. I don't want to see any property damage."

"Well then, how we supposed to get in?" Lula asked.

"I'm going in," Buggy said, pushing me aside. "I'm tired of waiting."

And he opened the door. It hadn't been locked.

I tiptoed in and looked around. "They have the buffet set out," I said to Lula. "*DO NOT* let Buggy eat anything."

"You hear that, Sweetums?" Lula said to Buggy. "We aren't going to eat any of the funeral food. When we're done here, I'll take you out for breakfast."

"I like breakfast," Buggy said.

I found the kitchen and set my casserole on the counter. There were several other casseroles there, plus bags of bakery rolls, and a couple coffee cakes. A professional coffee urn was ready to go and a full bar was set up next to the urn. I did a fast scan of the kitchen, moved through the dining room, and into the living room.

"What are we looking for?" Lula followed.

"A little chest. A pirate chest."

"You mean like that chest on the fireplace mantel?" she asked.

Holy cow, it was the chest. It was exactly as Joyce had described it.

Lula took the chest off the mantel and examined it. "What's so special about this chest? What's in it?" She turned it upside down and looked at the bottom. "It says 'Miss Kitty R.I.P.' "

The top to the chest dropped open, and ashes flew out at Lula and scattered across the living-room rug.

"What the heck?" Lula said.

I clapped my hand over my mouth. I wasn't sure if I was going to laugh, gag, or shriek. "I think Miss Kitty was cremated, and those are her ashes."

Lula stared down at herself. "Are you shitting me? I'm allergic to cat. I feel my throat closing up. I can't breathe. I'm makin' snot. Somebody do something! Call 911!"

She ran into the kitchen, grabbed the DustBuster off the wall by the pantry, and sucked the ash off herself.

"Freakin' cats," she said.

So much for Miss Kitty's final resting place.

Lula felt her face. "Do I got hives?"

"No, you haven't got hives," I said. "You can't be allergic to cat ashes. They're sterile. There's no dander."

"I feel like I have hives. I'm pretty sure I feel some popping out."

"It's all in your head," I told her.

"I'm very impressionable," Lula said. "My family's prone to hysteria."

I examined the chest, looking for a false bottom or secret message. I didn't find either, so I carefully placed the chest back on the mantel.

"Do I get breakfast now?" Buggy asked.

"I want to make a fast run through the house to make sure there aren't any more chests," I told Lula. "Keep your eyes open for visitors, and maybe you can DustBuster up what's left of Miss Kitty."

I did a cursory search, found nothing, and we were all out the door in ten minutes. Lula and Buggy left in the Firebird in search of a breakfast buffet, and I drove two blocks down and waited for the mourners to return from the cemetery.

Lancer and Slasher parked behind me. They didn't seem to be much of a threat for now, but I suspected that could change if their boss pressed the go button. And while I didn't feel immediately threatened, they were a constant reminder that I had a huge, horrible, scary problem.

It was almost noon when the cars filed by. I was sure one of the cars contained Grandma. I couldn't see her missing Frank Korda being laid to rest. I waited for the last car to arrive, and I gave it another ten minutes before I joined the crowd. I'd done a decent job of hiding my bruise under makeup, not to mention that after ten minutes, everyone would have knocked back a drink or two and not be noticing much beyond the shrimp salad.

I slipped into the house and located Grandma. She was sitting on the couch with Esther Philpot. They were drinking what appeared to be port wine, and they had a plate of cookies. I said hello and snitched a cookie.

"I didn't see you at the service," Grandma said.

"I couldn't make it," I told her. "I had a previous commitment."

"She's a working girl," Grandma said to Esther. "And she's got a gun. It's not as big as mine, but it's pretty good."

"What do you carry?" Esther asked Grandma.

"Forty-five long barrel," Grandma said. "What about you?"

"I have a little Beretta Bobcat. My grandson gave it to me for Christmas last year."

They looked at me.

"What do you have, dear?" Esther asked me.

"Glock."

"Get the heck out," Grandma said. "When did you get a Glock? Can I see it?"

"I wouldn't mind having a Glock," Esther said. "Maybe I'll get one next year."

They leaned in and peeked into my purse at my gun.

"It's a beauty," Grandma said.

"I should mingle." I looked around.

Grandma sat back. "There's little bitty cupcakes in the dining room, and the liquor's in the kitchen. I imagine that's where you'll find the widow. She was already three sheets to the wind at the service. Not that I blame her. A funeral is stressful, poor thing."

"Poor thing, my behind," Esther said. "She's not upset. She's celebrating. She was only staying with him for the house. Everybody knows that. Frank did some stepping out, if you know what I mean. There was Mitchell Menton's wife, Cheryl. And Bitsy Durham. Her husband is on the city council. I'm sure there were others."

"I guess Frank was having one of those midlife crises," Grandma said.

"And I imagine there are advantages to having an affair with a jeweler," Esther said.

I wandered into the kitchen, where Pat Korda was scarfing ham roll-ups and drinking something colorless.

"Vodka?" I asked her.

"Fuckin' A," she said.

I poured some into a tumbler. "Me, too."

"Here's to you," Pat said. "Whoever the hell you are. Looks like someone beat the crap out of you."

"Yeah, it's been one of those weeks."

Pat rolled her eyes and listed a little to the left. "Tell me about it."

"Sorry about your husband."

"Thanks. You want some ham? It goes good with vodka, but then, hell, everything goes good with vodka."

"I noticed the little chest on your mantel. The one that looks like a pirate chest."

"That's Miss Kitty," Pat said. "She was our cat. Frank used to keep her in the store, but I brought her back here when he croaked."

"It's an interesting chest. Is it one of a kind?"

"Frank got it at the pet crematorium."

So if the Pink Panthers didn't kill Frank Korda, and Joyce didn't kill him . . . who killed him? Maybe his wife?

"Do you ever wear pink?" I asked her.

"No. I hate pink." She took another slurp of vodka. "Frank was the pink guy. He had this whole pink thing. He used to tell his bimbos he was a Pink Panther. Hah! Can you imagine?"

"You knew about it?"

"Honey, wives know all kinds of shit. Frank had this whole routine. He got it from a Schwarzenegger movie. *True Lies.* Schwarzenegger was a spy, but his wife didn't know. She thought he was, like, boring. She was all hot for this other guy who was *pretending* to be a spy. So the wife's thinking of screwing the pretend spy, right? Anyway, Frank saw this movie and wigged out. He must have watched it a hundred times. Do you have a cigarette?"

"No. Sorry, I don't smoke."

"Nobody fucking smokes anymore. Just when I decide I need a cigarette, nobody smokes."

"About the Pink Panther Schwarzenegger routine."

Pat moved from the ham to the cheese. "Frank wasn't the most exciting-looking guy. Short, bald, glasses, not a muscle anywhere in sight. But he discovered he could pretend to be a big-time jewel thief and get laid. Go figure."

"How did you know all this? Did he tell you?"

"I knew he was messing around, so

I hired a detective. He put it together for me."

"But you didn't divorce Frank?"

"I thought about it, but what was the point? I'm comfortable. I like my house. And I had someone to take the garbage out and shovel the snow. And the best part was I had some dumb slut taking care of Frank's needs. I would have sent them all fruit baskets, but I didn't want to give myself away." She stared down into her empty glass. "Oh shit. Someone drank my vodka. Oh wait a minute, it was me!" And she did a sort of crazy-lady, semi-hysterical giggle.

"Do you have any idea who killed Frank?" I asked her.

"Probably one of his Pink Panther bimbos who found out the jewelry he gave her was fake. Personally, I'm not completely happy. I have to take my own garbage out now."

I left Pat Korda and returned to Grandma.

"I'm going back to work," I told her. "Do you need a ride home?"

"No, but thanks, I'm riding with Esther here. It's a shame you missed the graveside ceremony. That's the nicest cemetery. The deceased was laid to rest by a patch of woods. He must feel like he's always camping out now. I swear it smelled like campfire."

Esther nodded her head in agreement. "It did smell like a campfire. That's such a cozy smell."

I made a mental note to check the cemetery for Magpie.

TWENTY-ONE

I went home to change my clothes and discovered Joyce was back.

"That's it," I said to her. "I'm going to shoot you and bury your body where no one will ever find it."

"Relax. I just dropped in to get my chest. You went to Korda's house this morning, right?"

"Right. So I have some good news, and I have some bad news. The good news is the Pink Panthers aren't trying to kill you. Probably no one's trying to kill you. The bad news is, I found the treasure chest, but the only treasure in it was the remains of Korda's cat, Miss Kitty."

Joyce went pale. "I don't believe you."

"Believe it. It's true. Ask Pat Korda. She's got it sitting on her mantel. And just out of morbid curiosity, what did you *really* want with the chest?"

Joyce pressed her lips together and took a couple beats to get it together. "This is a real pisser," she finally said. "I actually think you're telling the truth. You haven't got enough imagination to invent something that hideous."

"About the chest?"

"What the hell, it doesn't matter now. Frank said he kept the safe combination in it. He said half the combination was on my key, and the other half was in the chest."

"You were going to rob the safe?"

"No. I was going to sell the combination. If I robbed the safe, I'd have to find a fence, and I didn't think chances were good I could depend on the Pink Panthers. I tried picking the lock to the store, but I couldn't get in. Then I thought of you. I figured you were dumb enough to get Ranger to open the door for you. Then you could get me the chest."

"How about the guy who bought the combination? How was he getting in?"

"Not my problem," Joyce said. "He could go in the front window with a bulldozer for all I cared."

It was comforting to know Joyce was still her old obnoxious, rotten self. Parts of my life were so beyond my control that it was nice to have consistency in others.

"Since we have everything settled, I guess you'll be leaving now and not coming back," I said to Joyce.

"Yeah, I suppose, but I need a ride. In case you forgot, my car got compacted."

"How did you get here?"

"Taxi. And I'm not taking one home. My income source just evaporated."

• • •

Forty-five minutes later, I dropped Joyce off at her town house.

"You're positive the Pink Panthers

aren't looking for me, right?" Joyce asked.

"Positive. Korda made the whole thing up. It was a line he used to get women to sleep with him. You weren't the only one. And if he gave you any jewelry it was probably fake."

"No shit. I found that out when I tried to pawn my necklace. I didn't get crap for it."

I drove away half afraid if I looked in my rearview mirror I'd see Joyce running after me.

I had a bunch of open files in my messenger bag that I should have started working my way through, earning rent money. But having resolved Lahonka, Buggy, and Joyce, I thought it was time to focus my energy on staying alive, and that meant I had to get rid of the photograph hunters. Raz was in the wind, and I had no good way to find him. Brenda was going to stick with her lame fiancée story, at least for now. That left Lancer and Slasher as the weak link. I was convinced they knew nothing beyond their instructions to follow me. I had to go farther up the food chain if I wanted real information.

I called Berger on my way across town. "Anything new on the photograph thing?" I asked him.

"Nothing significant."

"How about insignificant?"

"Two out of three people polled agree that the second sketch looks like Ashton Kutcher."

"Anything on Lancelot or Larder?" I asked.

"No."

"Would you tell me if you had something?"

A moment of silence. "Absolutely."

I knew from the length of the pause that his answer was actually no. I disconnected and called Morelli.

"Joyce is gone," I said. "I have my apartment back."

"Is that an invitation?"

"No. It's a statement. Would you like an invitation?"

"Maybe."

"Only *maybe*?"

"I'm not in good shape here. We're

getting ready to make an arrest in the Korda case."

"Really? Who?"

"I can't tell you."

"You're teasing me."

"Cupcake, you're breathing shallow and begging for more when I tease you."

"That wouldn't be now," I said to him. "Right now, I'm grinding my teeth and my eyes are squinty."

"I have to go," Morelli said.

"No! I need a favor."

"I'm hoping this has to do with teasing."

"It has to do with the FBI and the fact that three people are possibly trying to kill me."

"You have my attention," he said.

"Berger is no help at all. I think he knows something but he's not sharing. I thought he might talk to you."

"I'll get back to you."

While Morelli worked it from his angle, I thought I'd come at it from a different direction. I drove a quarter mile on Broad, turned right onto a side street, made another right, and found a parking place in front of the bonds office. Connie's car was there. No Vinnie. No Lula.

Connie was paging through *Star* magazine when I walked in.

"What's up?" I asked. "Where is everybody?"

"Vinnie is hiding at home. He's afraid DeAngelo will demand a Ferrari. Lula's off somewhere making coochy-coochy sounds at Moron Man. And I'm stuck in this hellhole. I can hear rats running overhead. Honest to God, I think they're planning an attack."

"I was hoping you could do some digging for me. We did a search on Mortimer Lancelot and Sylvester Larder, and I need to go deeper. They're working for someone. I want to know who it is. I'm guessing it's someone they met while they were security at the casino."

"That narrows it down to fifty thousand people," Connie said.

"I'm looking for someone shady."

"Okay, forty-nine thousand."

"Any ideas?"

"I can run another credit check, but

it's not going to show anything if they're getting paid in cash. You might do better if you went to the casino and talked to people."

"I'd like to take Lula with me, but I can't get her away from Moron Man."

"She says he's her true love," Connie said. "Something about a love potion."

I get that Lula would like to find her true love. And I get that she's giving it her best shot to turn pond scum into noodle soup. And I wasn't entirely discounting that Buggy was her true love, because I've seen some of Lula's previous boyfriends, and Buggy wasn't so far off the mark. But true love or not, I couldn't take much more of Buggy. Buggy had to go. If Lula could convince herself a love potion started this fiasco, she could damn well unconvince herself.

I called Grandma. "I need to talk to Annie Hart," I said.

"Tonight's bowling night," Grandma said. "She's gonna pick me up. I could invite her to dinner again if you want."

"That would be great. And tell Mom

to set three extra plates besides Annie's."

I called Lula next.

"Where are you?" I asked.

"I'm at the mall with Sugar Lumps. He needed a Dairy Queen Blizzard and a new leather jacket. And it's not easy getting a leather jacket for him, since he needs so much leather. You gotta just about use a whole cow for his jacket. Good thing I had my credit card limit raised."

"Remember when you thought you were a vampire, but it turned out to be an absessed tooth?"

"Yeah."

"And remember how this morning you thought you were having an allergic reaction to cat ashes, but you really were just fine?"

"Yeah."

"Do you suppose this attraction to Buggy is another one of those imaginary episodes?"

"I admit I'm an impressionable person, but I'm pretty sure Shrek is my true love."

"You mean Buggy?"

"Yeah, what did I say?"

"You said Shrek was your true love."

"Well, Buggy got a lot of Shrekness to him."

"Now we're getting somewhere," I said to Lula. "Maybe it's actually *Shrek* that's your true love."

"Something to think about," Lula said.

"I need to go to Atlantic City to do some research tonight," I said to Lula. "Are you on board?"

"Damn skippy. I love Atlantic City. Me and Buggy'll research the heck out of it."

"I'll meet you at my parents' house at six o'clock. We'll have dinner and head south."

• • •

Jeans and a T-shirt are perfectly okay gear for an Atlantic City casino, unless you want to get information out of a man. If information, free drinks, or dinner is on the agenda, it doesn't hurt to show some cleavage.

I went home, changed into skinny

designer jeans, a stretchy red sweater with a low scoop neck, and strappy heels. I added dangly earrings and a couple more swipes of mascara. I transferred my stun gun, Glock, cuffs, and all my normal girl stuff into a dressier handbag, and I was ready to go to work.

I arrived at my parents' house a little before six and parked behind Annie's car. Lancer and Slasher parked half a block down. There was no other traffic on the street. The seniors were still at the diner, finishing up the early-bird specials. Kids were home from soccer practice and piano lessons. Working moms were in the kitchen scarfing down Cheetos and wine from Costco while they frantically pulled dinner together. The men on my parents' street were zoned out in front of the television. No foreclosure signs on the front lawns. This was a neighborhood that was here for the long haul. Hardworking survivors who didn't care if their house was underwater. Nobody frigging bailed on the Burg.

Grandma was at the front door, waiting for me.

"You left the wake too early," she said. "The widow got snockered and passed out in the chicken salad and had to be carted upstairs. You don't see that every day."

"Where's Annie?"

"She's in the kitchen helping your mother."

We went to the kitchen and I snitched a corn muffin out of the breadbasket.

"We have a problem," I said to Annie. "Remember the little bottle of pink stuff you gave me?"

"Yes, of course."

"Lula drank it, and now she needs an antidote."

"Goodness. Did she have an allergic reaction?" Annie asked.

"No. She fell in love with a sandbag."

"How unusual," Annie said. "It was just a pocket-sized over-the-counter antacid. You were having digestive problems."

"Do you have any more?"

"I have some," Grandma said. "She gave some to me. I was saving it for when I saw my true love and needed it."

"Do you have a true love?" Annie asked Grandma.

"I'm hot for George Clooney," Grandma said, "but I think he mostly stays in Hollywood."

"My idea is to give more of the pink stuff to Lula, and tell her it's an antidote to the love potion she took," I said.

"That's a little deceptive," Annie said. "I don't feel comfortable with that. Suppose he really is her true love?"

"Yeah," Grandma said. "It would be like those time-travelers when they aren't supposed to mess around with history."

"Yoohoo," Lula called from the front door. "I'm here with my honey."

Grandma, Annie, my mom, and I traipsed out to see the honey.

"This is my big stud muffin, Buggy," Lula said, her arms partially wrapped around him.

"Yuh," Buggy said.

My father was in the living room, watching television, reading the paper.

He glanced over at Buggy, grimaced, and returned to the paper.

My mother and grandmother scurried off to the kitchen to get the food, and we all took our seats at the table.

"Have you and Buggy known each other long?" Annie asked Lula.

"About a week," Lula said.

Annie turned to Buggy. "And what do you do?"

"I'm a purse snatcher," Buggy said.

Lula looked over at Buggy. "He's a good one, too. He's real intimidating on account of he's so big."

My mother set a full rump roast in front of my father, and my grandmother came in with a cauldron of mashed potatoes. My father carved up the roast, and my mother and grandmother brought green beans, gravy, and applesauce to the table.

Buggy's eyes were darting from dish to dish. He was sitting next to my father, and he had a good grip on his fork, waiting for a signal that he could dig in, keeping close watch on my father, who still held the big carving knife.

My father selected a piece of meat and placed the knife on the table.

"Buggy," my mother said. "Help yourself."

"Yuh!" Buggy said, lunging for the meat platter, forking slabs of it onto his plate.

In seconds he had a mountain of meat and potatoes, beans, and applesauce. He poured gravy over the mountain until it slopped over his plate and ran onto the tablecloth. He shoveled the food into his mouth, chewing, swallowing, grunting, smacking his lips. Gravy oozed out of his mouth and dripped off his chin. Everyone sat in frozen horror watching Buggy eat.

"Isn't he adorable," Lula said. "Don't you just love a man who enjoys his food?"

"Get the antidote potion for Stephanie," Annie said to Grandma. "The one I gave you. The little bottle with the pink liquid."

"Okay," Grandma said, "but don't let him eat my food while I'm gone."

"What antidote is that?" Lula asked.

"I gave Stephanie a love potion a couple days ago," Annie said, "but I found out it's defective, so I prepared an antidote."

Grandma came with the little pink bottle. "Here it is," she said, putting it on the table.

"I was the one who drank Stephanie's love potion," Lula said. "How was it defective?"

Annie went blank. She didn't have an answer.

Grandma jumped in. "It'll give you worms," she said. "If you don't drink the antidote soon enough, you get worms and all your hair falls out."

"What about finding true love?" Lula asked.

"You gotta make a choice between true love and worms," Grandma said.

Lula did a shiver. "I don't want worms. Do you think it's too late? Will the antidote work on me?"

"Only one way to find out," Grandma said.

Lula chugged the bottle and felt her hair. "Anyone notice if I've been losing hair? Do I look like I got worms? I think I might feel some crawling around inside me."

"Anything else?" Annie asked. "Do you feel a little chilly?"

"Yeah, maybe a little," Lula said.

"That's a sign that the antidote is working," Annie told her.

Lula sat perfectly still. "I don't feel nearly so wormy anymore."

Buggy took a slice of beef off Lula's plate and shoved it into his mouth.

"Say what?" Lula said to Buggy. "You just took my pot roast."

"Honey Pot's hungry," Buggy said.

"Shrek wouldn't never have taken Princess Fiona's pot roast," Lula said.

"Well, I'm not Shrek," Buggy said. "I'm Honey Pot."

"You're no honey pot, either," Lula told him. "Who the heck said you're a honey pot?"

"You did."

"I don't think so," Lula said. "You must be mistaken."

"I want dessert," Buggy said.

"How is that to act?" Lula said.

"That's just plain rude. You don't go to someone's house and ask for dessert. What's the matter with you, anyways? I'm beginning to see you in a whole new light. Didn't your mama ever teach you manners?"

"I don't need manners on account of I'm cute," Buggy said.

"You been operating under a delusion," Lula said.

"Huh, well I'm going home if I can't have dessert. Give me the keys to your car."

Lula crinkled up her nose and squinted at him. "Excuse me?"

"I'm driving home. I want your car."

"Are you smokin' funny stuff or something? I'm not giving you my car. You're lucky I don't give you my foot up your ass." Lula looked around the table. "Excuse me. I meant to say up your *behind.*"

My father was smiling. Usually he ate fast, with his head down, tuning out my grandmother's ramblings. Tonight he was enjoying Lula giving the what-for to Buggy.

Buggy looked at my mother. "Is there dessert?"

"I made a pie," my mother said.

Buggy sat up straight. "I like pie a lot."

"You're a oaf, and you don't deserve no pie," Lula said.

"You didn't think I was a oaf this afternoon when you were doing nicky nacky on me," Buggy said.

My father gave a snort of laughter, and my mother knocked back a tumbler of whiskey.

"That was before I took the antidote," Lula told everyone. "I was under the influence of a potion."

"I like nicky nacky," Buggy said, "but it's not as good as pot roast."

My mother looked down the table at him, her eyes unfocused. "Thank you, dear."

"Maybe you should leave," I said to Buggy.

"Not until I get some pie."

"Will you leave if I give you half the pie?" I asked.

"Yuh."

Minutes later, he was out the door

with his pie, walking toward his parents' house.

"I'm worried about them worms," Lula said. "I'm pretty sure I've still got them."

TWENTY-TWO

"I don't know how I could have thought I liked that idiot Buggy," Lula said. "I tell you, you gotta be careful what you're drinking these days."

I was cruising around the casino parking garage looking for a spot close to the elevator. I'd taken the time to lose Lancer and Slasher before driving south, but I still had to worry about Raz, and possibly others.

I found something acceptable, and Lula and I took the elevator to the casino floor. I'm not much of a gambler, but I love being in a casino. I like the flash of lights, the bells ringing, the energy of the people, the theme park–fantasyland atmosphere. I'm willing to throw a small amount of money into the slots, but I have no illusion about winning. I can't count fast enough to play blackjack, I'm like death at a roulette table, and I'm the world's worst poker player.

"First off, I gotta play some slots," Lula said, taking it all in.

"We're working," I told her. "And you always lose all your money when you play slots."

"Yeah, but I feel lucky today."

"You always say that."

"It's on account of I'm a positive person. My glass is half full. You're one of them half-empty-glass people."

"Knock yourself out," I said. "I'll call you if I need you."

This was my first time in this particular casino. It was located at the far end of the boardwalk, and it offered no good reason why anyone should walk the distance. I wandered around, getting the lay of the land, paying attention to security. Like every other casino, this one had uniformed guards and plain-clothes guys who stood flat-footed, eyes glazed over from tedium. An ear-bud plugged them into some central command, and the promise of a stiff drink at the end of their shift kept them from shooting themselves in desperation.

I picked out a suit who looked like he'd rather be cleaning kennel cages than standing his shift, and I moved into his field of vision.

"Hey," I said. "How's it going?"

"Slow."

"Yeah, not a lot of people here. I guess it picks up on weekends. I haven't been here in a while. Lately, I've been going to the other end of the board-walk."

"You and everyone else."

"I used to talk to one of the security people here. He was real nice, but I don't see him here tonight. His name is Mortimer Lancelot."

"Morty," the guy said. "He doesn't work here anymore. Budget cuts."

"Bummer. What's he doing now? Is he at one of the other casinos?"

"No. None of the casinos are hiring. He went outside. I heard a rumor he got a job as a night watchman for one of the vendors. Real crap job. He was a senior guy here, too."

Progress!

"So who hired him? What's he guarding? Slot machines? Liquor? Vending machines?"

"I don't know. Are you interested in Morty?"

"Just making conversation."

"I get off in a couple hours. We could make conversation then if you want."

"Sure. That would be great. I'll be around."

I crossed to the other side of the casino and climbed onto a barstool. There were two guys working behind the bar. One was keeping the cocktail waitresses supplied, and the other was servicing the bar customers. At the moment, there weren't a lot of bar customers. Mostly me. I ordered a Cosmo and smiled when it was delivered.

"Not a lot going on," I said to the bartender.

He studied me for a minute. "You were looking for action?"

"No. I was looking for an old friend. I used to work with this guy years ago, and someone told me he worked here now, but I don't see him. Morty Lancelot."

"You're about six months late. Morty and a bunch of others got caught in a budget crunch, and it was adios."

"That sucks."

"Yeah, they got rid of everyone at the top of the pay scale. I'm still here because I work for peanuts. Literally."

He took a little glass dish, scooped peanuts into it from a tub under the bar, and set them in front of me.

"I used to have a more balanced diet when they had wasabi peas, but the peas got cut with Morty," he said.

"Do you know where Morty is now?"

"I heard he got a job with Billings."

"What's Billings?"

"Food purveyor. I see the truck at the loading dock every morning when I work days."

I finished my Cosmo and left a generous tip so the bar guy could get himself some peas. I roamed around a little more and eventually made my way back to the slots, where Lula was still feeding money into a machine.

"How are you doing?" I asked her.

"I won twenty dollars."

"How much have you spent?"

"Seventy. These machines are rigged. This is a crooked casino."

"I accomplished my purpose," I said. "I think I have a lead on the guys following me. Are you ready to leave?"

"Yeah, I'm broke. This was a exhausting day. At least I got a grip on the worms before I left your mama's house."

• • •

It was close to midnight when I pulled into the Burg. If it had been a little earlier, I would have gone to the cemetery looking for Magpie. As it was, Lula was asleep, and I was wearing four-inch heels. Not great for chasing a guy down through grass and gravestones. I eased to a stop at my parents' house and watched while Lula got into her Firebird and took off. I drove to my apartment building and did a scan of the parking lot. No Lincoln Town Car. No toaster car. No odd van. The big surprise was Morelli's SUV. I parked next to it, got out, and looked up at my apartment. Lights were on. Morelli had a key, left over from more committed times.

At least I didn't have to worry about walking in and finding Raz hiding out in my kitchen, I thought. Or Joyce. So how did I feel about finding Morelli hiding out in my kitchen? Warm. Nice and warm. How scary is that?

I let myself in, and Bob rushed to greet me. I gave him hugs and scratched behind his ears. I said hello to Rex, and went into the living room. The television was on, and Morelli was asleep on the couch. He was in jeans and T-shirt and socks. He was seven hours past a five o'clock shadow. He should have gotten a haircut a month ago. And he was incredibly sexy and cuddly as hell. I got the extra quilt from the closet and tucked him in. I shut the television and lights off. And I went to bed.

• • •

I woke up with Morelli's arm draped over me, and I didn't have to look under the covers to know he was naked. I ran my hand along the length of him, and his eyes half-opened.

"Surprise," he murmured.

A half hour later, Morelli was in my shower and I was in the kitchen pulling breakfast together. Morning sex with Morelli is fun and satisfying, but never stretches into marathon territory. Morelli has other things to do in the morning. Morelli has murders to solve.

I measured kibble into Bob's bowl, gave him fresh water, and told him Morelli would be out any minute to take him for a walk. I got coffee brewing and plated a babka my mom had given me the night before.

Morelli strolled into the kitchen the moment the coffee was done. He kissed me and poured himself a glass of juice.

"I stopped in last night to tell you we made an arrest on the Korda case," he said. "Where were you?"

"Atlantic City. I was looking for a lead on the two guys who've been following me."

"And?"

"I didn't have a chance to follow through, but I think they might be working for a food purveyor that services the casino. Billings." I took a chunk of babka. "Tell me about the arrest. Who's the suspect?"

"Carol Baumgarten. You probably don't know her. She's from Lawrenceville. We brought her in, and she totally cooperated. Claimed she never intended to kill anyone. She got tossed aside for Barnhardt, and she wanted to teach them a lesson. Her idea was to put them in the trunk, leave the car at the junkyard, and call Korda's wife to retrieve him. Problem was, Korda's wife never picked the message up on her cell phone, and Korda had a heart attack. By the time Baumgarten got worried and returned to the junkyard to rescue Korda, he'd already been compacted. So she panicked and started going through Stoli like it was water."

"How did you find her?"

"Cab records. She called a cab to take her back to her car at the jewelry store. I guess she followed Korda for days, waiting for the right time."

"I'm surprised you're sharing this with me."

"We have a taped confession and tons of physical evidence. Her prints were all over Joyce's car. And I'm sure there are DNA matches. The woman sheds hair like a cat. And with the way things operate in this town, every detail will be circulated at Mabel's Hair Salon and Giovichinni's Market today. I don't know how it gets leaked out, but it always does."

"Did you talk to Berger?"

"No. We've been playing phone tag. I'll try to hook up today."

Morelli left, and I went to my computer to get information on Billings. I found the company and scrolled through a bunch of pages. It looked like they distributed gourmet prepared food, specialty items, and premium meat and poultry. The warehouse and central offices were just north of Bordentown. It was a private company owned by Chester Billings. He wasn't exactly squeaky clean. He'd been charged with income-tax evasion three years ago, but he'd settled up and nothing more had come of it. He'd also been charged with possession of stolen goods, but nothing had come of that, either.

I plugged Chester Billings into a new search program that would give me some personal history. He was born in New Brunswick. Parents were Mary and William Billings. Sister Brenda. Holy cow. Brenda.

I put Brenda Schwartz into the same search program and read down. There it was . . . Brenda Billings. Brother Chester.

Okay, so I had finally made a connection. And it was interesting. But I still had no idea why the photograph was important. Or, for that matter, what I had to do to get everyone off my back.

I shut my computer down, took a shower, got dressed, and headed out. Lancer and Slasher fell in line behind me on Hamilton and followed me all the way. We parked in front of the bonds office, and I walked back to talk to them.

"I know who you work for," I said to Lancer.

"I didn't tell you," he said.

"No. I found out on my own."

"I guess it's okay then."

"You don't seem especially motivated to beat information out of me," I said.

"We're following orders," Lancer said. "We keep our eye on you and report back where you go and who you talk to."

"Razzle Dazzle is more aggressive."

Lancer snorted. "He's a freak. He used to hang out at the casino until they kicked him out. He had a way of getting the slots to pay out. Works for some Somali nutcase. Used to brag about how he could cut off a finger with a single slash of his knife."

• • •

Connie, Lula, and Vinnie were standing at silent attention when I walked into the office.

"What's going on?" I asked.

"We're listening," Connie said. "Do you hear that?"

I cocked my head and listened. "What am I supposed to be hearing?"

"They're squeaking," Connie said. "They're having a meeting."

"Who?"

"The rats."

Oh boy.

"I don't hear them no more," Lula said. "I'm not sure I ever heard them. I think the squeaking might have been Vinnie wheezin'."

"I don't wheeze," Vinnie said. "I'm the picture of health."

"Things to do. People to see," I said. "There's a warehouse I need to check out by Bordentown."

"They got good shopping at a flea market there," Lula said. "I wouldn't mind going with you."

"I wasn't planning on shopping."

"Yeah, but you never know when the urge might hit you," Lula said. "They got a kick-ass rib place there, too."

TWENTY-THREE

I ditched Lancer and Slasher in midtown Trenton, and got onto Broad. We picked Route 295 up in Whitehorse and went south.

"I'm feeling like those guys aren't trying real hard to tail you," Lula said. "Seems to me they don't got a lot of motivation."

"They're security guards who got promoted beyond their level of incompetence."

"Why are we going to look at this warehouse?"

"Lancer and Slasher are employed

by a guy named Chester Billings. Billings owns a gourmet food-distribution company, and his warehouse is in Bordentown. Turns out Brenda Schwartz is his sister."

"Hunh," Lula said. "What's all that mean?"

"Haven't a clue."

"So we're goin' pokin' around his warehouse?"

"Not so much poking around as riding by. I'd like to get a sense of the operation."

The Billings warehouse and office were in a light industrial park. I found the service road and wound my way through the complex, finally coming to Billings Gourmet Food at the end of a cul-de-sac. The buildings were relatively new. Grounds were minimally landscaped but neat. The office was attached to the warehouse. Maybe two thousand square feet for the office. A lot more for the warehouse. Large parking lot. I drove around back to see the loading docks. Two loading docks and two roll-up garage doors. Woods behind. I thought about the charge of receiving stolen goods. He had the perfect setup.

"Okay," I said. "I've seen enough."

Lula looked at me. "That's it?"

"Yep."

"We rode all the way down here to do this? You don't want to go in or nothin'?"

"Nope."

What would I say to big bad Chester Billings? I haven't got the photograph, but I'm pretty sure the guy looked like either Tom Cruise or Ashton Kutcher. And I'd appreciate it if you'd leave me alone. I couldn't see Chester Billings having a sense of humor about that message.

"I got the ribs place programmed into my phone," Lula said. "Just in case you're interested."

• • •

Ninety minutes and ten pounds later, we were back on the road.

"That was excellent," Lula said. "Nothing like lunching on ribs and fries and all that other shit to make me feel like a new woman."

I'd had absolutely no self-control. I'd eaten everything that was put in front of me, with the exception of the napkin, and I felt like *two* new women.

"What wild-goose chase we going on next?" Lula asked.

"I want to break into Brenda's house."

"Now you're talking! *WHAM.* What about the nosy neighborhood, and the fact it's daylight?"

"We'll be in disguise."

"A covert operation," Lula said. "I like it."

I drove back to Trenton, stopped at my mom's house, and borrowed a mop, a bucket, and a cleaning caddy filled with a bunch of cleaning products.

"This here's sexist," Lula said. "Why do we have to be cleaning ladies?"

"Because we look like cleaning ladies. Do you have a better idea?"

"I was just sayin'. No need to get huffy. Usually, we're 'hos when we go undercover. I'm good at being a 'ho."

"I didn't think 'ho would work here."

"I guess you got a point."

I found Brenda's little green house, and I parked in the driveway. We went to the front door and rang the bell. No answer. I felt around the doorjamb for a key. Nothing. I scanned the ground for fake dog poop or a fake rock. Nada.

We carted our buckets and mops to the back and tried the back door. Locked. I lifted the doormat and looked under. There was the key. We opened the back door and walked into the kitchen. A couple bowls and coffee mugs in the sink. A box of cereal on the counter.

"What are we looking for?" Lula asked me.

"I don't know."

"That makes it easy," Lula said.

It was a small, traditional ranch. Two bedrooms and one bath. Crammed with furniture. Probably whatever Brenda had loaded on a truck before the foreclosure police padlocked her out of her former house. There was a picture on an end table in the living room of Brenda and a young man. Her son, maybe. He was slim, with shoulder-length brown hair, wearing jeans and ratty sneakers and a brown T-shirt. They looked happy.

Brenda's bedroom was as expected. Her closet stuffed with clothes. Shoes lined up everywhere. A bureau crammed with undies, dressy T-shirts, sweaters. The top of the bureau loaded with hair products, nail polish, a professional makeup chest, a spice-scented candle. A jewelry chest containing costume jewelry. So far no pictures of her and Crick. No engagement ring in the jewelry box.

I moved to the bathroom. Medicine chest stuffed with over-the-counter decongestants, pain pills, laxatives, antacids, sleep aids, diet aids. Some makeup scattered on one side of the sink. Hairbrush, hairspray. Electric toothbrush. A second toothbrush, small tube of toothpaste, razor, and travel-size shave gel on the other side of the sink. Man stuff. Toilet seat up. Damp towel on the floor in front of the tub and shower. Definitely a guy here.

The second bedroom was being used. Bed unmade. Laptop on the bed. Men's flip-flops on the floor, along with tropical-themed boxer shorts. Backpack in the corner, partially stuffed with clothes. Nothing hanging in the closet. Nothing in the small chest of drawers.

"Somebody living with Brenda," Lula said.

"She has a twenty-one-year-old son. Jason. I'm guessing he's visiting. Doesn't look like he's planning an extended stay."

"That's nice he's visiting his mama, though. It's gotta be hard when your kid grows up and leaves."

I looked over at Lula. She never talked about kids.

"Would you like to have kids someday?" I asked her.

"I don't think I can have kids," Lula said. "Remember, I was hurt when I was a 'ho. I would have died if you hadn't found me and saved me."

"You could adopt."

"I don't know if anybody'd let me."

"You'd be a wonderful mom."

"I'd love the shit out of a kid," Lula said. "I'd try real hard. I never knew much about my own mom. She was a crackhead 'ho, and she overdosed on heroin when I was young. I was a better 'ho than her, on account of I never did the drugs like that."

I walked out of the bedroom, past a closet that held a washer and dryer. A few more steps down the hall, and I came to another door. I opened the door and peeked in. Garage. It looked like there was a car under a tarp. I switched the lights on, lifted the tarp, and gave a low whistle.

"That's a Ferrari," Lula said. "It's no ordinary Ferrari, either. It's one of them special-edition ones. This is a majorly expensive car. I bet Brenda has a orgasm drivin' this car."

"She doesn't drive this car," I said. "It hasn't got plates."

"Then I bet she has a orgasm sitting in it in the garage."

We grabbed our buckets and mops, I locked Brenda's house, and we got into my truck.

"I'm tired of fooling around with this," I said to Lula. "This is bullshit. I'm going to Brenda, and I want answers."

"Wham," Lula said. "Kick ass."

I motored out of Brenda's neighborhood, took Route 1, and turned into The Hair Barn's parking lot.

"I'm coming with you," Lula said. "I don't want to miss anything."

"There won't be much to miss. I just want to talk to her."

"Yeah, but if she won't talk, we'll rough her up."

"We will *not* rough her up."

"Jeez Louise," Lula said. "It's no wonder you go around in the dark all the time. You got a lot of rules."

Brenda was sitting in her styling chair when I walked into the salon.

"You came back," she said. "You decided to get something done with your hair, right?"

"Wrong," I said. "We need to talk."

"I don't need to talk anymore. I don't care about the photograph. You can keep it."

"I don't have it."

"Well if you *did* have it, you could keep it," Brenda said. "It's not important to me."

"What about Ritchy?"

"Who?"

"Your dead fiancé."

"Oh yeah, poor Ritchy."

"Talk to me about poor Ritchy. What was he doing with the photograph?"

"He just had it, okay? And then he didn't have it, because he gave it to you."

"Why did he give it to me?"

"That's a real good question. I think the answer is that he was an idiot."

"There's more of an answer."

Brenda stood. "I can't talk to you with that hair. It's disturbing. Look at your friend. She has amazing hair."

I glanced over at Lula. She looked like she was wearing a giant wad of tutti-fruiti–colored cotton candy.

"I take real good care of my hair, too," Lula said.

"You don't take care of your hair," I told her. "Every four days, you dye your hair a different color. You have indestructible hair. If you set your hair on fire, nothing would happen to it."

"I can't believe you two hang out together," Brenda said.

"It's embarrassing sometimes," Lula said. "She don't know much about dressing, either."

"Sit down here," Brenda said to me. "I'll get you fixed up. I don't have any clients for the rest of the day."

"Gee, thanks, but I don't think so," I said.

"On the house," Brenda said.

"It's not the money," I told her. "I sort of like my hair the way it is."

"Honey, your hair is *no* way," Brenda said. She cut her eyes to Lula. "Am I right?"

"Yep," Lula said. "You're right."

Brenda ran her fingers through my hair. "First thing, you need highlights. Big, chunky highlights."

"About the photograph?"

"Put a cape on and sit down while I mix this up," Brenda said. "We can talk when I come back."

Heaven help me, I was going to have to let her give me highlights to get her to talk.

"I don't trust her," I said to Lula. "She's crazy. What if she poisons my hair?"

"I'll go watch her," Lula said. "I know what I'm doing when it comes to hair and pharmaceuticals. You just sit in the chair and don't worry about nothin'."

They both came back after a couple minutes, and Brenda streaked gunk into my hair and wrapped it in foil.

"It's no big deal about the photograph," Brenda said. "I thought I needed it for a business transaction, but turns out it wasn't necessary."

"What about your brother? Am I off the hook with him, too?"

"You know about Chester?" She shrugged. "I don't know what's going on with him, except he's an asshole. I'm not talking to him. He's only my half brother anyway. We found out my mother was doing the butcher."

She picked up a different bowl of glop and streaked and foiled new gunk alongside the previous gunk.

I bit my lip and said a Hail Mary.

"I can see this isn't gonna be as interesting as I hoped," Lula said. "Bitch slapping's unlikely, so I'm gonna go sit and catch up on all your trashy magazines."

"You still haven't told me anything," I said to Brenda. "Chester hired two guys to follow me around. Why? Who's the man in the photo?"

"The man is no one. It's a composite. You know, somebody's nose and someone else's eyes. It's done on a computer."

"Tom Cruise and Ashton Kutcher!"

"I don't know. I never saw it," Brenda said. "Anyway, it's real clever. It looks like a photograph, but it's a computer program. You scan it into a computer, and the computer breaks the picture up into little itty-bitty thingies and sees a code. And then you can use the code to do things. Like open a car."

"I don't get why that's so special. You can open a car with a key. You can open a car with a remote."

"Yes, but this opens cars that have fancy doohickeys like GPS and security systems. You don't necessarily have to own the car to be able to unlock it, if you get my drift."

"You could steal a car with this?"

"Exactly, and after you open the car, you can start the engine and do all kinds of things . . . like work the gas and brake and steering without being in the car."

Lula looked up from her magazine. "So I could use that photo to start any car I picked out of the lot and ram it through your plate-glass window?"

"Maybe not *any* car, but I suppose," Brenda said.

"Nice," Lula said. And she went back to reading her magazine.

I was beginning to understand the potential value of the photograph. It sounded like the photo held a program that enabled you to hack into the operating systems of cars remotely. You could use it to steal cars. Or you could use it to drive an unmanned vehicle into another car, or a pedestrian, or a building. And if you filled the car with explosives, you'd have a remote-controlled bomb.

"Is this technology well known?" I asked.

"I guess a lot of people know it's out there, but not many people have hold of it. It's, you know, cutting-edge."

I thought about the megabucks Ferrari sitting in Brenda's garage.

"You used it to steal a car, right?"

"I used it to get my car *back.* Do you know who Sammy the Pig is?"

"Sure. Everyone in Jersey knows Sammy the Pig. He's famous. He runs the north Jersey mob."

"Well, my genius husband, who is now dead, decided he wanted to expand his business, so he borrowed money from Sammy. We were doing just fine with thirty-five car washes and a big house and platinum credit cards. I didn't want him to expand, but would he listen to me? No. He wanted to be the car wash king. He wanted to go national. He wanted car washes on the moon. So he got money from Sammy, and he started building car washes, and all of a sudden the economy is tanking and people are washing their own friggin' cars. And then Bernie starts having construction problems and labor problems, and he can't keep up with his loan payments to Sammy. So long story short, Sammy the Pig ended up owning Bernie's nuts. We lost everything. All the damn car washes, the house, the time-share in Jamaica that we never used. Everything. And three months ago, he took my car. He had no business taking the car. Bernie gave it to me for my birthday. Two of Sammy's guys came into the salon, took the keys out of my purse, and drove away with it."

"What kind of car was it?" I asked her. As if I didn't already know.

"A Ferrari. Red. And it was real expensive."

"Why didn't you just go get it back?"

"I was never able to find the papers for it. Bernie's records were a mess by the time he offed himself. And the registration was in the car. And what am I gonna say to the police? My husband was in bed with Sammy the Pig, and Sammy took my car to pay off the vig? Anyway, I sneaked over to Sammy's place and tried to steal my car back, but my key wouldn't work. It set off the alarm system, and the door wouldn't open. I guess The Pig had a new lock put in. Probably had a new VIN put on, too. He's got a bunch of chop shops. The truth is, the car might have been hot even when I got it. Bernie won it in a poker game."

Brenda unrolled one of the foils and looked at my hair. "Still needs more time," she said.

"But you got the car back, right?" I asked her.

"Yeah, I was complaining to this person I know, and he said he could override all the systems and get me my car. Only thing is, he was living in Hawaii, and he was worried about sending me information. So when my client Ritchy came in to get a haircut, and he said he was leaving for a conference in Hawaii, I had this brilliant idea that he could bring the information back for me."

"Why didn't your friend just mail it to you?"

"He said it wasn't safe. Turned out this wasn't safe, either. At least he was smart enough to do the photo thing. I guess you wouldn't want this code stuff to get into the wrong hands."

"Like your brother?"

"Yeah, he'd probably sell it to the Russians, or aliens from outer space, or whoever the heck the enemy is. I can't keep up with it. Or he could keep it and use it to hijack shit."

I looked at myself in the mirror and tried not to grimace. This was more than I'd expected. My whole head was covered in foil.

"Here's the big question," I said to Brenda. "Why did Richard Crick put the photo in my bag?"

"It was an accident. He was airsick, or maybe he was coming down with the flu or something. Anyway, he got off the plane for the layover and was too sick to get back on. He was looking through his bag for his boarding pass, to get it changed out, and he realized he didn't have my envelope. And he said he remembered you had the exact same bag. A black Tumi messenger bag. And he realized he stuffed the yellow envelope into your bag by mistake in his rush to deplane. He said your bag was laying on the floor between the seats, just like his. So he called and told me. He said when he thought about it, he knew exactly what happened. He thought maybe I could meet you when you got off the plane, but I didn't get his message in time. And then he was dead. What are the chances, right?"

Probably pretty good, considering the circumstances.

"How'd your brother find out?"

"He was with me when I played the message back. How was I to know he'd be such an asshole?"

"You told him about the photo with the code?"

"I'd had a couple Appletinis," Brenda said. "I get chatty."

"I love them Appletinis," Lula said. "I could drink a gallon of them."

"Over to the sink," Brenda said to me. "You're done processing. This is going to be awesome."

• • •

I'm always amazed at the way life plays out. How so often a single decision sets people on an irreversible journey. Richard Crick agreed to do a simple favor for a friend, and it led to his death. And the whole ugly chain of events was set in motion when Bernie Schwartz borrowed money from Sammy the Pig. And what was the ultimate result? Highlights from Brenda.

When your hair is wet, you really can't see exactly what the hairdresser from hell has given you. So when I left the shampoo sink and sat in the styling chair, there was hope. By the time my hair was blow-dried, ratted up, and sprayed, I was ready for serious alcohol consumption. The highlights were brilliant red and yellow, my hair looked like it had exploded out of my head, and I was at least six inches taller.

Brenda had tears in her eyes. "This is the most fabulous thing I've ever done," she said. "I'm going to call it Route 1 Sunrise."

"I never seen anything like it," Lula said. "This here takes her to a whole other level. She's not just another ordinary bitch no more. She's, like, Super Bitch. She's, like, got *fire* hair."

"And you see how I gave her hair some lift," Brenda said. "It gives her style some drama."

"I could see that," Lula said.

"What do you think?" Brenda asked me.

"I'm speechless," I said.

Brenda put her hand over her heart. "My pleasure. I'm glad I could help you."

Lula and I left the salon and climbed into the truck. I got behind the wheel, and my hair stuck to the roof.

"I can't drive like this," I said. "My hair's stuck."

"You need a bigger vehicle to go with your new look," Lula said.

I slouched in my seat and drove to the edge of the lot, where Brenda couldn't see me. I took a brush out of my bag and worked at my hair.

"I can't get the brush to go through it," I said to Lula.

"That's the way hair's supposed to be when it got some body. She kicked your hair up a notch. Wham!"

"You might want to dial back on the *wham* thing," I told her. "I'm not in the mood."

"How could you be Miss Cranky-pants when you got hair like that?"

"This is *not* my kind of hair."

"Yeah, but it could be. It could be a whole new you."

I didn't want a new me. I still hadn't figured out the old me.

TWENTY-FOUR

I was still idling in the shopping-center lot, trying to squash my hair, when Morelli called on my cell phone.

"I finally caught up with Berger," he said. "They've been reviewing security tapes from LAX, and they have Razzle Dazzle on one of them. There were no cameras in the vicinity of the crime scene, but they have Raz leaving your gate area. They checked the plane manifest, and two passengers didn't reboard at LAX. Crick and a Somali national, Archie Ahmed."

"Archie Ahmed? Is that Razzle Dazzle?"

"Yeah, apparently Raz has something like sixty-four identities. The Somali government uses him as an operative. Everything from running guns to recruitment to wet work. They probably drop a stack of passports off to him once a month. Berger got tapes from Honolulu International and identified Raz going through security. It looks like he was on your plane."

"I don't remember him."

"Put a hat on him, and he might look human," Morelli said.

"Did Berger say anything about his source? I mean, how did he know about the photograph?"

"Information from an overseas operative that a courier had passed a photo to you. Berger is going on the assumption that it's a photo of a hacker the FBI has been looking for."

"Wonderful. Anything else?"

"Be careful."

I took Route 1 back to Trenton. I turned off Broad and parked in front of the bonds office. Lancer and Slasher were across the street, sound asleep in the Lincoln. Connie was inside at her desk, wearing a disposable surgical mask.

"What's with the mask?" I asked her.

"This office reeks," Connie said. "I don't know what's wrong with it."

Lula tipped her head back and sniffed. "Rat fart," she said. "They probably got into the deli Dumpster. Smells like they been eating sauerkraut."

"You're an expert on this?" I asked her.

"I know a rat fart when I smell one. And there's more than one rat farting up there. You probably got a rat condo over you. Personally, I don't like rats. They got those beady eyes, and skinny tails, and they give you the plague."

Connie was staring at my hair. "Speaking of rats' nests!"

"Brenda thought I needed to glam up," I said to Connie.

"It looked good before Miss Prim and Proper here tried to comb it," Lula said. "She ruined the dramatic effect of the line."

"I like the color," Connie said.

"It's Brenda's specialty," Lula said. "It's called Route 1 Sunrise."

Connie adjusted her mask. "It takes the attention away from the black eye."

"I'm leaving," I said. "The rat farts are getting to me." I turned to Lula. "I'm going after Magpie tonight. Are you in?"

"Hell, yeah. And if we get done early enough, we could go to a club and test-drive your hair."

Oh boy.

• • •

It took half a bottle of detangler and two sheets of Downy fabric softener to untease my hair. I showered and dressed in jeans and a black T-shirt, my thinking being to not compete clotheswise with Route 1 Sunrise.

At seven-thirty, I grabbed my bag and a black hooded sweatshirt and went to the lobby to wait for Lula. Ordinarily, I'd wait outside, but Raz was still at large, and I didn't want to chance running into him in the dark.

Lula's Firebird cruised up to the door, and I jumped in.

"Where we going?" Lula looked over at me.

"All Saints Cemetery. It's behind the big Catholic church on Nottingham."

"I know that cemetery. It's real pretty. It's got hills and woods and shit."

Twenty minutes later, Lula pulled into the church parking lot, cut her lights, and crept to the back of the lot, where a single-lane road led into the cemetery. We got out of the Firebird and stood for a moment, letting our eyes adjust to the darkness.

"I smell campfire," Lula said. "Magpie's out there, heating his beans like a hobo."

I had cuffs stuck into my back pocket, stun gun in my sweatshirt pocket, Glock in my bag. I was carrying a Maglite, but I didn't want to use it and spook Magpie. There was a sliver of moon behind broken clouds. Enough light to see three feet in front but not much more. The church was lit from the front. The rear was dark, as was the graveyard.

"This is creepy," Lula whispered, following close behind me. "I don't like walking around cemeteries at night. All the ghosts come out at night. I can feel them breathing on me."

We were deep into the cemetery when a set of headlights flashed into the parking lot and instantly blinked out. Lancer and Slasher, I thought. In a strange way, it was comforting.

We were following the road, and I could see a dark shape ahead. Something large. Magpie's Crown Vic. Beyond the Vic, I could hear the crackle of wood burning and see the occasional red ember float skyward. This wasn't the first time I'd captured Magpie. We had a fairly cordial relationship, all things considered. He wasn't a violent person.

I stepped around the Vic and called out to Magpie.

"Hey, Magpie," I said. "It's Stephanie Plum."

His fire was small. Just enough to heat a can of beans or roast a hotdog. Magpie wasn't a big guy. He was 5'5" and slim. Definitely entranced by all things shiny, and very clever at stealing them. When his treasures exceeded his storage space, he'd sell them off for whatever he could get.

Magpie looked past his campfire at us. "How'd you find me?"

"Lucky break," I said. "You have a nice spot here."

"It's one of my favorites. It's so peaceful."

He was wearing the usual. Baggy jeans, a plaid flannel shirt, and about $30,000 worth of gold chains.

"You missed your court date," I said to him.

"Are you sure?"

"Yep. You have to go back with me to reschedule. You've already eaten dinner, right?"

"Yes. I was just enjoying the fire."

"It's a real nice fire," Lula said. "Keeps the spooks and ghouls away. And by the way, those are some lovely necklaces you're wearing. Not everyone understands the importance of accessorizing correctly."

"I have a whole trunkful," Magpie said. "I can't wear them all at the same time. They get too heavy. You can have some if you want."

"Thanks," I told him. "That's nice of you, but we can't take any. I'll put the cuffs on you, and Lula and I can put the fire out, and then we'll go into town. Do you want to ride in the Vic with me? Or do you want to ride in Lula's Firebird?"

"The Firebird!"

I was about to cuff Magpie when Raz jumped out of the shadows, knife raised. He looked certifiably crazy in the moonlight, bonfire flames reflected in his eyes, and his hair all Wild Man of Borneo.

"Eeeeee!" Lula shrieked. "It's the Devil. It's Satan!"

Magpie's eyes went wide, rolled back into his head, and he crashed over in a dead faint.

"It's not Satan," I said to Lula. "It's Razzle Dazzle."

Raz lunged at me. "Bitch whore. I burn you good with fire stick until you tell me."

"Hey! What'd you call her?" Lula said, hand on hip, lower lip stuck out. "You better be careful what you call her. We don't put up with none of that shit talk."

He snarled at Lula. "You shut pie hole or I carve you like pig roast."

"Was I just insulted?" Lula asked. "Did he compare me to a roast pig? 'Cause I don't like bein' compared to a pig. And what's with the knife? I mean, who uses a knife these days?"

Raz held his knife in his right hand and pulled a semi-automatic out of his pants with his left hand. "I also got big gun," he said to Lula. "I shoot you in eye and then I slice you and make bacon and cook you in fire."

And he squeezed off a shot.

"Run for it!" Lula yelled. "He got a gun! Satan's got a gun."

Lula took off and was immediately swallowed up in the black night. She crashed through shrubs, smacking into who knows what on her way to the parking lot, her voice carrying back to me. "Ow, shit, sonovabitch."

Raz turned the gun on me and fired. I jumped behind a tombstone, he fired again, and the bullet pinged off the marble. I bolted for a small patch of woods directly behind me. I had my gun in my bag, but no time to search for it. I saw him stumble forward, lit by the campfire. He was hampered by a bullet wound in one leg and a knife wound in the other.

I carefully walked toward the ambient light originating from the front of the church, avoiding the road. I could hear Raz shuffling behind me.

"Here kitty, kitty," he called. "I come get you, kitty."

An engine cranked over, lights flashed at the top of the hill, and Magpie's Crown Vic roared down the road, crossed the parking lot, and disappeared for parts unknown, presumably taking a revived Magpie with it.

My feet wanted to run, but my brain insisted I go slow. I couldn't chance running into a tree or a tombstone in the dark and knocking myself out. I'd managed to find my gun in my bag and had it in hand. I was almost to the lot. I could see the two parked cars. I no longer heard Lula in front of me, or Raz behind me. Just the sound of my heart thudding in my chest.

As I exited the wooded area, I saw Lula move in front of a car and wave at me, and I broke into a sprint across the stretch of open field. I reached Lula and bent at the waist to catch my breath.

I glanced at the Camry next to Lula's Firebird. "Is this his car?" I asked her.

"Looks like it. There's no one in it. There's an extra clip for his gun on the front seat."

I shot two rounds into each tire, Lula and I hustled into the Firebird, and she drove out of the lot onto the road and sat at idle. I called Berger and got him on his cell. I told him Raz was in the cemetery, and his car was disabled.

"You gotta admit, he did sort of look like Satan in the beginning there," Lula said.

"You freaked. You were squealing like a little girl."

"I got caught by surprise. And I was affected by the atmosphere. You know how I'm all sensitive to that shit."

"You yelled *run for it*! What the heck was that?"

"That was smart," Lula said. "He was gonna make me into bacon. He's a maniac. Good thing he can't shoot for snot with his left hand."

I agreed. He was definitely a maniac. And he definitely couldn't shoot left-handed.

"I want to stay here and wait for the police to arrive," I said. "I don't want to chance Raz somehow driving away. I want him caught."

"Sure. Just keep your eyes open for him sneaking up on us. And keep your gun out. I'm not bein' no breakfast meat."

After a couple minutes, I thought I saw Raz navigate the open grass to his car. I was sure he'd heard the shots. If it was me, I'd immediately check the tires. I couldn't see him in the dark lot. We had the window down, listening for footfalls. Lula and I had guns drawn.

"Bitching bitches" carried out to us.

"He looked at the tires," Lula said.

I saw lights on the road behind us, and a cop car drove up and turned into the lot. It was followed by two more police cars and a sedan with a Kojak light.

My cell phone rang. It was Berger.

"Is that you sitting out on the road in a Firebird?" he asked.

"Yes. I put a couple rounds in his tires, so he's on foot. He's not far away. I saw him go to his car a couple minutes ago. He's armed."

"Thanks," Berger said. "We'll take it from here."

"Do you want to stay around and see what happens?" Lula asked.

"No. I want to go home."

Truth is, I was afraid if I stayed in the area, Raz might circle around and come back and shoot me.

TWENTY-FIVE

Lula pulled into my lot to drop me off, and we spotted Brenda's car.

"That's Brenda's toaster," she said. "And it looks like Brenda waiting for you at the door. And she don't look good."

Brenda was hunched, arms wrapped around herself, head down.

Lula cut the engine, and we went to where Brenda was standing and chain-smoking, the butts littering the ground around her.

"What's up?" I asked her.

"I have terrible problems. I need you to help me. I don't know who else to ask. It's my son, Jason. He's been kidnapped. I was there when they grabbed him and dragged him away."

"Omigosh," I said. "That's serious. Did you call the police?"

"I can't. There are circumstances."

"Such as?"

"The police are sort of looking for Jason," Brenda said. "It's not like he's done anything bad. I mean, he hasn't killed anyone or anything."

"What *has* he done?"

Brenda lit up another cigarette. Now she had two going at the same time.

"He's a hacker," she said.

"I know about them," Lula said. "They go around giving people a virus. And they steal Sarah Palin's email."

"Jason isn't that kind of a hacker," Brenda said. "He would never do anything mean. He's just interested in the technology. He says it's like a chess game, and he's playing the computer. He's really smart. He's a genius."

"So why do the police want him if he hasn't done anything wrong?" I asked.

"He has a couple friends who are just like him. It's, like, a geek club. I guess for giggles they break into government computers and leave funny messages. They don't take information out, but the government doesn't like when their systems get hacked."

"The government got no sense of humor," Lula said.

"Anyway, Jason and his friends went underground a year ago. Jason says they aren't leaving any more funny messages, but the FBI is still looking for them. The thing is, the FBI doesn't know who they are or what they look like, so if Jason keeps a low profile, he might be okay."

I took a step back to get away from the smoke cloud surrounding Brenda. "Jason is the friend who sent you the photograph from Hawaii, isn't he?"

"He was trying to help me get my car. He's such a good boy."

"Do you know enough about computers to use the photograph?" I asked her.

"No. Jason has a friend here who was going to help me."

"Sounds to me like Jason come home," Lula said. "Why'd he do that if the FBI is lookin' for him? Why didn't he just send you another photograph?"

"When poor Ritchy got killed, and we found out Razzle Dazzle was involved, Jason knew he was in danger and had to move. Razzle Dazzle has been chasing after Jason for over a year. There are terrorists who would love to get their hands on Jason. And Razzle Dazzle would deliver Jason to them."

"I'm confused," Lula said. "Why did this Razzle guy want the photograph? Why didn't he just go get Jason?"

"Raz only knows Jason by his electronic imprint. I don't know what that means. Jason says Raz is like a stupid hacker. Eventually, Raz tracks Jason down, but he doesn't know his human identity or what he looks like. I think Raz thought Ritchy had a picture of Jason. I don't think he knew about the code. At least, that's what Jason thinks. So since Jason had to leave Hawaii anyway, he came home for a couple days to help me get my car and to visit with me. He was supposed to fly out tomorrow, but he got kidnapped."

My heart did a flip in my chest. "Razzle Dazzle?"

"No. My brother has him. Jason and I were eating dinner, and my asshole brother came in with his two thugs and snatched him. I don't know how he knew Jason was here. Maybe he heard Sammy the Pig had his car stolen and put it together."

Okay, I could breathe again. "At least your brother won't hurt Jason."

"No, but Chester could hold Jason hostage until he agrees to show him how to hack into who knows what. And then Jason could be implicated in a crime. Or if Jason stays here too long, Razzle Dazzle or the FBI might find him. I thought of you because you grab people all the time. I was hoping you'd help me. I figure Chester has Jason at the warehouse." Brenda squinted at me through the smoke haze. "What happened to your hair? It's all flat and back in a ponytail."

"Rain," I said. "I got caught in the rain."

"I didn't see any rain."

"It must have been a rogue cloud. It

drifted over me and *whoosh* there was a downpour."

"So are we gonna stage a big rescue?" Lula asked me. "We goin' in with guns blazin'? I would have worn my Ranger outfit if I'd known."

Lula had forsaken the black for gold. Gold tank top, hot-pink short spandex skirt, gold spike-heeled shoes. It was a wonder Razzle hadn't taken her out with one shot. She made a really good target.

"We'll go in with guns *not* blazing," I said. "These aren't hardened criminals."

"Chester might be a little hardened," Brenda said.

"You hear that?" Lula said to me. "A little hardened. No telling what we can expect. That means we need to take my Firebird, on account of I got extra ammo in my trunk."

"Extra ammo might be good," Brenda said. "You can never have too much ammo."

We piled into Lula's Firebird, and I called Ranger when we reached Broad.

"Checking in," I said to him. "I'm off the radar because I'm in Lula's car, but

I wanted you to know I'm making a sort of mercy illegal capture just north of Bordentown. I might need help."

"Babe, you're not off the radar. You're wearing my watch. I know exactly where you are."

I looked down at the watch. "I forgot."

"I'll have someone follow you. Let me know if you want him to go in."

"Thanks."

"It's good to have a Ranger," Lula said. "He's like a personal Spidey."

• • •

Lula hesitated when she got to the Billings warehouse lot. There were two cars parked. One was the bashed-in Lincoln. The other car was a Mercedes. Lights were on inside the building in the office area.

"What's the plan?" Lula wanted to know. "We can't be sellin' Girl Scout cookies out here. Girl Scouts are supposed to be in bed by now."

"Park at the back edge, where the Firebird won't be so visible," I told her.

"We'll try the front door. If that doesn't work, we'll see if we can get in through the loading dock."

Lula parked, and we all got out.

"Hold on," Lula said. "I'll get my ammo."

I pulled my Glock out of my bag. "I really don't think we need extra."

"Yeah, but this is good," Lula said, opening her trunk.

I looked inside and stopped breathing for a beat. "That's a rocket launcher!"

"Yep," Lula said. "It's the big boy. I got it at a yard sale in the projects. It's loaded for bear, too. See that mother stuck onto the end of it? It goes *KA-BOOM*!"

"No rocket launchers!" I told her. "Absolutely no rocket launchers. This isn't Afghanistan."

"We don't have to use it," Lula said. "We just knock on their door and show them this bitch. Then they wet their pants and hand over Jason."

"It could work," Brenda said. "I almost wet my pants seeing it in the trunk."

She had a point. I had to admit, I had

a moment when I first saw it, too. "I guess it might be okay, as long as we only use it to scare them."

"Show-and-tell," Lula said.

Lula shouldered her rocket launcher. I had my hand wrapped around my Glock. And Brenda had her cute little girl gun. We marched up to the front door of Billings Gourmet Food, and I tried the doorknob. Locked. We circled the building and tried the loading-dock gates and the roll-up garage doors. All locked.

"I'm not going home without Jason," Brenda said. "I'm going in."

"Me, too," Lula said. "I'm right behind you."

"How are you going in?" I asked them.

Brenda set off for the office entrance. "The front door. I'm going to ring the bell and ask for Jason."

"And if they won't give him to us, I'll shoot a rocket up their ass," Lula said, following her.

I had to run to catch up, and I checked the parking lot on the way. I didn't see a Rangeman vehicle. Not good, I thought. This smelled like disaster.

Brenda went straight to the door and put her finger to the bell. After a couple minutes, the door opened and Lancer looked out.

"Oh shit," Lancer said.

He tried to close the door, but I already had my foot in it.

"Where's Jason?" Brenda asked. "I want my son."

"I dunno," Lancer said. "He's not here."

Brenda pushed past him into the office. "Of course he's here. Where else would he be? My sister-in-law wouldn't put up with him in her house."

"Hey," Lancer said. "You can't come in here. It's not office hours."

Lula shoved past him, close on Brenda's heels. "S'cuse us. Outta our way."

Lancer eyeballed the rocket lancher and turned white. "I'm going to have to get tough now. I'm going to have to force you to leave."

"Do you got one of these babies?" Lula asked him, patting the rocket launcher.

"No."

"Then how you gonna force us to leave?"

"I have a gun," Lancer said. And he pointed his gun at Lula.

"I don't like when people point a gun at me," Lula said. "It makes me nervous, and it's rude. Do you see me pointing my rocket launcher at you? I don't think so."

"It's rude to break into people's private property," Lancer said.

"It's rude to kidnap my son," Brenda said.

We were in a small lobby. A hall led off to the right.

"I bet you have him down here," Brenda said, moving along the hall, little girlie gun held out in front of her.

Lula followed Brenda. Lancer followed Lula. And I followed Lancer.

Brenda opened a door and looked inside. "Warehouse," she said. And she moved on.

I did a fast scan of the cavernous space. Rows of boxes stacked one on another. Gallon tins of olive oil on wire shelves. More boxes. An eighteen-wheeler in the garage area. No Jason.

Brenda opened a door at the far end of the hall and yelped. "Jason!"

We all ran down the hall and looked into the room. Jason was working on his laptop. Slasher and another man were slouched into a couch, watching a small television.

"I'm sorry, boss," Lancer said. "I couldn't stop them."

"What do you mean you couldn't stop them?" the man said. "You have a gun, don't you? Shoot them."

Lancer hesitated.

The man stood, pulled a gun, and pointed it at Jason. "How about this, Brenda. How about I shoot your kid if you don't go home. He's doing good stuff for us here, so I'll only shoot him in the leg."

Brenda went beady-eyed. "Chester, you bastard. If anyone's going to get shot, it's going to be you."

And before anyone could move, she fired on Chester, tagging him in the arm.

"Kill her!" Chester yelled. "Kill her!"

Lancer trained his gun on Brenda, and I tackled him from behind. We went to the floor, and his gun discharged two rounds. One zinged past Lula, and the second cut off two inches from her four-inch stiletto heel.

"What the heck?" Lula said, toppling over, off balance from the two-inch heel difference. "I'm hit!" she yelled. "The asshole shot me. Woman down. Woman down. Call 911."

"You're fine," I said to her. "You just fell off your shoe."

"I see darkness," Lula said. "It's closing in on me. There's a tunnel of light. I see angels. No, wait a minute, there's no angels. Shit, it's Tony Soprano."

It wasn't Tony Soprano. It was Chester Billings, roaring like a wounded bull elephant, charging across the room at Lula and Brenda. He knocked the little gun out of Brenda's hand and grabbed the rocket launcher. Somehow in the scuffle the rocket got launched, *whooshing* across the room, punching a hole in the far wall, disappearing from view. There was an explosion that rocked the building. Plaster fell from the ceiling. Everyone was yelling and scrambling for cover. A second smaller explosion rattled furniture, and I could see flames lick through the hole made by the rocket.

"Fire in the warehouse," Lancer said. "The rocket must have hit a propane tank."

Smoke poured into the windowless room, and there was a rush to evacuate. Everyone ran into the hall and scattered. Lancer, Slasher, and Billings ran in one direction. Lula, Brenda, and Jason ran in another. I was the last out of the room. I stepped into the hall and the lights blinked off. I was confused in the dark, choking on the smoke. An arm wrapped around me, nearly lifting me off my feet, moving me in the opposite direction. It was Ranger.

"This way," he said, pushing me down the hall to a fire door.

He shoved the door open, and we were out of the building. I could hear emergency vehicles screaming on the approach road.

"How many people were in the building?" Ranger asked.

"Six plus me."

Ranger was connected to Tank in the other SUV. "Talk to me," Ranger said.

I could hear Tank on speakerphone. "Lula disappeared into the woods behind us. I shouted at her, but she kept going. Five more people came out of the building and scattered. A woman and a young guy panicked and ran in opposite directions when a flaming chunk of roof landed next to them. The woman is hiding behind the Dumpster. We tried to get her, but she shot at us. The guy is out there somewhere. Looked like he had a computer. Three men jumped into a Mercedes and took off."

"Everyone's out of the building," Ranger said to me. "Let's move, unless you want to talk to the police."

"No!"

He grabbed my hand and pulled me at a flat-out run across the lot, over a grassy median that separated Billings Gourmet Food from the neighboring business, Dot Plumbing. Two Rangeman SUVs sat at idle in the shadow of the Dot building. Ranger got behind the wheel of one, and the second followed us to the edge of the lot, lights off.

Flames were shooting from the top of the Billings warehouse. Police cars slid to a stop in the lot. Fire trucks rumbled in.

"Did you call the fire and police?" I asked Ranger.

"No. I didn't have to. The explosion blew the roof off the building. It could be seen for miles. And my control room heard the fire alert go in from Billings's security system."

"I don't see Lula's car in the lot."

"I had Hal move it. He's on the road in front of us."

Ranger pulled onto the service road and Lula jumped out of a clump of bushes, waving her arms and yelling. She had one shoe on and one shoe off, leaves were stuck in her soot-smudged pink-and-yellow hair, and her gold sequined tank top was blinding in Ranger's headlights.

"It's Lula Sunshine," Ranger said, stopping to let her jump into the SUV.

"Holy cow. Holy crap. Holy moly,"

Lula said. "That was freakin' scary. And look what that idiot did to my shoe. These are genuine Louboutin knock-offs. Where am I gonna get another shoe to match this?"

Ranger turned onto Route 295, and Lula sat forward in her seat.

"What about my car?" Lula asked. "We can't leave my baby here. It'll get ashes all over it. That sucker went up like a whatdoyoucallit? An inferno."

"Hal has the Firebird," Ranger said. "He's taking it back to Trenton."

"Really? Wow. Hal's a sweetie," Lula said. "I'm gonna have to do something real nice for him."

The corners of Ranger's mouth twitched into a small smile.

"Gutter head," I said to him.

That turned the twitch to a full-on smile.

A police car blew past us, lights flashing.

Lula had her nose to the window. "I think that was Brenda's kid behind the wheel of the cop car!"

• • •

A half hour later, Ranger and I were parked in my lot. Lula was gone. She'd retrieved her Firebird and was meeting Hal at a downtown bar to show him her appreciation.

"Thanks for rescuing me," I said to Ranger.

"I sent Hal and Rafael to keep an eye on you, and I went to check on a commercial account in Whitehorse. Rafael called to tell me Lula went in with a rocket launcher, so I skipped Whitehorse. I pulled into the lot seconds before you destroyed Billings Foods."

"It was an accident," I said.

He looked at my hair. "And?"

"Professional necessity. I had to get information out of a hairdresser."

"I knew the explanation would be worthwhile." He checked his watch. "I'd like to stay and seduce you, but I have to backtrack to Whitehorse. Someone managed to hack into the alarm system and clean out a computer store we're supposed to be protecting."

I squelched a grimace. I suspected I knew who'd done the hacking.

"How sophisticated are these hackers?" I asked him. "Suppose the photograph everyone was looking for had a code hidden in it? Like, could the photo look like Ashton Kutcher, but when you fed it into a computer it would break down into digital components? And those digital components could be a code a hacker could use to start a car? Is that possible or is it just fiction?"

"The technology is real. And it's an increasing threat to my business. They're not so much codes as messages that instruct another computer to perform a function, like starting a car or disabling a security system."

• • •

I woke up the next morning thinking about Razzle Dazzle. I had my phone in my hand to call Morelli, and a text message buzzed in from him.

I'm in meetings until noon. I'll call later. Raz slipped away last night. Be careful.

My equipment was loaded and charged and positioned in my bag for easy access. I stayed vigilant when I crossed the parking lot to my truck, and I drove watching my rear.

By the time I got to the bonds office, everyone else was already there. Connie was behind her desk. Lula was perched on a folding chair, doing the day's Jumble. Vinnie was pacing, checking messages on his smartphone.

"News of the day?" I asked.

"Vinnie just wrote a bond on Brenda," Connie said. "There was an explosion at her brother's warehouse, and she was arrested on the scene."

"They arrested her for just being there?" I asked. "Did they think she was responsible for the explosion?"

"No, a defective propane tank apparently exploded," Connie said. "I've been listening to police chatter."

Lula looked up from the Jumble, rolled her eyes, and made the sign of the cross.

"Brenda was there when the police arrived, one thing led to another, and she punched out a cop." Connie looked up at the ceiling. "Hey, something just dripped on my desk."

We all looked at the ceiling. There were big wet splotches, and it looked like it was buckling.

Lula sniffed. "It's the rats. They're relievin' themselves, and it's soakin' through. There must be a lot of them. When I was a 'ho, I used to do business out of a Chinese restaurant, and they had this problem. It used to drip into the hot-and-sour soup."

"There's no rats," Vinnie said. "There's probably a busted pipe. Somebody call the landlord."

"I know rats when I smell them," Lula said. "And there's rats." She got a broom from the corner and poked the ceiling. "Shoo!"

The minute the broom made contact with the ceiling, a piece of the ceiling broke loose and fell onto Connie's desk. A crack opened up above us, and there were some smooshy, groaning sounds. The crack stretched the length of the room, the ceiling sagged, the crack gaped open, and about a thousand rats poured down on us. Big rats, small rats, fat rats, startled rats. Bug-eyed and squealing. Nasty little rat feet treading air. Tails stiff as a stick. They thudded onto Connie's desk and the floor, stunned for a second and then up and running.

"RATS!" Lula shrieked. "It's raining rats."

She climbed onto her chair and covered her head with the Jumble.

Connie was on her desk, punting rats across the room like they were footballs. "Someone open the door so they can get out!" she yelled.

I was afraid to move for fear of stepping on a rat and pissing him off. I think I was screaming, but I don't remember hearing myself.

Vinnie lunged for the door, bolted out, and the rats rushed after him.

Minutes later, we were on the sidewalk, looking in at the office. Most of the rats had departed for parts unknown. A few rats, too dumb to find the door, were hunkered down in corners.

"I feel like I got rat cooties," Lula said. "I bet I got fleas. And I think one of them bit me on the ankle."

I examined Lula's ankles. No bite marks.

"It must have been one of those bites that don't show," Lula said, "on account of I'm coming down with something. I can feel it. Lord, I hope it's not the plague. I don't want the plague. You break out in them booboos when you got the plague."

"I don't see any booboos on you," I told her.

"Well, it's still early," Lula said.

Better booboos than Buggy, I thought, hiking my bag onto my shoulder. "I'm heading out. I'm going to look for Magpie."

"I'll go with you," Lula said. "Only I gotta get something to settle my stomach. I gotta keep my strength up in case I get the plague. I need chicken."

• • •

I cruised into the Cluck-in-a-Bucket drive-thru and Lula got a bucket of extra-crispy, a bag of biscuits with dipping gravy, an apple pie, and a large diet root beer. I helped myself to a piece of chicken, and I got a text message from Brenda.

Thanks for everything. I'll send you the formula for your hair.

I texted her back and asked if she was at the salon and could she do my hair.

Negative, she texted. *Arrivederci.*

"Change of plans," I said to Lula. "Brenda's running."

"How do you know?"

"I just know. I'm going to see if I can talk her out of it."

Forty minutes later, I was about to turn off Route 1 into Brenda's neighborhood when her toaster zipped out in front of me. There were four cars between us, but I knew it was Brenda.

"You want me to call her?" Lula asked.

"No. Let's see where she's going."

She took Route 1 to Route 18, and got onto the Turnpike heading north. It was clear where she was going. She was going to the airport, and Jason was in the car with her.

"Maybe she's just taking her kid," Lula said. "He's still hiding, right?"

"It's possible."

I followed her to the short-term parking garage and watched from a distance while she took suitcases out of the Scion. They walked toward the terminal, dragging their luggage. It didn't look to me like she even bothered to lock the car. I knew she was jumping bail.

I found a parking place, and Lula and I hustled to catch up with Brenda. A man was a short distance away, walking toward us. He was carrying a suiter, looking very tanned.

It was The Rug. Simon Ruguzzi. The skip responsible for all my problems in Hawaii. Our eyes met, and he dropped the suiter and took off.

Brenda was worth loose change to Vinnie. The Rug was worth big bucks.

I changed course in the middle of the parking garage and ran for Ruguzzi. I could hear Lula clattering in her heels behind me, and I was gaining on the guy in front of me. I got to within a couple feet of him, took a flying leap, and grabbed his pants cuffs. He went to the ground, and Lula rushed over and sat on him. I cuffed him and dragged him to his feet.

"How'd you know to run?" I asked him.

"You're famous," he said. "I saw you on the side of a bus, in an ad for the bonds office."

Vinnie's brilliant idea, and not a highlight in my life.

I loaded The Rug into the backseat and headed back to Trenton. I called Ranger from the road.

"I just captured The Rug," I told him. "I had a feeling Brenda was going to skip, so I followed her to the airport. I ran into Ruguzzi in the parking garage, and Lula and I took him down."

"Babe," Ranger said.

• • •

It was late afternoon by the time I met Vinnie at the coffee shop.

"Sorry about Brenda," I said. "I'm pretty sure she skipped."

"I was counting on it," Vinnie said. "She put her Ferrari up for bond. Now I can give it to DeAngelo."

"It's hot," I told him. "And it doesn't come with keys."

"Don't care," Vinnie said. "That's DeAngelo's problem. I'll send it to him on a flatbed."

I got a Frappuccino and got into my truck. Magpie would wait for another day. Truth is, I was rolling in money from my Ruguzzi capture. I stopped at my parents' house on the way home.

"Looks like you tore the knees out of your jeans," Grandma said.

I followed her into the kitchen. "Occupational hazard."

"Are you staying for dinner?" my mom asked.

"No. I need to go home and take a shower and change my clothes."

I'd been pelted by rats, plus I'd skidded across about five feet of cement when I tackled The Rug. I didn't think she wanted to know the details.

"I was hoping I could mooch some sandwich stuff from you. I need to go shopping, but I didn't want to go into Giovichinni's with this hair and the skinned knees, and my black eye is turning green."

"Green is good," Grandma said. "That's one of the last colors."

My mom fixed a bag of food for me and handed it over. She went to the cupboard where she kept her liquor stash, pulled out a photograph, and held it up. It was the photograph from the plane!

"Your grandmother had this in her room," she said. "I know you were looking for it. I found it when I went in to change the linens today."

"The guy in the photo is a hottie," Grandma said. "I pulled it out of the garbage. I didn't know you wanted it."

I tucked the photo into the food bag. I'd give it to Ranger for safekeeping. Or maybe for giggles I'd give it to Berger. He'd think he finally had a picture of the hacker he'd been after. As far as I knew, Berger and Razzle Dazzle didn't know the photo was a composite that hid a computer message.

"Gotta go," I said. "Thanks for the food and the photo. I'll find a hot replacement for you, Grandma."

Grandma took a little bottle filled with

pink stuff off the counter. “Annie dropped this off for you.”

“More Pepto-Bismol?”

“No. She said this is the real thing.”

• • •

I’d picked Morelli’s SUV out in my parking lot, so I wasn’t surprised when I opened my door and Bob bounced up to me. I scratched behind his ears and gave him a kiss on the top of his head. Morelli strolled in from the living room. The television was on.

“Suppose I came home with some hot guy, and you were here in your socks, watching television,” I said.

“It would be awkward.”

I set the bag on the counter and unpacked.

“Looks like you stopped off at your mom’s house,” Morelli said. “Oh man, is that chocolate cake?”

“Yes. And I have some sandwich stuff. Are you hungry?”

“Starved.” He opened a plastic baggie and snitched a piece of ham. “I have good news for you. Berger got Raz."

"Get out!"

"Actually, he was dead by the time he got him, but he got him all the same." Morelli opened another baggie. "Corned beef. This is the mother lode."

"How did Raz get dead?"

"He escaped from the cemetery, but he stole a car sometime during the night, and this morning one of Trenton's finest spotted him. There was a chase, and Raz lost control of his car and hit a bridge abutment."

"Jeez."

He looked down at my knees. "I heard you brought The Rug in. Looks like you tackled him."

"Yeah, I should take a shower. The blood's caking."

"I could help with the shower." He put the corned beef down and picked up Annie's little bottle. "Your mom thinks of everything. I've had heartburn all day." He unscrewed the bottle and drank it before I could stop him.

I stared at him. "Um, how do you feel?" I asked.

He thought for a moment. “Better,” he finally said. “Warm.” His eyes got dark and soft, and the corners of his mouth tipped into a smile. “Very friendly.” He reached out for me and pulled me into him. “Come here, Cupcake.”

ABOUT THE AUTHOR

JANET EVANOVICH is the #1 *New York Times* bestselling author of the Stephanie Plum novels, twelve romance novels, the Barnaby and Hooker novels and graphic novels, *Wicked Appetite* (the first book in the Lizzy and Diesel series), and *How I Write: Secrets of a Bestselling Author.*

Visit Janet Evanovich's website at
www.evanovich.com
Facebook/JanetEvanovich

or

write her at PO Box 2829,
Naples, FL 34106.